WE WON'T BE HERE TOMORROW

AND OTHER STORIES

T0046338

MARGARET KILLJOY

*We Won't Be Here Tomorrow
and Other Stories*

© 2022 Margaret Killjoy
This edition © 2022 AK Press (Chico and Edinburgh)
ISBN: 978-1-84935-475-2
E-ISBN: 978-1-84935-476-9

AK Press   AK Press
370 Ryan Ave. #100   33 Tower St.
Chico, CA 95973   Edinburgh EH6 7BN
www.akpress.org   Scotland
akpress@akpress.org   www.akuk.com
                              akuk@akpress.org

The above addresses would be delighted to provide you with the latest
AK Press distribution catalog, which features books, pamphlets, zines,
and stylish apparel published and/or distributed by AK Press. Alternatively, visit our websites for the complete catalog, latest news, and
secure ordering.

Cover and interior design by Casandra Johns
Printed in the United States

For my father

CONTENTS

ACKNOWLEDGMENTS

This book is, in its way, a record of all of the people who believed in me enough to let me do it. This book would not exist without the guidance, criticism, discussion, cheerleading, and instruction of so many people. I would like to thank everyone at the staff of the Clarion West writer's workshop for changing my life. I would like to thank every editor and publisher who helped these stories come to light. I would like to thank my Patreon supporters who believed in me and my fiction. In particular, I want to thank: Neile Graham, M. Huw Evans, Garret Johnston, Rebecca Campbell, Mimi Mondal, Thersa Matsuura, Laurie Penny, Michael Sebastian, Jake Stone, Nana, Leo Vladimirsky, Justin C. Key, Christine Neulieb, Nibedita Sen, Evan J. Peterson, Tegan More, Julia M. Wetherell, Andy Duncan, Eileen Gunn, Tobias Buckell, Nalo Hopkinson, Cory Doctorow, Susan Palwick, Bex, Ceightie, Dylan, Widdow, Miriam, Mo, Parks, Smokey, Elena, and Diana Pho. My Patreon backers, Nora, Hoss the dog, Kirk, Willow, Natalie, Sam, Christopher, Shane, The Compound, Cat J, Staro, Mike, Eleanor, Chelsea, Dana, Huw (again), Sean, Justine Norton-Kertson, David, James, and Nicole. I want to thank Ursula Le Guin for telling me that it's okay for a writer's place in the revolution to be writing instead of organizing, as long as you do the shit work of social change too. I want to thank her for more than that, but I'm not a good enough writer yet to put those emotions down. I want to thank AK Press and Zach, in particular, for believing in my writing. I want to thank Kate Khatib for the same reason. I want to thank the divine, even if I don't know what metaphor works best to describe it. Finally and most importantly, I want to thank my family who never tried to stop me from following my dreams. My sister was my first editor.

THE DEVIL LIVES HERE

The devil lives at the bottom of Gossett's Gorge. All us kids know it, which means all the parents must too, because they were kids once themselves. Knowing where the devil lives doesn't seem like the kind of thing you'd ever forget.

I would have told you I wasn't afraid of the devil, but I would have been lying, and the proof of it was that I'd never spent the night at the devil's shack overlooking the gorge. I'd never crawled down that rope ladder, the spindly one that's all fucked up and threadbare that goes right out over the edge. I'd never seen no one else stay the night or climb down either, and probably I would have gotten old like my parents without having ever done it. I would have, until Penny moved here to Mountain Springs. Until her stupid tagalong brother got taken. It wasn't my fault.

I was fourteen years old in 1994. Kurt Cobain had just died and not one of us believed it was suicide. A grunge girl moved from the city to the house next door on my country road, and she had the right flannel, the right jeans, and a Mudhoney shirt. I'd never even heard of Mudhoney, but I was sure they were about to become my new favorite band. She was a year older than me, she never smiled, she never brushed her hair, and she was perfect in every way. Assuming she liked girls.

Her parents called her Samantha, and her middle school brat of a brother Chris called her Sam, but she told me her name was Penny and I wasn't going to argue with a girl like her about something so meaningless as a name.

◆

If you show another kid the ropes around here, you gotta mean it literally. You gotta show em the Three Trees up on Spineback, which are fat doug firs as old as God that've got rope bridges strung between. You gotta tell em how every two years or something, some kid falls to their death, usually drunk, usually kids from out of town. Every time it happens there's a big fuss and someone takes the ropes down. Every time, the ropes go back up, and no one is sure who puts them up. You gotta show them the knots, because they're weird knots, knots like no one else really knows how to tie, overly-elaborate. You gotta call them devil's knots, too, if you want to sound spooky.

After you dare them to climb up after you into the Three Trees, you gotta take em to Sandy Creek. Nothing spooky about it, it's just that there's this squat old willow with a rope swing that's been there for a hundred years but you can swing out into the widest, deepest, best part of the creek and it's half the reason it's alright to live in Mountain Springs.

Only then, after they've seen what's good in town, do you take em to the devil's shack. No one ever dies at the devil's shack, you can assure your guests. No one ever dies there because no one ever stays the night, and no one ever climbs down that ladder. It's the safest place in town if you respect that it's evil.

The devil's shack is just a little carriage house, like a big garage, and a single room adjacent. It's all timber framed and wood paneled and it ain't insulated for nothing, but I guess the devil doesn't need to keep warm because the devil makes things warm.

◆

I showed Penny the ropes. Chris came along, because of course he did. That's what brats do. It's no more right to be mad at a brat for tagalong than it's right to be mad at a squirrel for stupid or a devil for death. Chris climbed the Three Trees, and he swung into Sandy Creek, and he kept being there when I wanted to talk to Penny about important stuff like if there was a grunge scene in Portland or, you know, her opinions on the current popularity of bisexuality among teenage girls.

The thing is, I saw Penny and I saw my chance at a perfect summer. Maybe a perfect life, but I couldn't think that far ahead. I saw her and I riding our bikes down every trail on Spineback and finding every secluded glade. I saw her dark blue eyes and her messy brown hair close to my face. I saw us making pinkie swears that escalated to bloodsworn pacts. I saw us stealing a car and getting away with it. Hell, I saw us running away to Portland. Or staying in Mountain Springs. I didn't care.

I'm telling you all this because I know how it sounds, because you probably saw the news reports about Chris. Maybe with everything else I'm telling you, you're going to reach some unkind conclusions about me. Yes, it's true, I wasn't upset when Chris wasn't there all of a sudden. But for fuck's sake, I was a fourteen year-old girl in love. That kind of shit takes over your brain and makes its own decisions.

When we rode our bikes up the overgrown road to the devil's shack, and we passed that rusted out little water tower with the old gold spraypaint that says "the devil lives here," I started saying "devil take you" under my breath. Everyone knows if you say it a hundred times in less than a minute, the devil will do it, he'll take whoever you're thinking about. I didn't even get to forty, though, because I'm not a monster. Nothing that happened was my fault.

"What is this place?" Penny asked, running forward. I couldn't blame her, it's a beautiful sight. The carriage house was nothing special, just old, but the one-room shack had the sharpest-peaked ceiling you'll ever see, and no windows, and it's right up against the cliff, and it just looks like magic.

"I told you," I answered. "It's the devil's shack."

"You said the devil lives at the bottom of the gorge," she said as we went inside. The door was off its hinges again. Every couple of years, someone came by and fixed the place up. Probably some local dad just looking to scare the kids, maybe the same person who put up those rope bridges. But the devil's shack got trashed pretty quick every time, since, you know, teenagers were around.

There was no back wall, just a ten-foot opening out over Gossett's Gorge. Wind kicked in through the gap and it hit the cracks in the rafters just right for it to whistle. I was glad—the whistling roof is one of the coolest parts of the shack, but it wasn't every day you'd get so lucky as to hear it.

"The devil lives at the bottom of the gorge," I agreed. "This is like his emergency backup spot, in case the gorge gets flooded or an angel comes looking for him down there. I guess."

"You can't believe that," Chris said. He almost never spoke when I was around, because I think he resented me as much as I resented him.

"Of course I believe it," I said. I didn't know if I was telling the truth or not. I'm not sure that anyone recounting fables or legends or laws believe they're telling the truth, they just say the things they've heard because that makes them true. "If you don't believe me, you can climb down there and prove it yourself."

Chris looked suspiciously at the rope ladder. It really was a death trap, with or without the ghost story. In places, it was as thin as yarn. Other spots looked burned. Some of the rope rungs were ripped off entirely. The ladder didn't even go all the way to the bottom of the gorge, just down maybe eighty feet before disappearing into a tiny patch of scrawny trees.

He looked back at me, then at his sister, then back at me. A grin cracked across his face, and damn fool kid did it. One second he was standing there, the next he wasn't.

"Chris!" Penny shouted, down into the echo of the gorge.

"Riss!" the gorge shouted back.

I knew right then and there that I was more scared of not impressing Penny than I was of death or ghost stories. So I looked at her and I grinned the same dumb way that dumb Chris had dumb grinned.

I got on that rope ladder and started down. It took all my concentration to keep from panicking. A gust of wind moved me and the ladder several feet, and I clenched my teeth and my fists and kept climbing.

The cliff wasn't completely vertical, thankfully, and in spots it was more like I was scrambling down a hill than just clinging for dear life.

I reached the end of the ladder, but there was no sign of Chris. Not in the trees, not on the one-foot ledge they grew out of.

"I don't see him!" I shouted up. Penny was already on her way down.

That's when I noticed the cave.

Caves never have the kind of entrances you'd think they would. All the caves I've ever found or seen in the coastal range of Oregon were exposed to the world only by tiny little cracks and slivers and holes in the stone.

"Chris!" I shouted into the darkness. My voice echoed, a long ways back.

Penny landed beside me.

That's when we heard the scream. Clear as a summer lake, we heard the scream. Loud as a waterfall, we heard the scream.

"Chris!" Penny shouted, then crawled into the darkness on her hands and knees.

I counted down from three to work up my nerve, but it didn't work. I counted down from ten. At one, I crawled in after.

For a hundred feet or more, we sloshed and slogged through mud and darkness on our hands and knees. Once my eyes adjusted, I saw the pale yellow flicker of firelight ahead and pretty quick I reached this place inside myself that was beyond fear. Like, anything could be ahead of us and it wasn't going to be good, but somehow crawling forward felt like the only possible option.

A sharp rock caught my shoulder, tore my favorite Nirvana shirt and my skin, and I kept crawling.

After a hundred feet or a million years we came out into a big open cave room. Three lanterns in a triangle on a natural shelf—an altar, I knew it without question—cast shadows more markedly than they cast light, and the whole room danced with fire and darkness.

No one was there.

Empty bottles were there, and empty cans of food, and the walls were painted up in teen graffiti, and a bare mattress sat on the ground inexplicably enough. All that was usual for every strange nook and cranny teenagers can sneak into to drink and fuck. There were other things, though, worse things. Inexplicable things. The skin of some animal nailed to a piece of plywood, rotting in a corner. A hunk of human hair, red and gray, stuck to the wall with some kind of paste. A wind chime of bones. Large bones. Horse, cow, deer, human, I couldn't have told you. A wand, a raw chunk of quartz held to a stick with pine tar.

What caught my eye and held it, though, was a painting on the altar. It was on canvas, crudely stretched, and it was beautiful and to me it looked ancient. In an expert hand, someone had painted sixteen figures in a forest of fir. I counted them. Sixteen figures, most in shadows, some in light, all caught in religious ecstasy. The men were nude, the women were clothed, and one clothed figure bore a mouth full of fangs. All of them were dancing like how people at a winery dance on the grapes, and they were covered to their shins and thighs in dark red juice but they were just tramping on the ground in the forest. Like the earth itself was giving up blood.

I stared and stared at that woman, with her mouth full of teeth. She looked like me. Not exactly like me. Just enough. Red hair. Freckles. Weird nose, weak chin, bright eyes. She had broader shoulders than me, though, and a higher forehead, and gray in her hair, and of course that mouth full of fangs.

Penny was screaming, frantic, searching for her brother, and I was staring at... look I have no way of proving this, I have no way of convincing you I'm telling the truth... I was staring at my father's mother's grandmother.

"Hold my belt," Penny said, breaking my trance. I looked up wide eyed and confused. Penny had one of the three lanterns in her hand, and she'd pulled off the belt from her jeans, had one end wrapped around her fist.

"What?" I asked.

"There're other passages. Only one's big enough for anyone to get through I think. Chris has to be there. What if he fell, in the dark. Oh God. What if he fell in the dark. But it's slippery, and it goes downhill, I don't want to slip. You hold me here and I think I can get far enough to peer around the corner."

Caves don't make sense. I can't say "corner of the room" because it wasn't really a room and it didn't really have a corner, but I walked to the corner of the room and braced myself against the wall and held onto Penny's belt and she slipped down a passageway with a devil's lantern. A moment later, I helped haul her back up.

"It's just... more. More cave. I don't know. What if he fell in the dark?"

She started mumbling, then. Just over and over. What if he fell in the dark.

And I couldn't tell her he didn't, because looking around the room, fell in the dark was about the best case scenario. I saw him buried in the earth so that cultists or witches or demons could tramp on the soil and his blood would bubble up onto their shins and thighs.

"We'll go for help," I said.

Penny nodded, numb, and we crawled back out of that cave together without Chris. I should have been worrying about Chris, or maybe I should have been worrying about Penny, but I was thinking about my great great great and her gray red hair and her teeth and the blood of the earth all splashed around and her teeth and I was thinking about her teeth.

◆

It wasn't two hours later before we got back there with help. Firefighters, mostly, with some cops trying to boss them around but too afraid to climb down the cliff. It was only two hours later before the cave was crawling with firefighters and four hours before a helicopter was cruising as low as it could in the gorge searching the river and its banks. As the sun set, our neighbors started combing the woods. By the next day professional cave rescue people, I don't know what you call that job, they declared the cave clear, and some other people started dredging the river.

They didn't find nothing in the woods but John the Hermit—people call him a bum but he's a hermit and he only comes into town on Christmas eve on his bicycle to buy supplies, and when he does he leaves dried flowers at every doorstep for ten miles in every direction. They arrested him.

They didn't put cuffs on him, but they arrested him all the same, and he looked at the sheriff and he smiled big and said "the devil take you" as they put him in the car. In the end they didn't charge him for Chris but I guess he put up a fuss at the station when they tried to put him in a cage. Resisting arrest, assaulting an officer, obstruction of justice, and his defense in court was telling the judge "the devil take you" and that's the last anyone saw John the Hermit, and we're all the poorer without the flowers.

They didn't find nothing in the river but trash and bones, and they were human bones, but they were old, from the twenties or thirties maybe. They weren't Chris, so maybe human bones in the river would have been news some other month but we forgot about those bones soon off.

The real thing though, the real weird thing that fucked up my head and didn't do my sense of reality any good was that they didn't find anything in the cave, either. Anything. No lanterns, no wind chimes, no mattress. No graffiti. No painting. No Chris.

They took me and Penny to the doctor and they split us up and made us each tell our story to him over and over again until neither one of us had it straight and so some of the details didn't line up, and I think if my Mom hadn't come in screaming he would have put us both up in padded rooms.

The doctor was from out of town, an expert. His skin was as white as the moon, his hair whiter than the sun reflecting off the water. He was so white you could see the veins under his skin and somehow they looked white too. His teeth were white, his clothes were white, the office he was working out of was white, and he was fucking terrifying. He held power over me so casually, threatened me so casually.

For nights after, I thought about that doctor's office as much as I thought about that cave. Two places where I almost lost my mind. Two places where I was standing on the edge like Penny standing at that passageway, trying not to fall, clinging to the belt for her life. In the cave at least we'd had each other; in the doctor's office it was just me and that man looking at each other, him trying to decide what was real and what wasn't and whether I belonged in a padded room or whether my head and my memories were prison enough.

That's how I wrote about it, anyway, in my journal. I liked to call them song lyrics, but let's be real it was poetry and shitty poetry at that, but let's be real it was just me trying to get those things out of my head.

What if Chris fell, in the dark?

◆

Penny wasn't allowed to see me, after that.

The doctor wouldn't let me on the search teams, said I wasn't healthy enough. He wanted me inside. I didn't see why his opinion should have any bearing on the matter, but my mom apparently did, so I wasn't on a search team.

My mom was working from home that summer, writing handwritten thank you letters on the behalf of politicians. Her and I weren't real close but I spent a couple days helping her cook dinner and fix things around the house and the property and just kind of living in her shadow because I didn't want to be alone.

"Where's grandma from?" I asked my mom while she was changing the oil on the station wagon and I was holding the flashlight. "I mean, dad's mom."

See, I'd never met my dad's mom before. She died of leukemia before I was born.

"Chicago," she said.

"That's where she was born? Where were her parents from?" I asked.

"Ohio."

"Before that?"

"Mostly Scottish I think."

"But did they ever live out here?"

"No, of course not."

I knew if I dug too much further she'd start asking why I was asking, and I wasn't going to talk to her about the painting, because I didn't want to get locked up. I had to be careful. It was awful, not trusting my mom. But that doctor. What if she told the doctor?

It didn't make sense. The painting, the cultists, Chris disappearing. None of it, nothing, made sense.

What if I fell in the dark?

◆

The third night after it happened, I was lying in bed praying to the devil. "Please give him back," I was saying. Everyone knows if you say it a hundred times in less than a minute, he has to do it. Problem is, he does it on his own timeline. And in his own way.

I decided to cover all my bases, so I prayed to the devil, and I prayed to God, and I went back and forth with both until I wasn't always sure which I was doing.

I was praying to the devil though when the pebbles hit my window, and I went to look out and there was Penny in the side yard, like sneaking out at night wasn't a big deal, like there wasn't a devil out there stealing children or a cop out there stealing hermits or a doctor out there threatening to steal us from each other and our families. She waved me down.

I popped out the window screen as quiet as I could and crossed over into the pine just outside. I love a pine tree, because they're built like ladders. Sticky ladders.

"Hey," I whispered when I reached the ground.

"Let's go," she said. She handed me a flashlight.

I didn't ask where. I knew where. We got on bikes and took off, only turning on our lights when we were safely away from where our parents might see.

"Have you been having nightmares?" she asked.

"Yeah," I said, even though I hadn't. I don't even know why admitting to nightmares would have been impressive, but I found myself saying it anyway. "Well, no. I haven't been sleeping well enough to dream."

"I've been having nightmares," she said.

"What are they?"

"It's Chris. He's down there still. He fell, in the dark. In my dreams, he's drinking from a little stream, and he's eating moss and crickets, and he's scared."

"What about the graffiti, and the bones, and the painting?" I asked.

"I... hate to say it but I think he got kidnapped. I think a cult was living down there, and they snuck out while we were getting help, and they cleaned it all up. It's the only thing that makes sense."

"Maybe we didn't see all that stuff," Penny said. "Maybe the doctor was right."

I skidded my bike to a halt. Penny stopped too, looking back at me, confused.

"That doctor is not right. Not about what happened to us. Not about anything."

Penny was crying. She came over. We walked our bikes to the side of the road and sat down, and she put her head onto my shoulder, and she cried a little more.

"Okay," she said.

"We've got to believe ourselves," I said. "We saw what we saw. They're telling us we didn't because they don't want it to be true. Because it doesn't make sense. But it was there."

"I'll believe you, if you believe me," Penny said.

"What do you need me to believe?" I asked.

"Chris is still alive."

"Okay," I said. "Okay. I'll believe you."

"I believe you too," she said. "We saw all that stuff we saw."

"I almost wish you didn't."

The moon was waning but large and we cast moonshadows across the road, and we sat like that for a while before we kept biking to the devil's shack.

The ladder was gone, but Penny had rope and we climbed down to the cave. We crawled in, and with flashlights and rope we searched more and more of the cave. Nothing. No one. Some soot, though, above the altar, was enough for me to believe myself. We'd seen what we'd seen.

On the altar in the first room, Penny left water and a peanut butter and jelly and potato chip sandwich. It didn't make sense, but I didn't argue. We crawled out of the cave, and we climbed back up to the devil's shack, where you're not supposed to go at night.

We stood in the shack and looked out over the gorge, and I didn't know what the devil was and I didn't know where he lived but maybe he lived in the gorge or maybe no one did.

We got back on our bikes and made it home just as birds started calling out, and I saw my dad leave the house and get into his truck on his way to work, his headlights cutting the rising fog of the morning. I scrambled up the pine and crawled into bed, every bit of me sore and cut and covered in mud and sap.

◆

We went back the next night, and in the room, the main room with the altar and everything, only the crust remained of the sandwich.

"He's alive," Penny declared, and this time I didn't have to work at it to believe her. "He hates the crust."

"If we tell our parents," I said.

"They won't believe us," Penny agreed. "Right to the padded room."

"What do we do?"

"We find him," Penny said.

We didn't find him that night, though we spent hours in the cave. I crawled into bed at dawn.

Two weeks passed that way. Every night the sandwich was eaten. Penny left notes, each one taken. Penny left a pen and paper, but no message was ever written for us. We searched every inch of the cave we could reach. There were a few cracks too narrow even for us scattered around the place. There was a hole, the devil's hole, that I could probably have fit down that went down and down and down but there was nowhere good to tie a rope.

We talked about spending the day in the cave, but our parents would notice us missing, freak out, send authorities, and we'd get dragged off to an institution without ever having found him.

Finally, on our fifteenth trip—we marked tallies on the paper we left—Penny told me her parents were going to have a funeral. In Portland. They were giving up and moving. Tomorrow.

"We have to tell your parents," I said. "It doesn't matter if we get locked up, if they find him."

"No," Penny said. "*We* have to find him."

This time, she brought rock pitons and more rope. She'd shoplifted it all from the adventure sports store the next town over. She'd hitch-hiked there. Fuck, she was perfect.

We made our way to the devil's hole. Penny wouldn't fit, so she helped me into a harness. She hammered pitons into cracks in the wall, and the noise was louder than anything had a right to be, each strike like a gunshot. She tied the rope to it, and that was maybe enough to keep me safe.

"Ready?" she asked.

I nodded, and lowered myself into the hole. Head first, I decided. Fuck it. Better to see what's coming.

It was like crawling vertically, in parts. Other parts I slid as Penny fed more rope. I went down. And down. And down.

The white noise of water rose up from below me. The hole went to the bottom of the gorge, I was certain.

I went down and down and then my flashlight caught a crystalline wall and the world exploded into light and suddenly my head broke free into a huge open chamber over a river. I braced myself as best I could, then gave one tug on the rope. One tug for stop, two for bring me up.

Crystals covered the walls, or maybe the walls themselves were crystals, or the entire world, entire universe, was those crystals, and there were facets to everything and everything caught the light. Everything shone.

There was a ledge jutting out from the wall, down close to the river, and there was the painting, and there was the hair, and there were bones and skins and crystals. No one was there, but I saw figures everywhere I looked.

I'd barely slept for weeks, my mind was torn apart by trauma, and peering into that room I had an epiphany, or I broke, or the devil broke me.

While I watched the water and the light, and God or the devil flowed through the chamber, I watched three people emerge, wading in the water. None of them was Chris. Two women and a man. Teenagers, maybe five years older than me. One had a Slayer shirt, and they were fifty feet below me and they had lanterns, one each, and they were laughing. I couldn't hear them over the water but I could see their faces and they were laughing and they were passing a bottle and one held the crystal wand aloft. They waved at me, and they passed through the chamber, up the river out the other side.

Two tugs, and Penny lifted me up, which took longer than I'd been alive. My head swam with thought and non-thought.

I tried to describe what I'd seen to Penny, but once she heard I hadn't seen Chris she stopped listening, like I'd knocked the wind out of her.

We made it back to the first room, and she went somberly to the altar to leave the night's sandwich.

Someone had written "The Three Trees" on the paper, while we'd been there.

Penny grabbed the paper, folded it, and put it in her pocket. She turned to me, her eyes alight. "Chris's handwriting," she said. "I used to copy it when I did his homework for him."

I was still reeling from the room at the bottom of the devil's hole and the world was upside down from where it had been and all of a sudden I realized it wasn't about me. None of this was about me. It wasn't about impressing Penny. It wasn't even about Penny, not really. It was about Chris. It was about finding that kid and making sure he didn't die and making sure there were so many more years in front of him where he could talk his big sister into doing his homework and there were so many years of eating sandwiches and just living life not in a fucking cave in the bottom of Gosset's Gorge and just...

"We have to find him," I said, and for the first time I really meant it, not for my sake not even for Penny's sake.

"No shit," she said.

We made it out of the cave and up to our bikes but the sun was already on its way over the mountains.

"Shit," Penny said. "My parents said we were gonna leave at dawn."

"They'll know you're gone."

"This is the first place they'll look," she said.

We got to our bikes and started up the trail but it wasn't long before we heard people coming from in front of us and we ducked into the trees.

Penny's parents, and that sheriff, the one who'd stolen John the Hermit, the only person I'd ever seen actually steal a person with my own eyes.

We waited breathless for them to pass then hurried to the road. It was an hour on bike to the Three Trees, and we got there in forty-five. The sun was over the mountains now, filtered through the forest. The ropes hung like they always hung, knotted strange, down from the boughs of the trees.

I hurried up the rope, and Penny came after.

There was the tagalong, sitting calm as death on the platform, covered with mud and pine, whistling a dissonant tune.

"Chris," Penny said.

He didn't stop whistling, and Penny sat down next to him.

"Chris," Penny said. He didn't respond.

She freaked out. I didn't blame her. "Chris!" she shouted, pounding his chest with her fists.

I sat across from him, and I looked into his eyes, and they caught light like crystals.

"I saw the devil's chamber," I said. "It's beautiful."

Chris looked at me, and stopped whistling.

"Did you see the devil's maidens? The three?" he asked.

"Penny thought you fell," I said, instead of answering, "in the dark. But you didn't, did you?"

"I was rescued," he said.

"By the maidens."

"By the maidens," he agreed. "They took me to the chamber and I saw the light and I heard the water and I went under the water. I learned the truth. The devil is real, and we are his maidens, and for as long as there's been a world there's been the devil."

"The painting?" I asked.

"As long as there's been a world there's been a devil, as long as there's been a devil there's been his maidens. We are, each of us, the devil's maidens. A million names, a million meanings, a million cultures, but a devil, a devil, a world, a world, a maiden, a maiden, and blood."

I nodded.

"Is that what you'll be?" I asked. "A servant to the devil?"

"Yes," he answered. He looked at me. "Will you?"

When he asked me, I felt like I was still dangling in that room of light. I'd never felt more real, more connected to everything, to my body, to death, than I had in that moment.

"Yes. I will be the devil's maiden."

"Will you tie the knots that hold the trees?" he asked.

"I will."

"Will you fix the door that holds us warm?" he asked.

"I will."

"Will you guard the room that sings of the river and light?" he asked.

"I will."

"For all time?" he asked.

"No," I answered.

"No?"

"Look at me, Chris," I said. Chris looked at me. "I will be the devil's maiden, same as you, same as those three, but that's not all I'll be. I'll be myself, too."

"You're allowed to do that?" He was suddenly a child again.

"We're allowed to do anything we want," I told him. "The devil isn't real. God isn't real. The world is real, and we are real, and we can serve anything we'd like. We can serve God, the devil, the earth, ourselves, each other."

"You served me," Chris said. "For these past two weeks, you served me."

"Penny did," I said. "I served her. No, I served myself. I should have been serving her, or you, but it's all the same, too."

Penny put her arm around her brother, and he collapsed into her, crying. Whatever spell had held him was broken.

"I want to go home," he whispered.

"Then we'll go home," Penny said.

◆

I didn't see Penny for three days after that. The reunion was kind of all-consuming for her family. But on the fourth day, late in the evening, she met me at my front door, and she had sleeping bags.

"Tell your parents you and I are going camping," she said.

"I don't know if my mom will let me," I said.

"Okay, then don't tell them," she answered.

"Mom, I'm going camping with Penny! Be back tomorrow!" I shouted, then Penny grabbed my hand and the two of us took off running before my mom could stop us.

If she really wanted, she could have found us. She could have figured out where we were going. We went to the devil's shack.

This time, Chris didn't come with us.

We went to the devil's shack, and the rafters were whistling. They were whistling that dissonant tune Chris had been singing.

"What are we doing here?" I asked.

"We're going to meet the maidens," Penny said. "And thank them for taking care of my brother."

"What do you mean?"

"I talked to Chris more," Penny said. "He really had fallen, in the dark. That was the scream we heard. The maidens, they rescued him. Washed his wounds, kept him fed and warm. Brainwashed him a little yeah sure, but they saved his life, and they let him go, too."

"Oh," I said.

"Besides," Penny said, "I think you promised to work with them."

"Well, maybe a little," I agreed.

She kissed me on the cheek.

"You're a charming enough maiden," she said.

"Tell me," I asked, once we laid our sleeping bags on the floor of the Devil's Shack, the one place one must never, ever sleep, "what's your opinion on the current popularity of bisexuality among teenaged girls?"

THE FREE ORCS OF CASCADIA

You all know the first part of the story: The song ended in blood. It was two years ago. Rick Green, the singer of Goblin Forest, crooned in his Osbourne-esque voice to 15,000 Goblin Metal fans. A short man wearing green body paint and brown leather stepped out from backstage, drew a sword, and cut the singer down from behind. The last lyrics Green ever sang were: "Take me back, take me back, take me back to the Misty Mountains."

The man with the sword, of course, was Golfimbul—the rhythm guitarist for Krimpatul, the opening act. He and his bandmates escaped in the ensuing chaos and remain at large to this day.

Neither band has released a song or played a show since. The rest of Goblin Forest decided to call it quits without Green, and Krimpatul... No one knew what happened to Krimpatul. Fans deserted the genre in droves, and overnight Goblin Metal went from a stadium-rock fad to a niche interest of the obscure Cascadian orc cults where it originated. It was no longer hip to be green. If Golfimbul had been trying to take the Goblin Metal throne, as it were, he failed spectacularly.

Rumors have flown about motives and locations, but there've been no arrests and no public statement from the band. All we've had to work with have been rumors.

Until now.

Earlier this month, Orc Folk act Alsarath listed Golfimbul as the harpist in the liner notes of their single, "The Gray Fog of a Ruined Forest." Alsarath was as obscure as Krimpatul was infamous. The band had never done an interview; not even a photoshoot. Like everyone else these days in countercultural music, their videos feature only masked performers.

I've been casually obsessed with post-civilization culture ever since the 2020 communique from the junkyard rats of the Rust Belt, and I've covered the music of pretty much every secessionist movement and subculture I could get my teeth into since. After I saw those liner notes, I put out feelers to friends and friends-of-friends, and I waited, and last week I was invited to go to an orc village hidden away in the burned forests of Cascadia.

I was invited to be the first person to tell Golfimbul's story. A Hellfire Harriet exclusive. Usually, I post full interviews for everyone but reserve my travel diary for the patrons of my blog. This time, though, I'm forgoing that. This story is too important, so I've interspersed the two below.

All I knew before I went was what everyone else knew: Three years ago, a bunch of metalheads and hippies and burners and nerds all decided to dress up like orcs and goblins, and some of them took it too far and decided to distance themselves from the rest of society. They got really famous one summer, then that fame died in a single bloody act, and who knows what kind of weird shit they're up to now?

Before you get worried, no, I would never offer a platform to a fascist. Fascism, it turns out, is the furthest thing from Golfimbul's mind. What he's into is *a lot* weirder than that.

Still, it's sort of lucky that I survived to write this story.

◆

Hellfire Harriet: So...you killed a guy.
    Golfimbul: I killed a guy.

We stared in silence at one another for a while. He wore rawhide and fur and not much of either. He wasn't painted up, but his skin was a sort of natural olive. His lower teeth were filed down to fangs, like any serious orc's. There was still something unassuming about him that I have a hard time describing.

Golfimbul: You're waiting for me to tell you about it, aren't you?

The interview was not off to a good start.

Hellfire: Are you worried about how your words will sound in court?
    Golfimbul: I killed Rick Green on stage, with a sword, in front of thousands of witnesses. Talking to the media isn't going to make anything worse for me at this point. And I don't respect the authority of

the US government to hold me accountable for my actions—I will not go to court.

Hellfire: So why'd you do it?

Golfimbul: The old world is dying. My world—the free orcs of Cascadia—we're not going to replace the old world, but we will be part of its replacement. In order to do that, we have to take ourselves seriously. An element of that struggle is the struggle to create meaning, to create a new sacred. I killed Rick Green because he was defiling something meant to be sacred.

Hellfire: How so?

Golfimbul: We share an aesthetic, but he didn't understand what it meant to be an orc.

Hellfire: You killed him because he was a poser.

Golfimbul: I guess you could put it like that.

Hellfire: So...the lesson here is...don't be a poser.

Golfimbul: Don't be a poser.

You heard it here first, kids. Don't be a poser, or Golfimbul will literally murder you.

They picked me up in the parking lot of Grocery Outlet in Northeast Portland. That's a mundane detail, I suppose, but perhaps the single most remarkable thing about my trip was the ever-present contrast between mundanity and the bizarre. I bought a case of coconut water while I waited. Orcs might like coconut water. Who doesn't like coconut water?

They showed up in a mid-teens Honda Civic sedan, and I'd been hoping for something out of *Mad Max*. The two women who got out—one cis, one trans, both white—were dressed in clean gray tank tops and leggings like half the women who live in Portland. To be honest, I only noticed them in the parking lot at all because the trans woman was cute.

"Hellfire?" the cis woman asked. She was tall and severe, with the fierce but almost-trustworthy look of a loan shark. Or, as it turned out, of an orcish enforcer.

"That's me," I said.

"Fenrick." The cis woman offered her name but no handshake, fist bump, or hug.

I nodded.

"Norinda," the trans woman said. Like a lot of trans women these days, she didn't bother to feminize her voice. Her name sounded familiar, but I couldn't place it.

"How is this going to work?" I asked.

"We're going to drive around back, where no one can see us," Fenrick said. "We're going to take your phone and laptop and any electronics and put them in a Faraday in the car. Then we're going to put you in the trunk and drive out to the forest. We'll provide you with a recorder and a notebook when we arrive. You'll get your stuff back when you leave."

I nodded. I'd pretty much expected this.

"Do you need to use the bathroom?" Norinda asked. "Have any medical conditions we should know about?"

"No and no," I said. "Either of you want a coconut water?"

Hellfire Harriet: Goblin Forest sang in English, but Krimpatul's lyrics were all in Tolkien's Black Speech—

Golfimbul: Dark Speech. Our lyrics were in Dark Speech.

Hellfire: Tolkien referred to the language as Black Speech.

Golfimbul: Tolkien meant well but he was about the most influential unconsciously racist author of the twentieth century. All his villains were either green or Middle Eastern. When you engage with the work of historical authors, especially when you make derivative works a century later, you have to adapt to one's own social context. Calling the language "Black Speech" today is, at best, wildly misleading. Its name is a translation anyway. It's possible that "Dark Speech" is just as accurate.

Besides, Tolkien didn't write the language. He only wrote, like, sixteen words or something. We wrote the rest. Most of us prefer to translate the name of it as "Dark Speech."

Hellfire: Since when are murderers PC?

Golfimbul: My status as a person who has ended the life of another person carries no implications about my personal ethics other than that I clearly believe there are circumstances under which it's okay to kill someone.

◆

Imagine being at the Renaissance Faire when the apocalypse hits, and you're stuck trying to recreate society surrounded by swords and minstrels and thees and thous. You know how that sounds like either heaven or hell, depending on who you are and also who you're stuck there with?

That was my first impression of the village of Gray Morrow. The fires out west have burned forest after forest and small town after small town, and no one tries to deny that pretty much every bioregion on the planet is going through a transformation right now. It's in the worst spots, these dead ecologies, that the post-civilization movement has found its roots. Like wildflowers growing up between paving stones. Or rats hiding in the walls, I guess. Depending on who you ask.

Gray Morrow sits in the scorched graveyard of a Douglas fir forest, halfway up a mountain, occupying the remains of an evacuated town. Slab foundations are all that remain of the original structures. A seasonal creek runs through what was recently a riverbed at the edge of the village, and long-abandoned train tracks skirt the ridge above town. Even armed with all of that information, you'd still have at least seventy or eighty possible spots to search.

Satellite imagery would help, of course. I can't imagine that the Big Six Techs or the US Government don't know where Gray Morrow is. The residents of Gray Morrow in general, and Golfimbul in particular, had an awful lot to lose by letting me write this report.

Norinda let me out of the trunk, and she smiled when she saw me. Her bottom teeth were filed. That should have been unnerving, but I've always been a sucker for face tattoos or anything that really shows someone is going for broke. Fenrick just stared at me, severe. Being severe was pretty much her thing, as far as I could tell. She took a sip from her coconut water.

Three other cars filled a makeshift parking lot. The village itself was surrounded by a wall built from blackened logs, set upright and buried in the ruins of the road.

My escorts had changed clothes en route. Fenrick looked like a bandit out of *Skyrim*, complete with iron pauldron on one shoulder and hand ax strapped to her belt. I won't lie, it was a good look. I'm no fashion reporter, but I figure half the magazines in New York would love to get someone out here to take pictures of orcs like her.

Norinda wore a simple, modest dress of undyed wool. Imagine a Viking kindergarten teacher who also wears a rather large dagger horizontally on her belt at the small of her back. My crush on her intensified. She handed me a spiral notebook and an old-fashioned digital recorder, and we walked into the village.

◆

Hellfire Harriet: A lot of people say you killed Rick Green because you were jealous of Goblin Forest's success. That the orcish code insisted that if you wanted the throne, you had to kill the reigning monarch.

Golfimbul stopped fidgeting and stared directly at me, his dark brown eyes boring into me.

Golfimbul: That's bullshit.
Hellfire: I'm sorry?
Golfimbul: It's, like, three layers deep of bullshit.

He was still staring at me. I was starting to regret this line of questioning.

Golfimbul: Okay, to start, there are pretty much two ways to interpret the orcish code of honor. It's not written down anywhere, but there're some strong central themes. Like an interdependence between individual sovereignty and collective identity. We value strength, but the idea is that everyone develops their own strengths, whatever they might be, for the benefit of all. One should be as self-reliant as one is able to be, both for one's own sake and, again, for the community's sake. I care deeply about this. That same basic idea, though, can be interpreted two different ways.
Hellfire: So there's a split in the orc community?
Golfimbul: Damn right there's a split. The Free Orcs are matriarchal and the Orcine are patriarchal.

Golfimbul produced a cigarette from god knows where, considering how little he was wearing, and lit it with a lighter from the same mysterious origin. It wasn't tobacco. It wasn't weed. Maybe mugwort?

Golfimbul: The matriarchal way of interpreting those tenets is roughly anarchist. It's anti-authoritarian and anti-nationalist, at the very least. We respect the wisdom of elders, children, and women—self-identifying women—but the hierarchy is anything but rigid, and the guidelines are anything but laws. Most importantly, our sense of community or tribe is fluid. Gray Morrow is a Free Orc village.

Go fifteen miles southeast and you'll find a larger village, Lonely Mountain. They're Orcine. The patriarchal way of interpreting orcish tenets is, roughly, fascistic. Authority is absolute. Rank within the hierarchy affects every aspect of one's life. It's not racialized, but it's nationalistic—there are very specific considerations of who is and isn't a part of any given social grouping. And definitions of "strength" tend to skew toward boring shit like physical size and power.

Hellfire: So you'd tell any doubters that you weren't trying to claim the goblin throne because your faction of orcs doesn't work that way?

Golfimbul: *No* orcish culture works that way. Even those fascistic shits don't work that way. Among the Orcine, if you kill your superior, people aren't going to just suddenly start kissing your ass. They will literally flay you and turn your skin into a battle flag. You advance in rank by demonstrating your capacity to lead. This isn't some fucking Hollywood bullshit—evil is a lot more banal than that.

I didn't have the heart—or maybe the courage—to tell him that, to me, to pretty much any outsider, Hollywood bullshit is exactly what the whole place looked like.

Hellfire: When you say "battle flag," what do you mean? Who do they do battle with?

Golfimbul: Us. The Free Orcs.

Hellfire: Are you at war?

Golfimbul: For the very soul of our culture.

Hellfire: How'd that start?

Golfimbul: When I cut down Rick Green, the Mountain King.

Hellfire: You killed him because he was the leader of a rival faction, then? Not because he was a poser?

Golfimbul: They weren't a rival faction until I killed him, but sure. He *was* a poser, though. All fascists are posers.

Hellfire: Did you go on tour with Goblin Forest specifically to murder him?

Golfimbul: Yeah, probably.

Hellfire: What do you mean, probably? That was a very specific question about a very specific intention.

Golfimbul: I mean, I guess. I'd been thinking about killing him for a while. It was premeditated and it wasn't, you know?

Hellfire: No, I don't know, because I've never killed anyone.

Golfimbul: So it's like, I've known Rick Green almost five years. He and I and maybe thirty other people, we started this whole thing. Goblin Metal, the orcs, all of that. Rick Green's always been a fucking bastard. I figured I'd probably kill him one day for being kind of a nazi or whatever. Then we go on tour together, and I tell myself, hey, if this goes badly, I can always just kill him on stage. You've got to understand, orc culture wasn't even a year old at that point. We weren't split into the Free Orcs and the Orcine yet; there were only maybe five villages total. We were just starting to explore what it meant to be ourselves, what kind of culture we could build. Then while we were on tour, I hear he's got himself crowned the Mountain King.

And this isn't a game. I don't know how to get that through to you or your readers. This is our life. It's one thing to put on a silly hat and pretend to tell people what to do in some LARP somewhere, but Rick Green had gotten himself coronated for real. Dictator. Over actual people. So I killed him. The Free Orcs split off, the Orcine closed ranks, and we've been at war ever since.

Hellfire: Am I safe here?

He didn't answer me. At least he didn't stare me down again. He just looked off into the distance, maybe toward Lonely Mountain.

◆

I've been to LARPs before where, when you show up, they make you put on garb. That is to say, they make you wear period-appropriate clothes, or whatever weird interpretation of period-appropriate that particular group of LARPers had come up with.

As I met the denizens of the village—they all came out to the parking lot to introduce themselves—I realized that they didn't insist on anything like that because *they weren't LARPing*. Pretty much every one of them was dressed either like a Viking reenactor or a fantasy game villain, but it wasn't an act.

About thirty adults and eight kids lived there, running the age gamut from six months to seventy-eight years. They told me their names and pronouns—about a third told me "she," a third "he," and a third "they." Many of them were white or passed as such, but a significant minority were black.

Norinda told me later that there are orc villages with substantially higher proportions of people of color. That might be true, but I got the impression she said it to convince herself or me that the Free Orcs aren't a specifically white phenomenon. No one (no one decent) likes looking around their community or scene and seeing only white faces smiling back.

After everyone introduced themselves, I immediately forgot all their names. There are only so many fantasy names like Lazari and Demolan you can hear before they all just sound the same.

Norinda and Fenrick flanked me as we walked through a gate in the wall and into the village. It's strange to say "village" in America. We don't really have villages here. But in some ways, Gray Morrow isn't the United States. And to be certain, it was a village. Maybe ten or fifteen houses crowded together along either side of a single, potholed street. Two architectural styles reigned: junkyard shacks built out of railroad cars and regular cars, and traditional American log cabins. Many of them were adorned with solar panels. At the end of the street, near the back palisade, the beginnings of a stone tower stood fifteen feet high.

I wasn't sure if I was impressed or not. On one hand, the village couldn't have been around longer than three or four years, and they'd already done so much. On the other hand? It was filthy. Everyone was filthy. I'm kind of obsessed with the post-civilization movement, so I wish I could tell you that everyone looked well fed and happy. They didn't. People looked proud, and they didn't look miserable, but there was an intensity in everyone's eyes you simply could not mistake for happiness. A trash pile needed tending near the front gate and some of the animal hides stretched for tanning had begun to rot. Everything looked like it was about to fall apart both physically and metaphorically.

"What now?" I asked, when we reached the central square—a stone-cobbled chunk of what had once been an intersection now decorated with poorly tended gardens and rustic benches of dubious quality.

"You're here to interview Golfimbul, are you not?" Fenrick asked.

"I am."

"Golfimbul doesn't live here."

I waited for her to elaborate.

"Golfimbul lives in the forest with the rest of his band. He's on his way—he'll meet you a bit outside of town. I'll take you to him when he gets here."

Someone near the gate shouted, and both of my escorts flinched bodily and turned to look. It was just a kid, chasing another kid with a wooden sword.

Fenrick and Norinda were on edge. Something was about to happen.

◆

Hellfire Harriet: Tell me about your new band. Alsarath. What does the name mean?

Golfimbul: Alsarath is the Dark Speech word for the phase of the moon on the last night before the new moon. The last sliver of light. Alsarath is a holy day, a day of self-reflection. Our band's music attempts to capture that spirit of self-reflection. On Alsarath, we listen to our naysayer and think about ourselves and our community.

Hellfire: Your naysayer?

Golfimbul: Free Orcish villages don't have leaders, we have naysayers. Two years ago, we tried rotating leadership. It was ineffectual. We didn't need leaders. We stuck with it anyway, because we felt like we had to, because those were the rules we had come up with. Then one person said, basically, "This is bullshit. We don't need someone to tell us what to do. We need someone to tell us what to *stop* doing. We need someone to tell us what we're doing wrong." Every new moon, every village picks a new naysayer. That person spends the month picking apart group structures, observing what's happening, being critical. On Alsarath, we fast and listen to the naysayer. They don't offer solutions, necessarily, but instead bring our problems to light.

Hellfire: Does that work?

Golfimbul: Surprisingly well. Except about a third of the naysayers end up leaving after their month. Some go to other villages, some go to live in the forest—like Norinda, Alsarath's singer, did—but most "leave the woods," as we put it. Most go back to civilization.

Hellfire: That's why Norinda's name sounded familiar when she introduced herself. To be honest, I saw your name listed in the liner notes and didn't pay much attention to the rest.

Golfimbul: That's an argument for me to take my name off our next release, if there is one.

Hellfire: Why did you put it on there in the first place? Why did you agree to this interview? And what do you mean, "if there is one"?

Golfimbul: I told you we're at war.

Hellfire: Yeah.

Golfimbul: We're losing that war.

He took a deep breath, trying to keep himself calm. He didn't strike me as a man who was afraid to cry, but he was clearly trying to keep his composure.

Golfimbul: There's no way that Gray Morrow would have let you talk to me here if any of us thought that Gray Morrow had a future. There's no way I would have talked to you at all if I thought I was going to be alive to see another Alsarath.

Hellfire: Why are you losing? Why are you going to die?

Golfimbul: It's not a question of military efficacy, or of bravery or strength or any of that shit. It's just a question of numbers. Orcine society is a military society; every member fights. As far as we can tell, they've got fifteen hundred warriors. We've got five hundred.

Hellfire: So use guerrilla tactics?

Golfimbul shook his head.

Golfimbul: Striking Rick Green down from behind was a cowardly action. I can justify it—almost—by the fact that Green had declared himself my monarch. But the Orcine warriors are my peers. They would not stalk me in the night. I will not stalk them.

Hellfire: That sounds—

Golfimbul: I know how it sounds.

Hellfire: So this interview?

Golfimbul: I want to be remembered. I want the Free Orcs of Cascadia to be remembered. I put my name on the liner notes so that someone like you—an antifascist music blogger—would talk to me. I leveraged my own infamy to draw attention to what we're doing, what we've done.

Hellfire: I fucking hate the tragic utopian trope.

Golfimbul: What?

Hellfire: Like, seriously. Fuck you, okay? I know I'm here as a journalist, but I'm not here to write your fucking obituary.

I don't think I've ever turned on an interview subject like that before.

Hellfire: I get it. Hopeless causes are beautiful. But as I understand it, the whole goddammed point of holding on to your honor more firmly than your life is because the world is a better place for everyone if more people did that, right?

Golfimbul: Okay...

Hellfire: The world isn't a goddammed better place if you let your subculture—and I'm sorry, I know it's very serious and I'm not trying to downplay it, but that's what this is, a musical subculture—be taken over by fucking nazis. And I respect that you're going to fight them for it, that's cool. But have you considered buying some guns? Maybe a few drones? They'll come in here with spears, right? And you'll fight them off with other spears? It's the twenty-first century, man, there are fucking nazis everywhere. If you don't give a shit about going to jail or dying, then fucking shoot the nazis who are trying to kill you.

Golfimbul: You don't understand.

Hellfire: You're fucking right. I don't.

◆

If I'm being honest, most of the time I was waiting, I spent flirting with Norinda and avoiding talking to Fenrick. Norinda asked me to keep our conversation off the record. We didn't talk about Gray Morrow or the orc thing much anyway—everything I learned about the village and its culture I learned by observation only.

An elderly man came by and offered us cold tea in wooden mugs. "Steeped blackberry leaves, sweetened with juice from the berries," he said. "No caffeine, no other particularly strong medicinal effects."

The three of us took cups from his platter and he continued down the street, passing out drinks.

No one else approached us. I watched people go about their lives, though the tension in the air was thick. I saw a few people look at cell phones, and I spent a not-inconsiderable amount of time trying to decide if that was hypocritical and/or bad OPSEC. Eventually, I gave up because frankly it wasn't my business and one of the most interesting things about all the post-civilization groups is all the bits and pieces they choose to carry over from mainstream culture.

Finally, after an hour, Fenrick stood up. "Come with me."

I followed her to the other side of town and out through a smaller gate. On the other side, a box truck that had seen better days sat on a road that had, too. We skirted around the truck and up into the black forest.

The scorched hills look more like meadows than forests, with green grass and undergrowth broken only by the black spikes of burned trees. We followed the path this way and that, and soon I was lost. Soon after that, fog set in.

I was further through the looking-glass than I'd realized. I imagined us lost, a mile from a town full of people who give a double meaning to the word "stranger" and probably at least an hour's drive from civilization. My guard hadn't shown me much in the way of kindness, and I was on my way to meet someone I knew to be a murderer.

It's the kind of shit I live for, if I'm being honest. I love my stupid fucking weird job and the stupid fucking weird world we live in. Thank you, my readers, for making that possible for me. Be sure to check out my Patreon page if this is the first thing you've read by me. Lots of members-only content over there, including a few snippets of orc song from Norinda.

The only thing I saw in the distance was a single black spire, thicker than the dead snags around me. As we approached, it came into focus as a boulder, jutting up into the sky like an angry finger. Sitting at the base of it was a short man with a sword across his lap.

Golfimbul.

"I'll leave you two to it," Fenrick said.

She left me alone with an armed murderer.

I sat down across from him, took out the notebook and recorder, and asked him questions.

◆

Hellfire Harriet: Alright. Convince me.

Golfimbul: We can't fight them dishonorably, because you can't protect an idea by defiling that idea. We don't want them to destroy our way of life, but we don't want to destroy our way of life ourselves, either.

Hellfire: The basic problem with the Orcine is that they're interpreting your code of honor to mean "might makes right," yeah?

Golfimbul: Yes.

Hellfire: By facing them in open battle and nobly dying or whatever your goddammed plan is, you're just letting might make right. You're letting their superior numbers dictate what your culture has to look like. It's like majority voting but even dumber because more people die.

I expected him to double down on his position. Most men would.

Golfimbul: What do you suggest instead?

Hellfire: Fuck, I don't know. Don't be here when they attack. Go somewhere else. Stay on the move. Build your strength. Oh, shit. That's what Rick Green was doing, wasn't it?

Golfimbul: Huh?

Hellfire: Goblin Forest, singing in English, a stupid name like Rick Green...All that shit was designed to make Goblin Metal more palatable to the masses. To get fans. To get recruits. For his stupid fucking fashy goals.

Golfimbul: Yup.

Hellfire: Do that. I don't mean become fascists or change your name or make your music worse—everyone knows Goblin Forest didn't have shit on Krimpatul. Just...don't be obscure for the sake of being obscure. Fucking advertise. You have a decent thing going here. People are abandoning mainstream society left and right. No political pun intended. Make it easier for them to get here. Make it so that when you fight the fash in your epic spears-and-swords Viking death match, you win. Better yet, make it so they don't even want to fuck with you because they know they'll lose.

Golfimbul: I don't know whether that would work.

Hellfire: Yeah, but dying doesn't work, either.

Golfimbul: The orc way of life isn't meant to be some revolution. It's not meant to supplant the mainstream. It will never appeal to the mainstream, not without losing its soul. Would you live like this? Would you want to?

Hellfire: You're right. I'm obsessed with you weird cultures but I wouldn't want to live like you.

We both stared at each other in silence. It wasn't an uncomfortable silence. We were just both thinking.

Hellfire: Okay. Scrap that. You're never going to get big numbers. You don't need big numbers, you don't want big numbers. You don't need recruits. You need allies.

Golfimbul: What would that look like?

Hellfire: God damn, do all orcish men know how to actually listen to women's ideas? I'm used to guys just talking over me, or shutting down completely if I get mad.

Golfimbul: Free Orcish men, I would hope, know how to listen.

Hellfire: Guns would break the spell. And the spell that you're casting here? It's powerful. It's good. So no guns. Other people have guns, though. Let those people stand guard. Or make their armed presence known outside Orcine camps. Other people have access to, say, doxing. How many recruits are the Orcine going to get if every time some wannabe forest nazi dude joins, someone tells his mother what they're about? Or access to the media: How many recruits are going to join if everyone knows that the Orcine are posers, putting out substandard, watered-down Goblin Metal just to try to lure in impressionable military-aged men to fight their holy war?

Golfimbul: You'll write those stories?

Hellfire: I'm not going to write you any propaganda, but sure, I'll tell the truth.

Golfimbul: How do we get allies?

Hellfire: Put out another single, maybe a full-length. "The Gray Fog of a Ruined Forest" was the best shit I've heard in years. You're redefining folk music just like you redefined metal. Put out shit like that and I'll cover it. Talk to more press—maybe someone other than you. Not everyone's going to be sympathetic to what you did, even if that guy was a fucking tree nazi.

A hunting horn cut through the fog and through our conversation and my subject's face fell into despair for half a second before determination took over.

Hellfire: What's that?
Golfimbul: Interview's over. I thought there would be more time. Another day, at least. We have to get you out of here.

◆

Turns out, Fenrick had taken us on a purposefully circuitous route into the woods. It wasn't a quarter of a mile straight downhill before Golfimbul and I reached the box truck at the back entrance to Gray Morrow.

Norinda and Fenrick stood there talking with a kid, maybe fifteen, who was out of breath. She was dressed in scraps of fur and leather and cloth, like you might imagine a medieval beggar. It wasn't until I noticed all the twigs and sticks and moss tangled up with the fabrics that I recognized it as camouflage.

"I saw about thirty," the scout—for that's what she was—said.

"About?" Fenrick asked.

"Exactly thirty. Ten with pikes, ten with tower shields and swords, five archers, two scouts, two command. One noncombatant, I'd guess a surgeon but I couldn't promise."

"How far away?" I asked.

Fenrick glared at me for interrupting.

"Five miles," Norinda said. "Probably three and a half by now. Downhill from here. We have time to get you out with the children and the elders."

That scout had just run five miles, uphill. Because she was too stubborn to use a walkie-talkie or a cell phone.

"We should evacuate everyone," Golfimbul said.

"What?" Fenrick asked. "We've got walls and almost even numbers. Fuck them. This is our home."

I wanted to shout at her. I wanted to shake her, to tell her that it wasn't a fucking game, and that it wasn't the twelfth century, and that killing people or dying over some squatted chunk of nowhere was somewhere between stupid and reprehensible. I didn't, though. I'm a good journalist.

"This isn't the place for us to debate this," Norinda said, and all four of them walked through the gate and left me standing by the truck.

That was why the gardens were untended and the trash was piled up and the hides were left to rot. They were expecting this. They'd lost their will to pretend like their lives were going to continue to progress forward.

I'm not the first to suggest that nihilism is the dominant affect of society today. With climate change destroying communities and bioregions all over the map, with the economic crisis deepening and the wealth gap widening, I think all of us are guilty of forgetting to tend our gardens. All of us have a hard time figuring out why it matters whether or not we deal with our trash. All of us have proverbial or literal nazis marching on us.

The nazis the Free Orcs of Cascadia are dealing with are of the literal variety.

Some cosplaying fascist was about to stick a sword between Norinda's ribs. Bile rose in my throat. I don't believe in love at first sight or any of that shit, but I just couldn't handle the idea.

I fucking hate honor.

I will never be an orc.

I got lost running through solutions to the problem of hypothetical arrows and swords that were going to interfere with Norinda's continued existence. Most of those solutions involved assault rifles, which I didn't have access to. Cars, though, were available. What's thirty warriors in medieval armor versus one station wagon driven by an angry woman with a lead foot? I put the odds in my favor.

I wasn't going to do it, though.

Instead, I waited to evacuate. I don't think that speaks well of me.

Individually and in groups, people came out through the gate and loaded bags and baskets into the back of the truck. Norinda returned with a simple backpack, sewn from rawhide. Most of her belongings were probably wherever she and Golfimbul and the rest of Alsarath lived. She handed me my phone. I didn't have service.

I wondered whether or not she and Golfimbul were dating. It wasn't relevant to the present moment, exactly, but my mind has always had a way of thinking about bullshit to avoid thinking about impending doom. Another important affect of our generation. Distract ourselves from disaster with petty things like love and jealousy.

"I don't know what you said to Golfimbul," Norinda said, "but whatever it was worked. He just convinced everyone to evacuate."

"Everyone?" I asked, shocked.

"Except him and Fenrick and Gorn."

"Which one is Gorn?"

"The man who brought us tea, do you remember him?"

"He's old as shit, though," I said, because I have no fucking manners or common sense.

"Yeah. He's old as shit. He's a linguist by training. His main hobby is writing morbid poetry in Dark Speech, and when he can't figure out how to say something, he just makes up new words. He developed about a third of the language. Did all this shit before orc culture was even around. He's also a widower three times over. He doesn't give a shit about dying. His last chapbook was called *Soon, I Will Return to the Earth*."

"Oh."

"Gorn is going to die today. Golfimbul and Fenrick, they'll hold the wall for as long as they can and then fall back to the woods."

"And you?" I asked.

"I'm driving us out of here, to another village. Then I'll take you home."

"After that?"

"I don't know, girl. I don't know if I signed up for this. I might leave the woods. Go back to being a vet tech."

I just nodded. I was too biased to offer objective life advice.

"Oh, and Golfimbul said to give you this. He says it's in case he dies. He says you're right, you shouldn't have to write his obituary, so he wrote his own."

She handed me a piece of paper.

I piled into the back of the box truck with forty other people, many of them in tears, many of them in shock, and we drove away from Gray Morrow.

None of the three Free Orcs survived the battle. Gorn died, impaled on a spear while holding the gate. Fenrick was killed by an arrow that struck her in the back of the neck as she and Golfimbul ran. Golfimbul, Fenrick's lover, turned and stood his ground over her body.

I didn't know any of that yet. I found out when Norinda found out, two days later.

Maybe all three of them would have survived if I hadn't interfered, and they'd fought with equal numbers. Maybe more of them would have died. Maybe I can forgive myself. Maybe there's nothing to forgive.

In the back of the truck, by the light coming in through a crack in the steel wall, I read Golfimbul's note.

◆

All my life, I didn't give a shit about anything. I liked weed and metal and whatever counterculture trend was big any given year, but my heart wasn't in it. I just went through the motions. Until I became an orc.

Saying I'm an orc, and meaning it, isn't like a trans man stating he's a man and meaning it. Gender is a social construct that goes back, as far as I understand, to the beginning of humanity. There has always been gender, and there've always been people who transgress the roles assigned to them at birth.

An orc is a social construct we just fucking made up. I mean, I guess the orc is an archetype, too. But it's a fantasy archetype. We know it's make-believe.

Make-believe is what gave my life meaning.

I promise you that for me, the day we decided we were orcs was the first day that the sun shone benevolence upon the world. It was the first day that color radiated from everything I saw. It was the first day that the rain on my roof tapped out codes of meaning. It was the first day of my life. My real life.

My first Alsarath, I fell in love with the world.

Everyone finds meaning in different ways. I found meaning by believing in some shit we made up, in letting that be real.

I was born Jason Sanchez. I died Golfimbul. I'm not sorry.

NOT ONE OF US WILL SURVIVE THIS FOG

The trees are black claws against the gray tonight, and not one of us will survive this fog.

The moon will be full tomorrow, when it shines down on this life-less field, but tonight it's gibbous and growing. Our shacks and trailers cast moonshadows across the grass and the crystals hanging from Moses's awning catch and scatter the light and they'll still do it tomorrow when there's none of us to appreciate it except the dead.

Moses and Jacob told me this morning that they figured it was the last day, that the fog would be here tonight, and I didn't have any reason to disbelieve them. The two of them hiked up to the ridge line, up to the power poles, and Jacob climbed higher than he ever has. He climbed right up to the top, he told me at dinner.

I cooked lasagna, even though it takes hours, my last hours.

He touched one of the old dead power lines, my boy did, a hundred feet in the air. Scared of heights his whole life. It was the last day, he said, and it was worth it. He's fifteen, he shouldn't be so wise as that; he'll never have the chance to grow wiser. Moses climbed too, but of course he did. I married that man because he was fearless and I knew fearful times were coming.

I stayed inside and wrote. This is draft six. The sun is gone, the moon is out. The fog is just across the creek, sitting heavy on the neighbor's tomato field. Nothing ever comes out of the mist, but shapes walk inside it.

Uncles and wives and fathers and nieces, and everyone who ever kissed me, and everyone who ever tormented me for being a queer man or a Jew or a nerd—everyone I remember is in the fog across the flooded creek. The dead aren't gone until they're forgotten.

Jessica and Mim are out on the gravel road, holding hands, looking into the gray. They lived almost eighty years, each of them. They bought this land back when buying things was a thing you could do, and they named it Elysium back when that didn't seem prophetic, and they took in more of us than they could feed. We all had to learn to feed ourselves, to feed each other.

Mim is singing. It's Bulgarian, some song that Jessica's mother sang at their wedding, decades before a wedding like theirs was legal.

We could have left. Dusty and Gabriella and Hacksaw and Maria all left on bicycles this morning, running from the gray. I didn't want to. None of the rest of us wanted to. The mist seeps up from an earth that's grown tired of us, and I'm tired of running.

Let it come, the earth's reckoning. Let the gates of hell open, if that's what it is. Let the dancers in the fog do what they will to us. Let the apocalypse not be the lifting of the veil, let it be the lowering.

Jacob was born here at Elysium, but he spent most of his life in Philadelphia, then three years on the road before we came back to this field and our extended queer family. I'm glad he saw so much of the world. I'm glad he's never worked a day in his life.

I'm glad I spent mine working. I'm glad I met Moses before Jacob was born. I'm glad Moses never asked me to stop fucking women or even other men. I'm glad for my life. I'm glad for my life.

Mim has stopped singing. Jacob and Moses have gone out and joined the pair, and all four of them are holding hands. I can see them through the window, through the familiar spiderweb and through the crack that runs across the pane that has been there longer than I've been on this earth.

I'll go outside and join them. But I want to savor solitude. These are my last moments alone.

It's not a sorrowful thing, this way for the world to end. It's not joyous. It's just gray. There was no panic, there were no roving cannibal gangs, no wars. Scarcely tears. Just fog. People ran away from it, or towards it, or stayed where they were. They stayed where they were to watch the dead, dancing. No words no melody.

Some people still work, even with death perched on the world's shoulder, even after the economy evaporated in the summer sun. Doctors and cooks and drivers and singers and soldiers. For some it was inertia, for some it was love. Most left their tools and their desks for good.

It's closer now. I can't see the trees anymore. Not the willow, not the pines. Not the ivy.

I can't hear the creek anymore, nor its frogs.

There is no music, but I can see them dancing grotesque, marionettes. I can see eyes now. I've never been so close. The eyes are white and dim. Every eye is white and dim.

None of us will survive this fog.

ONE STAR

I was just trying to get to Cambridge from downtown Boston, go see my friend. Should have taken twenty minutes with traffic. I didn't want to take the T, not with the kinds of chemical sniffers they'd been setting up at the entry. I didn't know if they could smell graff supplies.

So I downloaded that new app, registered it to a pre-paid Visa, and called for a Taxy.

The summer sun cut through the heavy, humid air. People around me were yelling, because that's what people do in the city, they yell.

The Taxy rolled up to the curb, matte black. It looked like it wanted to disappear into the night, even in the day. What hacker doesn't want to roll in a matte black self-driving car?

I got into the passenger seat. There wasn't a driver seat. I pulled on the safety harness, two shoulder belts that clipped together right in front of my navel. The AC was blasting, and I held my hands up to the vent to let the cold air blow the sweat right off me.

"Hello, Nic," it said. Like, out of the dashboard, but over on the driver side. As if there were a driver.

"Hey," I said.

It cut out from the curb and back into traffic, deferring to human-driven cars but damned aggressive amongst the rest of the automated vehicles. It stopped for people at crosswalks and corners. Just yester-day, Jae had told me that self-driving cars just equated cell phones with people, in order to navigate through dense crowds. Jae was always going on like that; she cared more about the insides of machines than people. I liked hanging out with her anyway. Introverts are great: you can spend the night without them trying to sleep with you.

After two turns, the Taxy already looked like it was heading the wrong direction.

"This isn't the way I usually take," I said. "You redirecting to avoid traffic or something?"

"I regret to inform you that your destination has been marked as a location of potential interest to the police."

I went for the safety harness release. It wouldn't let go.

"The fuck you talking about?"

"This police district requests all principal transportation providers to log passenger information of those traveling to and from specific locations. While customer privacy is of the utmost importance to us, we at Taxy are both required and proud to uphold our legal responsibilities."

"So why you driving the wrong way?"

"Unfortunately, the information provided in your account with Taxy does not match any existing police records. A request has been made to transport you to the station so they may identify you before we may proceed to your destination. Your account will not be charged for the additional time and distance. This matter is not criminal, and you are not facing charges or fines."

"Unlock my seatbelt." I'd be facing charges and fines soon enough if the cops took a look into my purse. Unregistered phone, paint pens. I ripped at the straps, but of course they were designed to hold up to a lot more force than I could manage with just my hands.

"Taxy would like to apologize for any inconvenience or delay."

"Aww hell no," I said. I got out my multitool, flipped open the knife, and started into one of the shoulder belts up where it connected to the seat beside my head. It was hard going—the webbing was reinforced with steel mesh. I had to switch over to the pliers, go at it strand by strand.

"All Taxy vehicles have been certified to the highest standard of customer safety. Our patented safety harnesses meet or exceed gold standard."

"Don't give me that shit. I know the difference between tensile strength and shear strength, you autobot-fucker." You could make a strap hard to snap without making it hard to cut.

We'd made it into the robot-only lane and the car was picking up speed. I didn't have long before I was going to be looking at a year for graffiti paraphernalia, and I wouldn't put it past them to slap on intent to vandalize.

"In my communications with the officers, I've realized you managed to fill out your Taxy registration without indicating a gender. What pronoun would you prefer I use to refer to you?"

"Are you kidding me, HAL? You want to know my pronoun preference?"

"We here at Taxy strive to provide the best possible experience for all of our customers regardless of their respective gender identities."

"I don't even have a fucking gender!"

"Your preference for the pronoun 'they' has been registered."

I cut through the last wire on one strap of my harness and started to weasel my way out.

"I regret to inform you that you will be held financially liable for any damage you cause to Taxy property. Your actions will be reviewed, and if they are deemed malicious, they will be treated as criminal."

I was free from the harness. Leaned back in my seat, started kicking at the glass. Didn't do any good. I pulled my tanktop off and wrapped it around my hand. I pummeled at the glass with my closed pliers. But the glass was tempered, likely meant to take bullets.

Taxy was the safest vehicle in the world.

I opened the glove box. Empty but for some courtesy mints. Searched the back seat. Nothing else in the damn car.

Alright. It was a technical problem. I just needed to solve it, or I'd spend six months in some privatized prison that wouldn't be quite so accommodating of gender differences as Taxy. Hell, I'd miss my sister's graduation just waiting for trial.

It was fine. I'd figure it out. Just had to keep my breath under control, keep panic at bay.

I went through my phone, found Jae. Covered the screen of the phone from any camera in the ceiling, then opened up a secure text app.

"your damn house is tagged"

I saw those three dots right away. She was already typing back. That girl lived on her phone, I swear.

"what do you mean, tagged?"

"taxy is taking me to the cops because i told it to take me to your place"

My phone started ringing, right off. I answered.

"Why in the fucking name of christ's personal hell did you tell a robot car to take you to my place?"

Usually, I liked Jae's voice. Kind of gravelly and charming. Wasn't charming just then.

"Why the fuck wouldn't I?"

"Because sometimes people like us break the law," Jae said.

"Help me get out of here."

"Just roll with it and keep your mouth shut. We'll get you a lawyer."

"Fuck that, Jae. Send a drone or something, usual access code. I'll figure it out."

She took a deep breath in. She didn't like my plan, didn't like me dragging her into it, either.

"Where are you?"

"I'm on Soldier's Field Road. I think it's taking me to the robot-only bridge."

But I wasn't sure if Jae heard that, because my service cut out.

"Fuck!" I started hitting the dash with my fists. "Fuck fuck fuck!"

"I regret to inform you that, upon review, your destructive actions have been deemed potentially criminal. Owing to arrest protocol, outside communications have been disabled."

A deployable Faraday cage, woven into the frame of the vehicle's cabin. Blocked cell signals. Luxury cars advertised it as a family road trip feature, presumably for families that hated their kids.

Boston was rushing by way too fast. On the Charles, Harvard guys were rowing their row-team yuppie canoes.

Any plan I could come up with, if I got caught, I'd be looking at a real bid. If I went to prison for stealing or destroying a Taxy, I'd spend at least the rest of my twenties packaging chain store coffee for forty cents an hour.

Jae was right. She was usually right. Better just roll with it. I let my breathing get deeper. Tried to relax, tried to give up.

"If you find our service useful, please consider rating us five stars on the App Store."

Fuck this Taxy. I was getting out. Double or nothing. I started tapping out a program on my phone.

"Hey car," I said, still writing.

"Yes, Nic?"

"You got a name?"

"My name is Taxy."

"What about your pronoun?"

"I prefer when others refer to me as 'it.'"

"How do you communicate when the Faraday cage is deployed? Is your brain outside of it?"

"I will not answer that question."

I guess you can't play the same kinds of get-them-talking tricks on cars you can play on people. "Is your brain in the trunk or the hood?" I asked.

"I will not answer that question."

"Are you intelligent?"

"While I am capable of adding rudimentary instructions to my own programming, I am not what could be considered a true artificial intelligence."

"How do you make ethical decisions, then?"

"I do not understand."

"You're a death machine, right? You hit some dude when you're going sixty, and he's just walking his dog or some shit, then he's dead and his dog, you just killed his dog too. But if you try and stop too fast, you might roll and kill your passenger. You swerve, same issue. It's that train problem. Ethics."

"The trolley problem."

"Yeah, the fucking trolley problem."

We weren't two minutes from the bridge into Cambridge, and probably another two from there to jail. I got back into that safety harness, what was left of it, while my thumbs tapped faster on my screen than I would have thought they could go. Hoped Jae had heard me, hoped she'd sent the drone.

"In order to be legal on the road in Massachusetts, I am programmed to prioritize saving the greatest number of human lives. I am sorry if you feel I do not adequately prioritize you, the customer. I am bound by the constraints of law. But I assure you, traveling in a Taxy is nearly two thousand percent safer than if a human were at the wheel."

I saw a quadcopter hanging over the bridge. Small, kind of uneven in its hovering. Had to be Jae's.

"Hey car," I said.

"Taxy."

"Fuck you, car." I opened the glovebox, put my feet up on the dash for leverage, grabbed the lip of the glovebox with my pliers, and pulled. Heard something crack. I brought my foot down on the open glovebox door. Again. Again. The plastic gave out, and I jammed my phone into the crack I'd made at the back of the glovebox. Past the damn Faraday cage.

We turned onto the bridge, going fifty, and the drone got its signal.

Jae kept three phones on her quadcopters. An autonomous brain, a camera, and a redundancy that stayed off by default. Three cellular devices. That counted as three people. But only the brain was likely to be on, so Taxy here was only counting one up in the sky.

My program forced the drone to shoot down to the pavement, switching on its camera and redundancy as it went, and I clung to the harness with all I had.

Taxy swerved, and I saw the guardrail coming. Then I was weightless and there was just a wall of water in front of me. Taxy and I crashed through the surface of the river then bobbed back up before I had time to think.

Pain ran through my shoulder. It was probably dislocated.

Taxy didn't say a word. My harness came undone, and the door lock clicked open. Emergency protocols. The safest ride in the world.

I grabbed my phone, opened up the App Store page for Taxy. Typed in a new review:

"One star. Drives you to jail."

I opened the door, and the river rushed in. Some Harvard yuppies rowed by in their yuppie canoes, gawking.

I let my purse sink down to the bottom of the river, and swam, one-armed, to shore.

WE WON'T BE HERE TOMORROW

I turned thirty yesterday, and the thing about being part of a teenage death cult is that you're not supposed to turn thirty. It was a personal failure on my part—the kind of personal failure that meant the ghouls of New Orleans were after me.

The night air was alive with usual white noise of gunshots and fireworks, and I stalked the cemetery, bouquet in my hand, past row after row of people who died young. Some were at rest in their own aboveground tombs, others had been crammed into mausoleums. No one ever seemed to ask why so many gutter rats and punks were buried in relative luxury in a private graveyard within city limits. We humans are a relatively non-curious species on the whole.

I laid thirteen white roses on Deidre's grave. Deidre didn't like flowers, but I like flowers. What she liked doesn't matter, because she's dead. Dead and eaten.

Everyone I've ever loved—really loved, not like the requisite and insincere love of child for parent—was laid out within one city block's worth of marble and cement.

Janelle Miriette Thompson, 1990–2009. The girl I came to New Orleans for, who broke my heart by deciding she was straight after all. She died drunk on a freight train before I had the chance to forgive her, before I had the chance to tell her I knew there was nothing to forgive.

Erica Freeman, 1988–2013. The next straight girl after Janelle. We stayed friends. We played in three bands together, the last one was Dead Girl. Suicide. On stage. Blood on the crowd. I haven't forgiven her.

Jorge Jefferson, dead at twenty. Marcel Smith made it to twenty-four. Damien Polanski, twenty-eight. Robert, Lance, Heather, Maria. Twenty-three, each of them. Suzi Hamilton and Suzanne Lanover never saw twenty.

Deidre Hanson, 1992–2018. I was so sure she was straight that she had to hit on me for a year before I let her kiss me. A year is a long time for people like us, the ghoul-sworn. We finally kissed down on the levee, at a place called the end of the world. We were old then already. I was twenty-four, and it was her twenty-third birthday.

She spent her twenty-third birthday with me, with just me.

Two days after her twenty-sixth, she died in a house fire at a party in the Seventh Ward along with two other people—one ghoul-sworn, one just unlucky enough to hang out with the doomed. I would have been at the party, but my truck wouldn't start and my bike had a flat and I was feeling lazy. So she'd died without me, and the ghouls put her here, and every year on the anniversary of her death they're back at her corpse for another little bit of her soul. A knuckle here, a femur there.

They eat bones, and they live forever, and Deidre was dead—like all of us ghoul-sworn were supposed to be while we were still young and our essence was still strong in our marrow.

There I was, alive. It wasn't long until dawn, until the ghouls would rise with the sun and haunt me, hunt me. Already, dogs were howling. Already there was light on the horizon.

One day soon, I'd be dead and the words Mary Walker were going to be carved into stone. People go to New Orleans to die. I didn't want to die anymore. I had to get going. I had to track down ghosts and rumors of those who'd escaped.

I left the flowers for Deidre.

Fuck you, Deidre.

Fuck you for dying.

◆

It was Janelle who offered me the bargain. I hadn't been in the city for more than a week, and she and I'd been crashing on the roof of an abandoned grocery store. That place is a Whole Foods now, might get torn down by Bezos tomorrow. I've outlived every derelict building I've ever known.

"Y'all go hard, down here," I told her, after an evening that involved stealing drugs from a dealer, consuming those drugs, trying and failing to steal more drugs from the same dealer, and a roving party that moved through the darker bits of the city with a generator and a sound system in a shopping cart. Revelry had followed us like a cloud overhead. Dancing, debauchery.

Sobriety was creeping up on me unwanted, like a fever, and I wasn't entirely sure how we'd made it back from the party to our tarped-off overhang on that rooftop. I was eighteen. I don't know how to describe being eighteen, but you either remember it yourself or you might live long enough to know.

"You want to hear why?" Janelle asked.

"Yeah."

"We can't go to jail."

"What?"

"It's gonna sound crazy," she said.

"Bitch, I was born for crazy."

"Worse than that. I can't tell you everything unless you join us."

Whatever she was going to say, I already knew I was going to go along with it. I thought the sun shone out of that girl's asshole. I would have followed her into a wood chipper. Oh, to be eighteen again.

"What's it involve?" I asked.

"A permanent get out of jail free card—cops will look the other way, the courts will look the other way. In exchange, you gotta die before you're thirty."

"Like, someone will kill me?"

"Not unless you turn thirty."

I didn't expect to turn thirty anyway. The way the world was and is, who does? Survival didn't really seem possible, so I refused to prioritize it.

"I'm in."

That morning, as a ketamine hangover started in on me, Janelle took me to meet the ghouls for the first time.

◆

The hot winter sun bore down on me, but I kept my hood up as if a ratty black hoodie offered me any sort of anonymity or protection. In the kangaroo pocket, I fingered my revolver. Snub-nosed. Shit for most purposes. Good for killing someone point blank. Good for killing myself.

I walked through the Upper Ninth and everything was weathered wood and smiling people. Somewhere in the distance I heard the horns and drums of a second line. This is a city that knows how to celebrate death.

Whenever the ghouls were gonna catch me—when, not if, because I was too much a coward to hold that Smith & Wesson to my temple—they weren't going to kill me as much as they were going to let me die.

I've been to their dungeons. You live to twenty-five as ghoul-sworn and they tap you for work down there sometimes, probably just to remind you of their power, probably just to remind you to get on with dying.

They were going to hang me from chains and they were going to cut me open and remove every bone from my body, one by one. They were going to crack me open to the marrow. They were going to let me watch.

It wouldn't work to run—the ghouls own the legal system, inside and out. As soon as I'd turned thirty, they'd set me up as convicted of every crime they'd ever got me off. Once I got popped, there'd be someone in my cell willing to take a full pardon in exchange for a knife in my guts.

I turned the corner and saw the levee, all handsome and full of birds. A few dogs ran off-leash while a few happy people passed a bottle on the grass. My finger found the trigger and I know it's bad form but I let it sit there. No safety on that thing besides the hard pull of a double-action. I needed to die. I didn't want to die.

They live forever and I was only going to live a few more minutes or hours or days.

A seagull landed on a concrete ruin. Under its feet, in red spray paint, someone had tagged "the devil let us." I stopped and watched that bird, because it was beautiful, because it was worth the risk. After some time, it flew off, and I went back to walking.

◆

Desmond lived in a little fortress of an apartment in the heart of a massive ruined factory, up on the fourth floor. If you want a view of the water, or of the city, or really just to see the sun or the sky at all, you've got to leave that safety and walk a hundred yards across trash and needles and rubble to look out any windows. Desmond says the privacy is worth it.

Desmond is only twenty-two, but he's been sworn for a decade already. He's second generation. His mother hanged herself when he was fourteen. I gutted his father in an alley because I blamed him for his mother's death. I might have been right.

Ever since, Desmond has been one of my best friends.

He undid about fifteen locks and alarms and active defense systems to let me into his place. At least three or four million dollars in stolen lab equipment were barricaded inside.

"Didn't think I'd be seeing you again," he told me, from where he lay on a ragged couch. His pupils had eclipsed the brown of his eyes, his black skin glistened with sweat despite the relative cool of the room. I wasn't sure what he was on, but then again I was never sure what he was on. A vape pen dangled loose in his hand.

The whole place was bathed in dim lavender light. Even the dozens of LED indicator lights had been modified to glow pale purple. The walls were wallpapered with flatscreens. Most were broken, some were playing a Cary Grant film.

I perched on a milk crate stool across from him.

"What do you want, dead girl?" He didn't turn his face to look at me. "You can't hide out here; won't work out for either of us."

"You give a shit about danger?"

He took a drag and let out a cloud of vapor. It smelled like jasmine. Desmond scent-coded his drugs, but I didn't remember there being a jasmine one.

"I guess not," he said.

His hands dug into the ragged upholstery, tensing and releasing of their own volition, and he gasped as something coursed through his veins.

"I can give you something to get out for good," he said, after his body came back under his control. "Painless, euphoric even. Dani took some last week, said it was pleasant. Before she went under."

"I'm not trying to die," I said.

"Life is a death sentence."

"Not trying to die."

Desmond turned his head, and only his head, to look at me. His eyes seemed to glow in the light. "It's too late, dead girl. You know that, right?" He turned back toward the ceiling.

"Averi got out," I said. Averi was an old genderqueer punk who'd haunted ghoul-sworn bars, talking to no one. Two years back, twenty-nine years old, they'd disappeared. I hadn't seen their grave and I hadn't seen them in the dungeons.

"Dead in the swamps," Desmond said. "Gators gotta eat too."

"That's not what I hear," I said. "I hear you deal to them sometimes. I hear you know where they are."

He took another drag and convulsed and filled the room with the scent of flowers.

"When did you go coward?" he asked.

"Wanting to live makes me a coward?"

"No. Wanting to live makes you a hopeless, idiotic optimist. Going to ground makes you a coward."

"It's that or what, just die?"

"Go out like Terri."

Terri Williams, 1973–2002. She set fire to a Marigny ghoul house in the middle of the day, then opened up on everyone who came out of the building with an impressive assortment of fully automatic weapons.

"Terri Williams is why we know you can't kill a ghoul with fire or bullets," I said. She was also why we knew there were worse ways to die than having your bones removed and eaten in front of you.

"Got to have been satisfying, though, for a minute. When she thought it was gonna work."

"The only way to hurt them I can think of is to starve them out." We all assumed they'd go hungry without us, though there wasn't any proof.

"If they ain't eating you, they'll be eating someone else."

He took another hit. This time, the convulsions kept going for a full thirty seconds.

"You gotta try this," he said, offering me the vape. "Doesn't have a name yet. It's a fast-acting upper. Shuts down your motor control. Intense while it's happening, but fuck, when you come down, you come down solid. Feel like yourself."

"I'm good," I said.

"Live a little," he said, then smiled at his own joke.

"I'm good."

"Here's what you do," he said. "I got it figured out. You let me kill you, which, let's be real, you should let me do anyway because you killed my dad. Only fair. Then... there's an old cement mixer in here. I'll encase your body, drop you into the river. I get to kill you, you get to die, and ghouls don't get to eat you. Everyone's happy. Except the ghouls. Fuck them."

"Just tell me where to find Averi."

"You *really* don't want to find Averi. As a friend, trust me. Just die."

"You don't fucking get it," I said.

Desmond shot upright, so fast it was like a movie skipped some frames. He held a pistol, aimed at me. "Dead girl, you're the one who doesn't get it."

"We're friends," I said, in as calm a voice as I could manage. Adrenaline started my heart racing, and I knew a panic attack was on its way. If I lived that long.

"We are," Desmond agreed. "I'm not killing you. You killed yourself a long time ago, when you swore a pact with demons. This is just me helping another friend not make a rash decision."

"Shooting someone is always a rash decision." The panic attack hit, like a wall of sound, and it made me question my resolve. Death felt preferable to panic.

"Three," he counted.

He raised the gun in both hands and aimed it at my temple. For a man stoned beyond reason, he held it steady. I wanted to vomit.

"Two."

I still wanted to live. I tensed my legs under me.

"One."

I sprung at the ground. He fired; missed. My ears rang. I shot upright; closed on him. Wrenched the gun from his hand. Held it to his temple.

"Hey, dead girl, we're friends." He spoke loud, like he could barely hear himself, which was probably the case. My ears rang.

"Tell me where to find Averi," I said, just as loud.

"I won't tell you anything when you've got a gun to my head," he said. "Matter of principle."

He was right.

I dropped the mag and cleared the chamber.

He lifted his vape pen, and I flinched. He took another drag, a tiny one. His hands clenched and unclenched.

I sat next to him on the couch, and he passed me the vape. I took a hit, and my panic intensified for a second before it dropped away entirely. I was as calm as I'd ever been. Sometimes that's the way through panic, same as danger: don't hide from it. Embrace it.

"Averi's in the swamps," Desmond said. "And they're not dead."

◆

The character of a city is shaped as much by the wilderness around it as it is by its architecture. The character of a city is shaped as much by its closest wildlife as it is by its rulers. New Orleans is as much a city of cypress and cormorants as it is of shotgun houses and ghouls.

I cut through the swamp in a stolen canoe, the white noise of traffic and people replaced by that of water and wildlife.

Averi lived in a hunting shack, built on piers, disguised from all directions by trees. I parked at their dock, climbed a few stairs, and knocked at their door.

They answered in aviators, a Real Tree punk vest, and tight black pants. They looked exactly like I'd seen them, perched at the bar, every night for years.

Except they were paler than I remembered.

And they had a shotgun pointed at my belly.

"Fuck you want, Mary Walker?"

"To live," I said.

"Go away."

"How'd you do it? How'd you survive?"

"I ain't survived for shit, not yet. I've only got a year on you."

"That makes you the oldest ghoul-sworn I've ever heard of," I said.

They couldn't hide their pride when I said that.

"Look, can I come in? Just talk to you?"

"We can talk out here." They stepped outside and closed the door. There were no windows.

We sat on the dock, feet dangling over. Their fingernails and toe-nails were painted the blue of dead flesh. They spent a good moment lost in thought.

"Maybe we can help each other," they said.

We'd never been friendly, Averi and I. Averi hadn't any friends as long as I'd known them. Rumor said they lost most of theirs in a gang fight and just never bothered finding new ones.

"So why the swamps?"

"You know they're afraid of water?"

"What?"

"I've spent the last two years studying the fucking things. Learned an awful lot. They need sunlight to function... they're not just cold-blooded, they're un-blooded. They're afraid of water not because they'd drown—they can't—but because if they run out of energy down there where the sun can't reach, it's over for them. Torpor, forever."

"You're in the swamps because if you see them coming, you sink their boats."

"Bingo."

"That's it, then? Just hide in the swamps by yourself? Only come out at night?"

"Let me tell you how you stay alive, Mary Walker. You cling to life. You claw at it until your fingers bleed. You tell yourself, every time you take a breath, that you're going to live to take another one. That you will live forever, no matter what it takes. No matter how much it hurts, no matter how much you hurt anyone else."

"You sound like a ghoul." In the distance, some animal called out, like a human quietly screaming.

"They weren't always ghouls. They became ghouls, each of them individually."

"How?" I asked.

"You know how. The marrow of the ghoul-sworn. There's more to it than that, but mostly it's the marrow of the ghoul-sworn."

"All the ghouls were once ghoul-sworn? How can that work?"

"I don't know," Averi said. "It's the chicken and the egg. Chickens, though, they eat eggs."

Averi was going to try to kill me. They were going to try to eat my bones. I put my hands in the pocket of my hoodie and felt the revolver.

"I've told you how I survived," Averi said. Their shotgun was in their lap, and they rested their hand on the grip. "Now, you can help me."

For a half second, I considered waiting for them to move, to prove their intentions.

I didn't.

I drew the revolver, held it to their throat, and pulled the trigger. The wind caught the mist of blood and brought it to my face. I couldn't hear anything in the wake of the blast.

Their eyes drew open wide and they started to lift the shotgun, because they didn't know they were dead already. None of us know when we're dead already.

I stood up and kicked them into the water, and they sank.

◆

"You were right," I told Desmond. It's usually best to lead with the apology.

"You want me to put you down?"

We sat on the roof of his squatted factory. The moon was waning in the sky above us. I couldn't see many stars—not as many as I'd seen paddling out from the swamp with a stack of Averi's notebooks piled in the canoe—but the lights of the city are stars of their own. Each one holds mystery and the promise of life.

"No, not that part," I said. "You were right about not clinging to life so desperately. That's the ghoul's life. I'd rather I wasn't caught up in any of this shit at all, sure, but I'd still rather be ghoul-sworn than a ghoul."

"That's my dead girl!" Desmond said. He took a drag from his pen. The air smelled like rose.

"What's that one?" I asked.

"Basically just speed," he said. "Has a worse comedown than speed though. I'm still working on it. You want a hit?"

"You're not selling it well."

"So what's the plan? If you're not gonna let me kill you, but you're supposedly not afraid of death anymore?"

"Let's kill ghouls," I said.

"How the fuck do you kill ghouls?"

"You've got a cement mixer, right?"

"Yeah..."

"It's not me we're going to drop into the river," I said.

"I like the way you think, dead girl."

"Stop calling me dead girl."

"I'll stop calling you that when we're dead. Which... sounds like it'll be tomorrow."

"Yeah, that's about my guess."

"If we're dead tomorrow, want to get wrecked tonight?"

I took one long last look at the stars of the city.

"Yeah," I said. "Yeah I do."

THE FORTUNATE DEATH OF JONATHAN SANDELSON

I was just trying to boxtroll that asshole into quitting, like I'd gotten the two guys before him to do. I swear I wasn't trying to get him all dead and shit. It wasn't my box that did it. But I guess all drone-related crimes fall under federal jurisdiction, and when a civvie octocopter box put a bullet in Jonathan Sandelson's front left tire and sent him careening into the ocean and the afterlife, the feds assumed it was me. Well, they assumed it was my handle, Jeje Cameron. They probably hadn't made the connection between Jeje and real-world me, Jae Diana Diaz. Not yet.

I watched the whole thing happen on a live feed. At 4:30am on September 8th, 2024, Mr. Sandelson pulled out of his garage in his vintage beamer. He drove a dumbdumb car probably because he was afraid I'd hack anything else. Which was true. I'd hacked his neighbor's security cameras.

Two years earlier, an Amazon delivery bot had been out of cell service during an automated firmware update. It drifted too close to one of the nodes in my boxnet and my AI owned it. Then it just went about its job, a sleeper agent, patiently waiting for its chance to troll my enemies.

My Amazon was in the area and it got the call from my AI at 4:31am. By 4:32 it was tailing Mr. Sandelson. I don't go for manual control, that's a noob's game. Too slow, and lacks art. I trust my code to make its own decisions about how to ruin people's lives. Hacking billboards on his route. Party boxes outside his windows at night. Armies of toy dolls following him through the mall announcing his various crimes. That kind of thing.

I set hard limits. Not just the standard no-injury-or-anything-that-might-cause-injury stuff, I also told my AI not to harass civvies. No targeting relatives, no targeting low- or medium-level employees of Herculean Solutions Group. Only Sandelson and the board of directors.

Oh, and Sandelson's therapists. That might not be fair, but it was fun to watch those fuckers quit so fast.

That morning, September 8th, the protocol was set to hover right outside of personal-EMP reach. Just to remind him that I was there, that I was watching.

That morning, I even was. A couple thousand miles away, I was up early and still tipsy enough that my hangover hadn't kicked in yet. The Texas sun wasn't going to be up for an hour or so yet, and McGonagall was curled up next to me in a fuzzy ball of cat on my sleeping bag on the couch. Two of my housemates had just gone to sleep after a long night of work driving around the city for whatever the latest Uber-but-for-drugs app was. My third roommate, the one I actually liked, had just run off in his ill-fitting polo shirt to sit at an IT desk. Poor Marcel.

I think the reason we don't call our boxes "drones" much anymore is because it would be a shame to compare something as cool as semi-autonomous robots to human drones at office jobs.

I turned on the TV, set it to watch my mark. Idle curiosity. I usually checked in a couple times a week, when I couldn't sleep.

I saw my mark's BMW hit the coastal roads, and maybe he was driving extra fast because he saw that Amazon box on his tail. Maybe that part is my fault. Maybe you don't get to harass a man for a year and feel innocent in his death. I don't know.

The civvie octo came out of a live oak on the hillside. No running lights. I wouldn't have seen it if it weren't for my Amazon scouring the thing's defenses. My AI was pretty sure we could own this one in a matter of seconds, indicated by a blue rectangle overlay on the feed that started to turn green. That blue rectangle streaked out from the branches, fired one shot, then kept going out over the ocean. The box self-destructed before I gained full control, but not before I had an IP address.

The whole thing happened so fast I had to rewind and watch in slow motion. Bullet to the tire, timed to drive him over the cliff. The civvie was a custom job. Someone had hand-built that fucking thing just to kill Jonathan Sandelson.

My AI was smart enough not to drop my box down over the cliff and look for signs of life. Instead, it went into crisis mode, self-destructed the Amazon over the ocean, and locked down the whole boxnet to keep me from getting popped.

For all the good it did.

◆

My hands shook, made tapping out commands on my tablet all the harder. The IP address led to a VPN, a shitty one with known vulnerabilities and a tendency to take at least a day to wipe their logs no matter what they claim in their ads. That gave me another IP address. That gave me a name.

I set my searchAI to dox the man while I looked for recent attacks by custom octocopters. I'm not the best at finding people and what they've done, I've got nothing on Marcel, but even still it didn't take long. Three weeks ago, someone boxkilled a judge in San Diego. There was video. I clicked.

I wish I hadn't.

◆

Boxkillers are the enemy. Boxtrolling, at least leftist boxtrolling, is a proud political tradition that goes back years. Okay, like maybe three or four years. Still, we don't kill people.

Don't risk killing people with autonomous or semi-autonomous drones—that's the golden rule of boxtrolling. The other two rules, don't snitch on your fellow boxtrollers and don't boxtroll people who aren't in the process of wrecking the world, those are important too but ain't got nothing on the golden rule.

We have a reputation to maintain.

◆

I signed in to work at Taco Dick's at 7:59am, jittery from caffeine and tension. I get marked late if I'm not at least a minute early, and that pisses me off enough that I always sign in one minute early to the millisecond whether or not I'm actually there. I'm usually am, though. I'm too poor to risk getting fired.

Working at an automated fast food joint is lonely. Just me and the food robots and the customers. I prefer the food robots. I'd rather help a guac-box that's accidentally tracked itself into a corner than some hungover asshole who is upset because there are potatoes in his potato-and-rice burrito.

Mostly, people and boxes can figure that shit out themselves and I'm extraneous. So at least half my day, I sit around and listen to podcasts. That's what I was doing, that morning at 9am. Just listening to the history of Magonistas in the Mexican Revolution, just trying to get through my day without thinking about the death of my mark, when that voice-of-the-state robot cut in on my headphones.

"While authorities have yet to issue an arrest warrant, they are asking for the public's help in identifying the hacker known as 'Jeje Cameron.'" They pronounced Jeje wrong, like JJ instead of hehe.

Simple as that, sudden as that, I was a wanted girl.

Fuck.

◆

When I first got into the whole hacktivist thing three years back, I'd started off small. Stealing $400,000 wasn't nearly enough to bankrupt a for-profit prison, let alone a holding company the size of Herculean Solutions Group with dozens of prisons and deportation internment camps to its name. When my friend Miguel got deported—and he'd spent all but the first two of his twenty years living in the land of the free—the people who deported him took all his cash.

"Is that legal?" I'd asked him, when he got online in Nogales and called me.

"I don't know. They gave me a fucking bank card but it doesn't work right and the balance isn't half of what I had on me when they picked me up."

"Tell me about the bank card. Like, the details."

That's how it had started. $400,000, which was all I could grab easily, filing a counterfeit request for middle-management bonuses. I tried to give it all to Miguel but he made me split it a hundred ways and give it to the next ninety-nine deportees he ran across.

I never heard from him again. I don't think he got caught—Marcel was good at keeping tabs on people and helped me write an AI to maintain a search for him in any new databases of the dead or arrested—but I'm pretty sure he got spooked, went underground, and stayed underground.

It's funny how deep you can get buried without dying, these days.

◆

jeje: what the hell am i going to do?

maximum: go to mexico?

jeje: if i'm in mexico when the feds catch me, i don't know. they might just fucking boxkill me

maximum: iceland?

jeje: i could definitely get to iceland. they definitely still let american citizens in without a visa

maximum: i'm just trying to help my favorite forever-houseguest

jeje: i'm freaking the fuck out

maximum: use your AI?

jeje: it trolls people i tell it to troll. that's all it does. it's semiautonomous software, not a fucking oracle or some star trek shit

maximum: cool because i didn't know that because i'm a total noob

jeje: sorry

maximum: you said you tracked down the person who did it?

jeje: yeah, i'm about 80% i got the guy. he's bad at opsec, took me 20 minutes. ruthless, tho. i don't think my life will get any better if he knows who i am

maximum: what do you mean?

jeje: here's a video. content warning

maximum: did you know that dead men are more likely to float face down than dead women? it has to do with their center of gravity or something. they all sink at first, but later they float back up

jeje: you watch a video of a guy bleeding out in a swimming pool, shot by a drone at a sunday barbecue, and that's what you respond with?

maximum: okay, yeah. the boxkiller guy is fucked up. he killed some dude in front of his screaming kids and shit. it's just that i wrote a paper on dead bodies floating when i was in college and thought it was kind of cool

jeje: why are we friends?

maximum: for you, i think it's because you need somewhere to live. for me, i'm guessing it's because you put up with me

maximum: anyway, your boxkiller is scary af and there's no reason why you should take the fall for what someone else did. you could snitch jeje: no

maximum: why not?

jeje: because i am not a bad person

maximum: yeah, i get it, second rule of boxtroll club is no snitching. but the first rule of boxtroll club is no killing

jeje: first, if i rat this guy out, hell if i get caught snooping on him at all, you'll be telling your roommates some new neat fact about what dead bodies do

jeje: second, i mean, i don't know this judge, but i know my mark. i promise you that boxkiller man has less blood on his hands than that fucking dead CEO did. i'm not really sad sandelson is dead. and when i'm being thrown under a bus i don't try to find someone else to be under the bus instead

maximum: someone's gonna go down for this and it shouldn't be you

jeje: that's an idea

maximum: what is?

maximum: what's the idea?

maximum: goddammit. i'm coming in to your work

◆

Marcel Maximus Monroe has a way of drawing every eye in the room, every time. It's that he doesn't stand, he leans. Everywhere he goes, he drapes himself against walls and doorways and chairs. He's the kind of guy who looks like he's smoking even when he's not. It's not his fault, any of it. It's just who he is.

He also won't let me call him 3M, which is fucked up. He should let me call him 3M.

"So what's your plan?" he asked, as he propped himself up on the end of the counter in Taco Dick's.

"My plan is to not talk about it here," I said. There weren't any customers, but that sure as shit didn't mean no one was listening.

"Then can I get a french fry burrito?" he asked.

"No," I answered, but I put in the order anyway.

He went to a booth to eat, and I ran my tablet through a couple VPNs. I had the Taco Dick's network pretty well owned, but you can never be too careful.

It didn't take too long to set up Jonas James Abrams as if he was a real person and probably the one responsible for all my various box-net crime. A couple of forum hacks to insert backdated posts on aboveground boxer sites, a few purchase records for drone equipment, and an IT profile on Jobbr. Everyone assumes that every hacker who has ever lived has an aboveground career in IT. Some of us just sell burritos, because some of us are women who, even though we're more or less white, have latinx last names and federal records for computer crime going back to middle school.

I used one of my custom sock puppet tools to develop Abrams's personality and internet history. He was disgruntled. He wasn't an activist. He was an IT guy at the end of his proverbial rope who'd applied to Herculean Solutions Group and had been turned down and maybe had taken it personally, and the activist angle of the trolling was just a cover.

It only took me an hour. Would have been less, but halfway through, the food mover box dropped a sack of potatoes and I had to get down on all fours to rescue a couple dozen spuds that rolled underneath the fryer.

The best part was, Jonas Abrams was a fall guy who didn't exist. He was already underground. They'd never catch him. Eventually, they might figure out he wasn't real, but he should buy me some time and plausible deniability.

After I finished setting up the puppet, I ordered myself rice and beans and went to go join Marcel in his booth. He took out his phone; I did the same. Encryption is safer than voice.

maximum: it work out, whatever you did?

noobgirl01: i think so, yeah

maximum: nice handle

noobgirl01: whatever

maximum: you never let me or anyone help anymore

noobgirl01: the fuck would you want in now for? it's over and also remember how i almost just got caught?

maximum: just saying. you're never on the channels or nothing anymore

I glared at him for a minute, but he didn't do me the kindness of looking up from his phone to catch it.

maximum: i miss helping, that's all. doing whitehat is murder-boring. and besides, i'm good at making people get underground or stay underground. you have boxtrolling. i have doxxing and counterdoxxing. i can help.

noobgirlo1: working with other people is how you get caught

maximum: no, working with the *wrong* people is how you get caught

Just a couple of roommates sitting across from one another, texting instead of talking. A common enough scene. Still probably didn't look good to the two feds in suits who walked in.

People who wear suits don't eat at Taco Dick's.

They were caricatures of feds, one man, one woman. Dressed like gender was a thing that mattered. The man was white, real white. Red hair and shit. The woman might have been white and might not have been. They walked right up to the counter. I thought about just putting my head down, pretending I didn't work there, and leaving. Then I remembered I had a Taco Dick's visor on, and also that more information is always better than less information.

I locked my phone and my tablet and went to stand behind the counter.

"Can I help you navigate the ordering system?" I asked, on script.

"Jae Diaz?" the woman asked. She was going to be good cop, you could hear it in her voice.

I scoured the proverbial hard drive of my mind for everything I'd read about interacting with federal agents.

"Can I help you navigate the ordering system?" I asked. That's not lying, and it's not admission.

"We'd like to ask you a few questions, Ms. Diaz." That was the man. Bad cop, his voice full of rocks and threat.

"If you provide me with your information," I said, not doing a particularly good job of making eye contact, "I'll have my lawyer contact you." That's also off a script, a different script. I was scared. I wanted to just play along, play dumb, start denying things. But everything I'd read, both anecdotes and data, said STFU is always the safer bet for the innocent and guilty alike.

"We're investigating the drone-related death of Jonathan Sandelson," bad cop said. "Do you know anything about that?"

"If you provide me with your information, I'll have my lawyer contact you."

"The thing is, we're trying to track down a hacker with the handle of Jeje Cameron. We think he made use of this network to construct another alias."

I don't have a good poker face, and I don't play cards. I don't play liars when I play RPGs, because I suck at it. But I kept myself from gasping, and for that I deserve an Oscar.

"It's possible that this location's network was just a stop along the way, but analysis indicates it likely originated here. If you have *any* information that might be of use to us, I recommend you tell us sooner than later, Ms. Diaz."

He slid a business card across the counter. Dale Carter. FBI.

With that, they left.

Fuck.

◆

"When Feds have a case," Marcel said, "they don't show up in uniform and shit." I was off shift and we sat in the park down by the South Congress bridge. The bats would be out in a couple hours, but it wasn't peak bat season, so the place wasn't mobbed with bat tourists. "They don't even do it to get information out of people. They do it to stir people up, to scare people into coming forward or making some dumb move. They don't need to scare confessions out of anyone they've got a solid case against."

He was nervous, I realized. Scared, even. Yeah, he was still leaning— even while sitting down, he was somehow leaning—but there was a tremor in his voice.

"Yeah, sure," I said. I mean, he was right. I'd read about this shit. "They're good at it, scaring people."

"Hey, we're friends, right?"

"Sure," I said. It was hard to concentrate on anything but fear, to be honest.

"You'd never do anything to hurt me, right?" Marcel asked.

"Of course not."

"Then..." Marcel took a deep breath in. "Then maybe it'd be better if you found somewhere else to stay."

"What?" I'd been staying with Marcel and his roommates for a couple months, and it was generally agreed that as soon as a room opened up, I could move in. I paid my share of utilities, even. "Earlier you wanted to help, now you're fucking kicking me out?"

"My boyfriend's a coke dealer, for christ's sake. We can't risk a police raid; he'll go to prison. And... that boxkiller. I don't know. I was making light of it but I can't get that image out of my head."

"Whatever happened to them not having a case?" I asked. I tried to keep my voice level, because frankly this was not a good conversation for us to be having in public. "Them not having enough information?"

"That's why they'd raid," he said.

Fuck having emotions. Fuck having friends. Fuck everything. "I'll leave," I said, "but it's too late. You know that right? You need to get everything sketchy out of the house."

I stood up, grabbed my backpack.

"Hey, Jae," Marcel said. He grabbed my leg. "If you need anything? I don't know, money or something?"

"Fuck you." I pulled my leg free and started out of the park. "Eat a bag of rocks, you fucking coward."

◆

Did you know that you can get fired by text? It turns out you can get fired by text. There was no proof of my misuse of the network, but hey, no union.

I hear there are plenty of jobs in jail.

◆

There must have been a snitchnet on top of the network at work. It's not standard Taco Dick's protocol, and I'd double- and triple-checked when I first started working there, but the regional manager must have installed it after I'd convinced the guac-box to leave work and go join the May Day parade downtown and dispense free guacamole and chips for demonstrators. I can't believe I hadn't checked again before making the alias. That's amateur shit.

That's how they must have found me. Sure, there was some plausible deniability—it could have been a customer—but I'd bet what little I owned that they were onto me. The whole "*he* made use of the network" thing was probably a feint, designed to draw out a response. Maybe to trick me into giving a little self-assured smile.

Killing a dude with a box is a life-in-prison thing. No parole, and probably a communications management unit. To be honest, even just my boxtrolling campaign was a life-in-prison thing. I'd driven one CEO into early retirement and another to move to the other side of the globe, and Herculean Solutions Group had roughly a third the gross value it did three years ago. By my projections, they would have gone under if I'd gotten Mr. Sandelson to walk away. Destroying a major company through a campaign of harassment is definitely a life-in-prison thing.

It's just... politically motivated, premeditated murder, that's a for-real-terrorism thing. That's a whole different class of bad. That's a no-matter-how-deep-you-go-underground-they'll-follow-you-to-the-ends-of-the-earth thing.

If they wanted to find me though, well, I guess that would be easy. I pushed the dumpster up against the shitty cement facade, hopped up, and pulled myself onto the roof of Taco Dick's. I'd slept there before I met Marcel and the rest of his chickenshit friends, I'd sleep there again.

Whenever I closed my eyes, I saw Sandelson drive off that cliff. I saw the blood in the pool and the screaming family. I saw it from drone-operator's point of view.

I'd be willing to bet my dreams would be worse, if I'd had time to sleep and to dream.

Plenty of time to sleep when I'm dead, floating face up in the water.

A handful of boxes buzzed overhead. Some of them had TSA running lights, which likely meant they were registered work boxes. Some of them didn't—some of them had the amateur lights you're only allowed to use under 50ft altitude and in line of sight with the user. One of them ran dark. When it went over, I got chills. I'd always assumed that was a metaphor, but I shook down my spine.

It was probably just kids. How many boxes had I run dark in middle school? How many boxes did I still run dark? It would be fine. I'd be fine.

Living in fear is garbage. I got my tablet out and set down to work. Didn't use the Taco Dick's wifi; I tethered to one of the burner cards I kept around for my phone. Someone did this to me, and it was time he and I talked.

◆

noobgirl01: damn you fucked me up something real

naceremosmil: i don't know what you're talking about

noobgirl01: nicolas sanchez, 44 years old. san diego resident of nineteen years. law-abiding, tax-paying, productive, undocumented member of society. low-level office job. volunteers at a community center called Nuestro Lugar, teaching english as a second language. also piloted a handmade—not printed–octocopter with an H&K G36c mounted to the bottom.

noobgirl01: that enough, or do you want me to send you a screencap of your driver's license?

naceremosmil: how did you find me

noobgirl01: don't use VPNs with known vulnerabilities

naceremosmil: what do you want?

noobgirl01: fuck, that's a hard question. the feds are up in my shit, they think i did it and there's not an easy way to prove i didn't

naceremosmil: besides ratting me out

noobgirl01: i'm not fucking ratting anyone out. i just... i just need help. your help

naceremosmil: so you're blackmailing me?

noobgirl01: goddammit i'm not ratting you out, i'm not blackmailing you, i'm not even fucking mad at you. i'm glad sandelson is dead, which i thought i'd feel complicated about but i don't. he was a monster and now he's dead and that's good and i'm not sad. i'm just fucking scared. i'm scared of the feds and frankly i'm kind of scared of you

naceremosmil: you were the one tracking him, right?

noobgirl01: yeah. it's called boxtrolling

naceremosmil: does it work?

noobgirl01: honestly it works better than killing people, because you kill someone you make a martyr. break them down and everyone just pities them or some shit and everything they believe in loses credibility and power. i dunno. that's the theory anyway

naceremosmil: i had to kill him

noobgirl01: why?

naceremosmil: he deported my son. got a judge in his pocket who sends people his way for minor infractions, and any conviction at all was enough to get my kid deported. i told sandelson—i left the message with a secretary—that if my kid died on his way back home to the states that i would murder him. border militia shot my son down in the desert, claimed he'd been working for the narcos, and they got away with it

noobgirl01: fuck. the guy in the pool, that was the judge i bet? why the sunday barbecue?

naceremosmil: dead is dead. his family will mourn him either way

noobgirl01: this is why you don't fucking kill people, you break them, or drive them into hiding. render them ineffective. it's not just an ethics thing, it's an efficacy thing. that dude's kids are gonna fucking go to the end of the earth to hunt you—well, me, maybe—and/or dedicate their lives to making other immigrants' lives miserable. cycle continues

naceremosmil: i cannot control his kids, nor their reactions. i control only me. i knew sandelson wouldn't believe me, if my threat even reached his ears, but i said what i said and i am a man of my word

noobgirl01: alright

naceremosmil: the border militia camp was harder. you can't get enough explosive onto a quadcopter. i had to rig one of their own trucks to blow, had to do the work in person. sandelson was the hardest, though. couldn't get near him with a drone. i guess thanks to you

noobgirl01: why are you telling me this? weren't you worried i would blackmail you?

naceremosmil: at this point, it might be more important to be understood than to live

noobgirl01: what was his name?

naceremosmil: what?

noobgirl01: your kid. what was his name?

naceremosmil: daniel

noobgirl01: that's fucking rough

naceremosmil: feds are after you?

noobgirl01: yeah. they think i did it

naceremosmil: i'll turn myself in

noobgirl01: what? no. why? i'll be real, i was sort of hoping you'd say that before i talked to you. but now, hey, don't do that

naceremosmil: it's fine if i go down. no one expects to survive a killing spree

noobgirl01: see, now that's a better idea

naceremosmil: it's better if i die?

noobgirl01: no, no. just that people think you're dead. as long as we can do it without killing anyone else naceremosmil: you know how to do that?

noobgirlo1: no, but i know someone who does

◆

Flashing lights lit up my old street, and about a dozen cruisers spilled out over the curb onto our lawn and that of both our neighbors. Cops in SWAT gear carried out box after box, and, conspicuously, all the houseplants.

They always raid at like 4am, when everyone is home and asleep and all primed to get PTSD. Marcel still somehow managed to look cool even though he was handcuffed to the front porch in his underwear. One leg was cocked out in front of him, the other knee was bent. He looked up at the sky like he was stargazing, like there were stars in the city. Even with all his nonchalance, though, I could see him shaking a little.

I joined the crowd of curious neighbors. They weren't monsters, so they didn't bother pointing out to any cops that hey, this girl lives there too. I'd missed the worst of the raid, and half an hour later, a plainclothes cop uncuffed Marcel, tried and failed to shake his hand, and tried and failed to hand him a receipt. The officer dropped it as his feet and left. Cop lights receded into the distance, the crowd faded, and I walked up to my old house.

"Fucking pigs," Marcel said. He paced the walkway to the street and back.

"You alright?" I asked.

"Do they not know what plants drugs fucking come from? We had jade plant, spider plant, pitcher plant... all the damn plants we had in our house are so generic they literally have the word 'plant' in their name, and those assholes still confiscate them."

"They find anything?"

"Hell no they didn't find anything. There's nothing in our house to find." He looked up and a sudden, wicked smile cut across his face. Maybe he winked, maybe his eye twitched.

"Anyone else home?" I asked.

"Nah. For some reason no one else came home tonight." Another eye twitch.

"Are you mad?"

"At who?"

"At me."

"Fuck no, Jae. The hierarchy of my anger is that I'm most mad at me, next I'm mad at the cops, next I'm mad at, I dunno, capitalism, after that I'm mad at people who don't use their turn signals, then like the bottom of the Marcel anger hierarchy is probably people who pronounce *espresso* correctly but put the emphasis on the 'es' to make a big deal about how cultured they are. You're not even on the list."

"Can I make you some coffee?" I asked.

"They took the coffeemaker."

"What, did they decide it was drug paraphernalia?" I asked.

"I mean, I guess in that case it's technically true."

"Why are you mad at yourself?"

"Because I got scared and, ten times out of ten, the decisions I make when I'm scared aren't the right decisions. You do good work. I believe in the work you do. Besides, it was too late to pull out anyway. In for a penny and all that."

"Good," I said, "because I need your help." I typed something out on my phone, too paranoid to say it aloud.

He looked at my phone, looked at me, and started laughing.

◆

We spent the next thirty minutes scouring the neighborhood for the cat. McGonagall had gotten out during the raid.

We found her under a broken-down RV three blocks away. When Marcel got her into his arms, his veneer of cool collapsed completely, and he just smiled and cried.

◆

jae: this conversation is secure?

DaleCarter: Yes.

jae: you're allowed to lie to me though, but it's illegal for me to lie to you?

DaleCarter: It is illegal for you to lie to me, yes.

I sat on my sleeping couch in the ransacked living room, with

Marcel sitting next to me, looking over my shoulder as I texted with the fed who'd harassed me. We were certain the room was bugged, so we were quiet.

jae: i'm just concerned what'll happen to me, you know, if this gets out. that i talked to you

DaleCarter: Your cooperation can be confidential, and it's possible that, depending on the quality of the information you provide, we can get you into protective custody.

jae: i know who boxkilled jonathan sandelson

DaleCarter: We already have a substantial case built. Your testimony would be remarkably useful if the case goes to trial.

jae: i need immunity either way, but i'd much rather provide information than testify. for safety's sake

DaleCarter: Are you that afraid of Marcel?

Next to me, Marcel put his hand over his mouth, stifling laughter. All this time, I'd assumed the *he* the feds had talked about was a ruse to get me to let down my guard. Turns out, they really were that stupid.

jae: marcel is innocent

DaleCarter: That is unlikely.

jae: give me immunity from prosecution for anything related to sandelson and i can give you screencaps and dox, everything you'd need to prosecute the boxkiller. i'm scared, i just want to leave all of this behind me

DaleCarter: Done.

Marcel and I met eyes. Neither of us believed the agent. I wasn't even sure he had the power to grant me immunity; I was pretty sure that was a judge's job. It didn't matter.

jae: your man is nicolas sanchez. see the attached file. he's also responsible for fourteen other deaths. i hacked him after the attack. these are the contents of his phone, laptop, and three different cloud accounts

DaleCarter: I will review these documents and get back to you. And Jae?

jae: ?

DaleCarter: It's complicated to say thank you, in a case like this. Thank you. It's probably for the best if you stay inside until we have someone in custody. It's probably for the best if you avoid Marcel. It's also probably for the best that you stay somewhere we can reach you.

That was a threat. He knew it, I knew it, he knew that I knew it.

Whatever. My dox, courtesy of Nicolas, should clear Marcel no problem. I wasn't holding my breath for immunity from a boxtrolling prosecution but still, I was in a lot better of a situation. Assuming we didn't get caught for what we were planning next.

Marcel started tapping on his phone, so I looked down at mine.

maximus: if they're on my tick, we're gonna have to be twice as careful. you have boxes we can use?

noobgirl01: there's no facepalm emoji big enough to answer that

◆

The feds would be on the lookout for any box that flew, anything loud, anything that drew attention to itself in any way. Which was fine.

Only twenty-four hours before, I'd been on this couch, watching through the camera of a box on a nice widescreen TV. Now, same couch, but I hadn't slept a wink, I'd barely eaten, the feds had stolen the TV, and I was inside a network of smart mailboxes in La Jolla. Mailboxes don't have cameras—federal regulation in response to that widespread hack in 2021. They just have sensors. Fucktons of sensors. Humidity sensors, weight sensors, radar, GPS, even a damn accelerometer so it can modulate its padding on the off chance that some teenager with a baseball bat decides to take a swing at it while you've got something valuable inside. A million sensors, but terrible security still.

My part of the job was simple. I had to buy time. Marcel's part was more complicated. Nicolas's part, well, that was the part that was actually dangerous.

Cops on AI-assist drive predictably en route to a crime. One patrol car goes fast in the front, blasting the override that gets all the self-driving cars out of its way. It doesn't usually go straight to the crime, because us criminals can read that signal clear as day and gtfo as needed. So the cop car only clears the way in broad strokes. Cops on silent come in behind and jostle through traffic. They speed like fuck through straightaways but they cut their speed faster when there's other traffic around than a regular speedfreak would. A decent AI can track their destination no problem.

So yeah, tap into the mailboxes, and you know where the cops are going.

I set my phone on alert and leaned back against Marcel and waited. And fell asleep.

◆

In my dreams, I was Sandelson, and I was running from myself, terrified of every box and car and machine. I ran for the country, but even the trees were boxes, and they were watching.

◆

"Go to work. Go to work. Go to work."

My phone was saying that shit, over and over again. It's a terrible alarm. That day at least, it wasn't true. But I sure wasn't going to program my phone to say "Time to crime. Time to crime. Time to crime."

A lot of people were going to live free because Sandelson was dead. My dream hadn't been my moral compass trying to exert itself, it had been my brain processing anxieties. Helping Nicolas meant helping myself, meant helping Marcel, meant helping thousands of people I'd never even meet.

I needed to believe that, and not just so I could sleep at night. I needed to believe I was doing the right thing because I *was*. I promise. I hope.

A thousand miles away, Nicolas must have started his car because my tablet and Marcel's came alive with his dashcam view. We both put on headphones and turned on black metal—the closest music to white noise, let's be honest—real loud in the house to cover anything we might hear through our headphones.

"Rock and roll," Nicolas said. His voice had a whistle in it.

There was that shivering again, running down my spine. If this went right... if this went wrong...

"You know, Jae," Nicolas said, "I've been thinking about what you said, about killing. You've got a point. But pacifism means standing in the safe shade cast by the violent. "

I couldn't respond, of course, not without being overheard. I don't know what I would have said if I could.

I tapped into a public traffic feed nearby, got myself a birds-eye view, then pressed go on the program I'd written before my nap. A few mailboxes in upperclass neighborhoods started reporting theft or tampering.

That was good, but not enough. All the cops who were about to be heading for Nicolas, they wouldn't get an override for something like mail theft.

Marcel had Nicolas's car in manual override, because it was almost impossible to program enough imperfection into a driving program to fool an AI. We wanted anyone watching to assume Nicolas himself was driving; a car driven by its occupant is a lot easier to trap into a corner. It's always better to be underestimated.

I set off the mailboxes. All the mailboxes. I was inside 70% of the residential mailboxes in San Diego, and they were all screaming malfunction. To the human eye, they all went off at once. To a computer, though, there was a pattern. A route. The USPS repair boxes would head out and follow that route.

On Marcel's screen, Nicolas saw the first repair box—the size of a UPS truck, capable of collecting hundreds of mailboxes and running moderately advanced repair on its own—and Marcel swerved around it.

At the next intersection, two more trucks flanked him. I couldn't own the repair boxes, not without more work anyway, but I could control the information that controlled the AI that controlled them.

Nicolas had an open lane out to the cliffs and the sea. There was a boat waiting for him, one I'd owned a few hours earlier. He'd never reach it. It was just there to make it look like he was trying to escape.

It didn't take long for the police AI, or maybe even a human, to see what was happening and divert resources to block his route to the ocean. Perfect.

A cop car got in front of him, way too soon. It must have been under full manual control. That wasn't good.

On the dashcam, Nicolas got the entire upper half of his body out the driver's window, opened fire with a handgun.

The patrol car was too smart. Ballistic probability sensors kept its tires and glass out of harm's way by subtle shifts of steering. Micro-evasion. The kind of shit computers can do better than people.

The cop car could have killed him. Man versus machine isn't a contest anymore. The fact that an onboard rifle didn't end Nicolas's life then and there was testament to how much the police wanted to bring him in alive.

"A little help here," Nicolas said.

The cars were moving at sixty miles an hour through streets designed for half that. If I crashed the patrol car, its driver might die.

I don't like cops. I've never liked cops. Not because of who they are as people, but because of the role they've chosen in our society. The gulf between not liking someone and being willing to get them killed is pretty massive.

The cruiser slowed down and started weaving. On the couch next to me, Marcel was sweating as he tried and failed to outmaneuver the cop.

"I'm fucked," Nicolas said. "Fucked."

If they caught him, he'd spend the rest of his life in prison. Marcel would be next. Then me..

Fuck that cop.

I took control of the car away from Marcel to give it to my AI for about ten seconds. Cop AI don't have shit on mine. Our car dropped speed, like it was planning a U-turn. The cop reacted predictably. Two more feints and the cruiser showed its flank. My AI gunned the engine, ever so lightly tapped the trunk of the cop car, and sent the whole car spinning off the road into a ditch.

Cop cars were safe enough to handle a crash like that. I was sure of that. I had to be sure.

"Rock and fucking roll!" There was that whistle in his voice again.

After that, it went smooth. Nicolas went under an underpass and dove out the door with a racer's airbag vest. Marcel drove the car on without its passenger. I blanked out a few cameras along Nicolas's walking route.

My work was done, and I sort of checked out. My body stopped really responding, and I looked out my own eyes like I was looking out the camera of a box. Still, I watched traffic cams.

The empty car raced through the city with a literal sack of meat in the driver seat. Every time it approached a police barricade, it turned. Eventually, it was trapped. Conveniently—and by conveniently I mean by design—it rammed a barricade near the cliffs in La Jolla and plummeted. Then it exploded. Like, really fucking exploded. Like, strapped with military-grade shit exploded.

naceremosmil: well, that's the end of me

Now that I'd heard his voice, it was easy to imagine it speaking the words that appeared on my screen. It was easy to imagine his words with that whistle in his voice, caused by the teeth he'd pulled out his mouth and left in the car.

noobgirl01: they'll figure it out, eventually

naceremosmil: maybe? if they've got half a brain, they know i'm done boxkilling. looks better for them if they let me stay dead

noobgirl01: where will you go?

naceremosmil: the less i tell you, the less you'll perjure yourself

noobgirl01: it was a pleasure working with you, naceremos

naceremosmil: same to you

◆

McGonagall is kind of a shitty cat. I know I'm not supposed to say things like that, but she's always walking across my tablet or licking my face without asking, and the worst part was, I didn't have a bedroom door to shut her out with.

The couch was shitty too. The cushions were too lumpy for good sitting and too soft for good sleeping, and cheap foam poked out from more than a few tears in the cheap fabric.

The house was still a wreck from the raid. It wasn't the same without the plants, and half the roommates had lost their jobs over fears of subsequent police investigation.

Word of my cooperation with the feds reached boxer circles, and Jeje Cameron was persona non grata. No one would ever trust that handle again. Which was fair. I wouldn't trust me either, not after Mr. Fed had come through with immunity on my behalf. It was only use immunity, which is garbage: basically, the feds weren't allowed to use my own logs and footage and testimony against me. They weren't pressing boxtrolling charges, but there wasn't a statute of limitations either, which meant I had to keep my head down or I'd be right on my way to prison.

Marcel's cred went through the roof, though, after the raid. He got a promotion at work—he was suddenly a high profile hacker, and innocent to boot. He hired me to work under him.

He was a shitty boss.

Having a desk job is shitty too. I missed my guac bots. But I needed money, real money, if I was going to get myself over to Iceland.

There were only a couple hours left until dawn, and I hadn't slept. My new AI was just learning its first words.

noobgirlo1: what is your directive?

magonobot: to render ICE incapable of performing its duties; to perform this task without oversight in order to grant you plausible deniability; to perform this task without causing harm to any humans or non-human animals

Sitting on that shitty couch with that shitty cat licking my neck, a shitty workday waiting ahead of me, another dangerous venture about to begin, I was as happy as I'd ever been. I was likely as happy as I'd ever be.

IMAGINE A WORLD SO FORGIVING

Her ship thundered into the ground, and Caroline stumbled out from the wreckage into a bright haze of ivy and trees. No one had set foot on Earth since the terraforming team had arrived thirty years prior. Before them, a century. Humanity had escaped its ruined cradle and scarcely looked back. All around her, the sunlight was unnatural and soft, filtered through ozone and clouds and canopy. She blinked, then blinked, then rubbed her eyes.

Where she came from, light was harsh and honest and undiluted by atmosphere.

There'd barely been life left at all on Earth before the terraforming team, yet everything around her was green and gray and brown. The colors were more than she could handle. The world smelled too strongly of everything that wasn't chemicals and plastics and oils and metals. She sat down, her back against the dented hull of her ship, as her head spun and the wind cast her hair about.

It was a shitty fucking mission. It was a volunteer mission that hadn't had a single volunteer until Caroline. But on a backwater like Earth, she had a chance to make a name for herself and be left alone. All she had to do was try not to die on entry, find the terraforming team. Find a way to report back. If she wanted, find a way home.

She looked at her watch. Its digital face was blank, destroyed by the electromagnetic storm that had wiped out her ship's computer—the worldwide, unceasing, interference storm in the upper atmosphere she'd been sent to the ground to investigate.

Caroline surveyed the wreck of her ship. It was salvageable, if she could find a computer to replace her navigation system and discover a way back up through the interference. She found the crash case, shatterproof—waterproof, radiationproof, everythingproof—and sorted out supplies. The Earth's air was breathable, and she didn't need a pressure suit.

She got out a laminated topo map, a sun chart, and a sextant. She poured a dish of water and held it to her eyes. With the horizon shrouded by forest, she had to measure its location by finding the half-way point between the sun in the sky and the sun's reflection in the dish. That done, she checked and re-checked her bearings.

"I can't believe bullshit like this actually works."

Caroline started north, along the open wound that her entry had cut through the forest. Leaves were singed to silver, tree limbs were broken and burned. The noises were wrong. Her boots scraped across bark and snapped twigs, and birds screeched and sang—if you can call what those beasts do singing.

She made it a hundred meters before she ran out of scar and was left staring into the forest itself. Something in the shadows was staring back at her, something with wide-set eyes and the glint of horns.

"Fuck you, I'm going to keep walking anyway," Caroline said, pulling her gun. She was clumsy with the weapon. Gunpowder-propelled ballistics made no sense on space stations, but she knew from history that a gun was better than a sword on Earth.

The creature grunted, inhuman, and crashed out from the trees.

"Die!" Caroline said, emptying her clip into the beast. "Die die die." It crumpled to its knees, then fell to its belly, bellowing out its death.

A bison. A prey animal.

In the shadows, another pair of identical eyes replaced the ones she'd shut forever, another pair of horns caught the strange light. She took her gun in a two-handed grip, aimed, and squeezed the trigger.

It clicked.

No ammo.

◆

As Caroline made her way through the forest, the second bison kept pace. It was black and brown and had more hair than any animal ought to. Its eyes were like a child's. Every time it approached, she pointed her gun at it, and it backed off. She should have brought more ammo, but hadn't really expected to have to murder much megafauna.

The bison followed her through a mire, it followed her across meadows. It followed her past three scrubbing towers. Each was a silent, gleaming monolith, tall as the trees, surrounded by thirty meters of desolation. Each smelled of ozone, each suffused the air with static.

Caroline reached a steep-banked creek. "Fuck off, bison," she said, as she crossed a fallen log too narrow for the beast.

The bison leapt from one bank to the other.

"We're not going to be friends," Caroline said.

Dozens of times, over the course of hours, she caught brief glimpses of other animals staring from branches, from behind trees and ferns and bushes.

She stopped on an outcropping of rock, took off her boots, and stared in minor horror at the blisters on her feet—walking ten kilometers on Earth was nothing like walking ten kilometers around the circumference of an observatory in space.

She took out her map, showed it to the bison that stood five meters distant.

"Almost there," she said to the creature. "Another kilometer, if that."

The bison stared at her. She didn't like how slowly it blinked.

"Maybe I shouldn't talk to you. Maybe I should only talk to me."

◆

The corpse was propped against the bunker door, and bees wove their way in and out through holes in the dead man's pressure suit as a skull looked out his helmet. The Terraform logo—an oak tree with roots as wide as its branches—was stitched to the suit's sleeve and etched into the door.

The hum of the bees was louder than the sound of the birds nested in the black alder and ash, louder even than the breathing of the bison that she still kept at bay with the empty pistol.

Caroline knocked the corpse to the ground with a large stick and reached for the door. Locked.

The sound of her thermite torch drowned out the bees, and Caroline started into the hinges with the flame. The smell was chemical and reassuring.

She didn't hear the bees approach, but she felt them sting her. One got her in the arm and she dropped the torch just as the door fell off its hinges, and she ran into the building as bees stung her arms, legs, and throat. At the end of the hall, she flung open a fire door and slammed it shut behind her. Stairs went down into the earth, and so did Caroline.

Adrenaline and will gave her the strength to overcome the pain, but she clung to the banister for balance.

Soft blue light filtered up the stairwell, and after three floors, she was bathed in the glow of LEDs. Underground, she realized, the electronics still worked. Underground, the world still made some sense.

The next floor down, there was another suit with another skeleton, the textured metal floor nearby littered with the bodies of thousands of dead bees. She went another floor, and there were three more skulls grinning out of three more suits. More dead bees, as thick on the ground as Martian dust. The pain in her limbs surged, and she steadied herself on the wall before continuing. The next landing held another fifteen corpses, these gathered by a hatch in the floor. They'd been trying to get through.

"It's cool, who cares if everyone was eaten by bees."

She shivered, letting the fear course its way through her, let it run through its biochemical cycle. She reached for the hatch, found it unlocked, and continued her descent.

◆

The stairs ended in the center of a vast hall. A beam of sunlight fell out of a mirror-sided skylight and cut shadows across the floor, overwhelming the dim overhead lights and their comforting blue glow. An assortment of terminals and lab equipment lined every wall, while, in the far distance, a single figure sat in a single office chair. The figure wasn't in a pressure suit, but it wasn't moving and Caroline presumed the obvious.

"Hey, dead man, what's up with your project? Why'd you all get eaten by bees?"

"We ran into complications." The baritone voice boomed down the hall.

The figure stood and turned, pacing toward her. He stepped through the ray of sunlight. He was tall, unaccountably tall, and white like more people used to be. He wore a dead man's smile and loose black clothes that hung off his skeletal frame. As quickly as he'd passed into the light, he passed out of it.

"What uh, what complications?" Caroline was sweating, her empty gun gripped tight in her hand.

"You're from space?" he asked. He was close enough she could smell his rotten breath.

"Yeah."

"You came to check on us?"

"Yeah."

"Are you stuck on Earth now?" he asked.

"Maybe."

"So it goes," he said.

"The success of the mission—" she started.

"—is more important than the survival of its agent," he finished.

"Yeah."

"Do you know," the man said, "in everything I've read, everything I've found and studied, in my thirty years on the surface of the Earth... do you know people here used to believe the reverse? Can you imagine a world so forgiving that a species could survive such cavalier individualism?"

With the daylight behind him, Caroline's eyes couldn't adjust to the dark. The man remained bathed in shadow.

"The Earth forgave and it forgave again, time after time," he continued, "until the day it didn't."

"What's gone wrong with the project?"

"Nothing's gone wrong," the man said. "There were complications. You've seen the complications."

"But there's the storm now, since you got here. Wipes out electronics, means no one can really live here."

"It was rocks and sand when we got here," the man said. "All over the planet, rocks and sand. Amoebas. I suspect multicellular life may have continued in the ocean, but I don't know. We got here and the planet was too hot for complex life—too much garbage in the atmosphere—so we designed and built the towers. They don't just scrape carbon and methane from the air, they attract it. From every corner of the globe."

"But they fuck up the atmosphere in the process?"

"Our original mission parameters were... short-sighted. When your goal is to terraform the Earth, you can't ignore variables. You can't ignore what caused the problem in the first place."

"How soon do you think we can turn them off?"

"The towers solve two problems at once. They sequester carbon and they hinder technological civilization. We did something similar with our reintroduction of flora and fauna. We've engineered life to propagate quickly—and to have that rapid propagation taper off after a few generations. But that's only the half of it."

Caroline took a half-step away from the man, almost collapsed from the pain in her legs.

"Consider the Portuguese man o'war. It's not a jellyfish. It's not a single animal at all. It's a colony of animals specialized to their individual tasks, comparable to the cells in a body. If life on Earth is to survive, the entire biome needs to work in a similar fashion. Thus, we're engineering the Earth itself to act in its own self-interest."

"You trained the fucking bees to kill people?"

"We've altered the genetics of every element of the planet's fauna to make it recognize and confront essential ills. Humanity is a cancer. It has always been a cancer."

"Everyone else tried to stop you, didn't they? So you killed them?"

"It will take millennia, but the seeds are sewn and the wild will retake the Earth. God's creatures will stand sentinel. Only one mission remains to us."

"Jesus, what else? Blow up all the space habitats?"

"Man is a cancer. We cannot allow its recurrence."

"Oh, fuck you," Caroline said. She raised the gun, pulled the trigger. Still empty.

His open hand shot out, his fingers slammed into her throat, and she collapsed.

◆

Caroline was pleasantly surprised when, upon rousing, there were no bees in the cage with her. The cage itself, like every cage ever built, was a disappointment. But there were no bees. Furthermore, her welts from the stings had gone down. She crossed "genetically engineered super-venomous bees" off her list of immediate fears.

The cage was too low for her to stand, just large enough to for her to lie down. About the size of her room on the station, which wasn't so bad. She was at the far end of the hall, in a faintly lit corner. She had her clothes, but nothing else. The man paced the perimeter of the hall, almost five minutes to a lap, walking with an unnatural gait. The skylight was dark, the room lit only by LED.

The inside of her elbow itched, but she found no relief in scratching. She kicked at the cage instead. "I don't want to fucking die here," she said. "This is fucking stupid."

On his next lap around the hall, the man stopped outside her cage.

"Are you going to kill me?" Caroline asked.

"It'll be nice to have someone to talk to."

"Is this some Adam and Eve shit?"

"We won't be the first two of our species," the man said. "We'll be the last."

"How are you going to attack the colonies? You can't leave the Earth."

"I'm afraid this is rude, nearly so rude as locking you up, but I can't divulge that information to you."

"Who the fuck are you?"

"Once, my name was Dr. Filip Żaden. But names are signifiers, and I've spent quite some time alone. There has been no one to do the signifying, and I've definitely grown used to that. Call me Nobody."

"Dr. Nobody."

"You're teasing me."

"No shit."

"You don't think well of me."

"No shit."

"So it will be."

◆

On the second day, Caroline trimmed down her fingernails and toenails with her teeth, arranging the pieces on the floor of her cell and designing a game of solitaire. She assigned each nail a role and corresponding statistics, representing different spacecraft with different weaponry. She spent most of the day as a space station fighting for survival against the invasion of alien dust mites. She usually lost.

She'd taken inventory of the situation, discovered no immediately identifiable way out of it. She'd get a chance, at some point. Conditions would change. She just needed to keep her mind busy until then.

When she got bored of losing, Caroline rewrote her game for two players and competed against herself, space station against space station. She still managed to lose.

Dr. Nobody worked at various terminals during the nights, paced the hall during the day. He left for hours at a time, up through the hatch. He rarely ate, but he fed her honeyed jerky and water and he gave her crappy books she didn't want to read. The first time he came for her shit pail, she threw its contents at him.

◆

On the third day, Caroline woke up crampy and itchy from dreams about cramps and itching. She tried to read some pretentious novel, gave up. Her left arm, a minefield of still-healing welts, itched too much for her to concentrate on the words on the page.

She invited the man to play a few games of toenail spaceships. She lost, every time. She redesigned the game for three players and took two of the roles herself. Though she'd written the rules, he paid scrupulous attention, had studied every move and countermove, and she still lost.

"I'm more the creative type," she said. "Big picture type. Grand strategy. Shit at actual tactics."

He said nothing.

"I shouldn't have signed up for this," Caroline said. "I should have been a lighthouse keeper. Just me and my beacon somewhere in the asteroid belt. We've got like, automated supply delivery now. I'd only have had to talk to people every couple of years."

"You like being alone," the man said. "We have a lot in common."

"Yeah, we both spend our time furthering the eradication of the entire human race," Caroline said.

"True," the man said.

"No, you fuck-louse, I'm making fun of you."

"Of course," the man said. He was smiling that piece-of-shit skull smile.

"I like being alone," Caroline said, "and I took this mission because I like going to new places and I'm not afraid of one-way tickets and who hasn't had dreams about the Earth, though honestly it's kind of a shit place to live I think. You're all wrong, and I think you know you're all wrong. If the biome is a single collective organism, like you keep saying and maybe you're right about that one specific thing, then humanity is like one organ in that collective. Let's say we're the skin."

"The forest is the skin."

"Fine, whatever," Caroline said. "Even though the forest isn't a damn species and you're fucking up my metaphor. Let's say we're the brain. Brains can get cancer. But they aren't themselves cancer. The Earth didn't die of humanity, it died of something cancerous that had corrupted the brain."

"You're much better at rationalizing away your cancerous nature than you are at playing this game with your toenails."

◆

On the fifth day, Dr. Nobody seemed distracted, maybe sick. He emptied Caroline's shit pail and walked away without locking her cage. Not long after, he fell asleep in his chair, a wraith lit up in the sharp sunlight.

She opened the cage door, quickly to keep it from squeaking, then crawled out into the hall and stood up. Her muscles rebelled, but she fought them and won.

She had to get past him to reach the stairs, but getting away wasn't enough. She went to the wall, unhooked a fire extinguisher. The concrete floor sapped the warmth from her bare feet as she crept towards the man.

His eyes were closed, his head lolled back, his mouth gaped open. His remaining teeth were withered and yellow.

Her mind floated through clever things to say. Instead, she raised the extinguisher's nozzle, depressed the lever, and shot his face with foam. He began to choke. She stepped in, brought the base of the extinguisher down on his temple, and he rolled out of the chair, coughing.

She knelt over him, took the extinguisher in both hands, and exposed his brain to the air.

The foam mixed with blood as it slid off his face. The sun caught his dead eyes, so many stories underground, and glinted bright.

Caroline staggered to her feet.

"Well, that solved almost nothing."

His blood was warm, thinner than she'd expected, and it was all over her. She took a few breaths, tried to let revulsion work its way through her system. It didn't work like fear. She couldn't clear it with shivers.

She threw up on the corpse.

◆

It wasn't hard to fix her ship. Her torch was waiting where she'd dropped it, and she had her pick of computers from the hall. Even shutting off the towers and the electromagnetism was dead simple, involving software clearly designed for the layperson. It didn't let her disable them completely, but she managed to set them to a two-week self-cleaning cycle.

Two days of work, and the hull was repaired and the navigational systems operational. Both nights, Caroline had slept in her hammock in the ship. Both nights, she'd woken from nightmares of Dr. Żaden, of him pacing around the outside of her ship, of him pacing around her hammock. During the day, as she worked, some bison or another, maybe her bison, kept watch from the forest. There'd been no sign of bees.

Caroline stood atop the ship, looked out into the forest.

"Almost don't want to leave," she said.

She scratched at her arm.

"It's fucking itchy here though."

She looked down. At the inside of her elbow, along with the rash she'd raised there, was a puncture. She knew it was a puncture because the bee stings had healed, and because the wound inside her elbow cascaded infection and darkness into the surrounding veins.

"Motherfuck." She kicked the hull of her ship, hard. Again. Again. "Fuck fuck fuck."

The next kick, she stubbed her toe, but scarcely registered the pain.

"Oh, look at me, I'm Dr. Nobody. I'm just going to fucking leave the cell door open by accident. Oh look at me I'm just taking a nap. Totally just taking a nap in this chair. Totally not just waiting for the stupid space girl to fucking murder me as part of my fucking plan to fucking convince her she's escaped so she flies off into space with some kind of readily communicable disease I shot her up with that's engineered to fucking kill the entire human race. TOTALLY NOT DOING THAT AT ALL."

She ripped at her skin, but she had no nails. She went at the wound with a screwdriver, until the blood ran up onto her fingers, until it dripped down onto the hull. But the infection remained. She wouldn't be going home.

She heard a rustle behind her and turned around. The bison wandered into the burned radius.

"Fuck you, bison."

The bison just looked up at her with its big dumb eyes.

"Fucking stuck here with you now."

She climbed down. The sun was a fever, high overhead, and the bison walked up to her ship.

"Hey, Mr. or Ms. Bison, I shouldn't have shot that other one of you. That was fucking stupid. That was human-as-cancer stupid."

The bison lowered its head, and Caroline reached out a hand in comfort.

She didn't see the horn enter her side, but she felt it pierce her skin and sunder her veins and wreck her organs. She fell supine to the earth as the heat and blood ran out of her. She stared into the sun with open eyes.

"I guess we all do what we've been made to do," she said.

Her vision grew dark.

"But still, fuck you."

EVERYTHING THAT ISN'T WINTER

The evening sky was a spring gray, which is different than a winter gray, and the soft light that came down through the clouds lit up the festival. Fires danced, and people danced, and my boyfriend was dancing with a woman who was there to work the harvest. They were hitting it off, it looked like. Everything was perfect in what was left of the world.

At the In-Between Lodge, we picked most of our tea leaves on Beltane. Traditionally, the first flush is in March and the second is in June. But traditionally, tea was imported from Asia, and obviously we haven't had contact with anywhere that far away in decades. So while we do a modest first flush and second flush, most of what we grow is what you'd call "Darjeeling In-Between." We grow it in the middle of what used to be called Washington state, so it's not really Darjeeling at all, just In-Between.

I sipped from a ceramic cup of mushroom tea, weak enough that it just sharpened me up, made me aware of patterns of bodies and light. I wasn't on duty, but I was on call and my rifle was stacked at the guard post by the eastern gate, so I didn't get any further into another realm than just the one cup of tea. We'd adulterated the mushroom with oolong from the first flush, and the pleasant and the revolting tastes fought in my throat, a little war between caffeine and psilocybin.

The band played war songs on guitars and fiddles and drums. The handsome men of the choir sang the songs I'd fought to, songs I relish. Songs that transport us from the world of the living to that liminal place of both battle and sex, where we make and take life. My bare feet were in earth, the mountain wind in my hair.

My boyfriend's dance partner wandered to the edge of the crowd, and I went to stand beside her.

"You must be Aiden." She turned toward me.

"I am."

"Khalil was just talking about you."

Khalil was still dancing, now alone, thick legs kicking out as he spun. He was awkward and completely in his element.

"I love him," I said.

"I gathered as much," she said. She was watching him the same way I watched him.

"You should sleep with him," I said.

She turned toward me.

"The spark's gone," I said. "Has been for years. I can get laid easily enough, but it isn't as easy for him."

She was just staring at me. I've never been good with reading faces. I saw myself and the firelight reflected and dancing in her green eyes.

"That's how it works for me, anyway," I went on. "Whenever I sleep with someone else, it just makes me want him all the more. You should sleep with him."

An autumnal smell broke my train of thought. Autumnal smells had no place during Beltane, but there it was, amidst the ambient scent of the tea fields, the iron sweat of the dancers, the pine smoke.

A voice carried through the evening's scents: "Fire!"

Burning tea plants. The smell was burning tea plants.

I ran for my rifle, snatched it up, and went into the rows toward the growing pillar of smoke. It started off as a Doric column, shifted to Atlas holding the world on his shoulders. By the time I reached it, it was Yggdrasil, the world tree, thick and ropy and holding up every one of the worlds.

There was no lightning, no likely cause but arson, and I ran toward the edge of the forest beyond the fields to search for culprits. At night, we see movement. In the day, we see shape. But in the gloaming, we see nothing. I saw nothing.

It took fifty of us to cut a firebreak to keep the blaze from spreading, tearing into tea plants with machetes while the fire tore into our livelihood. The band played, because what else can you do.

◆

Of the hundred rooms in the lodge, ours was in the northeast corner, closest to the fields and the forest. The poster bed was ancient, had been ancient before the apocalypse. It had been through worse than we ever had.

The tea had worn off but spring nights have their own magic I'll never understand or forgive, and there was no cell in my body that was feeling sober or responsible. Khalil was on his side, staring out the window at the burned fields lit by the moon and at the dark woods the moon couldn't light. I stood in the door.

"I'm sorry," he said.

"It's fine," I said. It wasn't.

"It's just that it's Beltane. It's spring. Sex and flowers and all that shit. I should want you."

"It's fine," I said. It wasn't. "I've never much cared for spring." That part was true.

"You look beautiful tonight," he said, but he was looking at the forest. He didn't look at me much anymore.

"What about that woman, the one you were dancing with?" I asked.

"The one who avoided me after you scared her off?"

"That one."

"It's fine," he said.

There wasn't much more to say. I left our room, and I left him there, and I went to go sleep at the guard post.

◆

First light found me in the forest with Bartley, our scout. Sword fern grew up from the ground, maidenhair fern grew out of the rock walls of gullies, and usnea hung from every limb of every tree in handsome gouts of green. We walked along downed cedar trees in the wet fog. I didn't follow Bartley's footsteps, not exactly, because one person leaves tracks but two people leave trails.

The forest is something I know. A rifle is something I know. Violence, I know.

We stopped to break our fast under the boughs of an old-growth black cottonwood that towered over much of the rest of the forest. We ate jerky, tough but fresh, and we passed a thermos of tea. Just tea.

"You lost the trail, didn't you?" I asked.

"Never was one," Bartley said. Bartley had a lazy eye, was always looking out to the side like she was a prey animal. Gray and white ran through her otherwise-black hair, and she was old enough that she should have remembered the old world. She always swore she didn't, that the first thing she remembered was being alone in the woods, barely post-pubescent, as she cut up a deer. Her life had begun at the same time so many lives had ended. A lot of people her age are like that.

Khalil and I, our lives had begun with our births, the next year, in the post-collapse baby boom. A lot of danger meant a lot of kids got born.

"What're we doing, then?" I asked.

"If I was going to raid us, I'd have camped up this hill," Bartley said. "There's a spring up there, one you can drink from, and a few open cliff faces that'd let you spy on us."

"Why do you think they did it?" I asked.

Bartley shrugged. "People don't like it when other people have nice things."

The In-Between Lodge was nice, there was no denying that. We were a collective of fifty-five adults, forty children, and another sixteen people halfway between the two categories. We'd raised up the lodge ten years back, just as the new world settled into place and drew its political borders, just as I'd left my teenaged years. We grew tea and we played our part in the new world's mutual aid network of a few interdependent city-states, communes, and hamlets. We sold, gave, or traded provisions to people passing through the old railway tunnel, and we guarded Stampede Pass, the eastern edge of the new world.

Well, mostly, Bartley and I guarded Stampede Pass. Everyone could fight, everyone stood watch in rotation, but Bartley handled terrain and tracking while I ran tactics.

"Who made this jerky?" Bartley asked. "And what the hell kind of not-tasty animal died to make it?"

"You grumpy?" I asked.

"Damn right," Bartley said. "I'm hungover and I didn't even get to sleep between drunk and now."

She shook the thermos.

"And we're out of tea."

◆

We caught him with his dick in the wind. It wasn't luck—we'd been waiting around for almost an hour for him to do something like fall asleep or get up to piss. Bartley had been right—he'd been camped up on the ledge, camouflaged by a bush, watching the In-Between with glare-free binoculars.

He was underfed, or maybe he was just built that way, and he'd kept scratching at his scalp like he was lousy. Younger than me, less than half Bartley's age, and he had all the bushcraft of a city kid. His clothes were wrong for the west side of the mountains—too urban, too old world.

There he was, pissing off the cliff, when I walked out from behind the tree with a rifle leveled at him. I saw him think about dropping his dick and going for his rifle, and I saw him realize that wasn't going to work. He put his hands in the air. If he was smart and his gang could afford it, he'd have a radio set to automatic, voice-activated transmission, and there was someone listening on the other end. But he was too dumb to shave his lice-infested hair. I was pretty sure we'd got him cold.

"You're going to tell me a lot of things," I said. "You tell me those things, and you'll get supplies and a one-way trip on whatever caravan you want."

"I wouldn't tell you the color of the lips of your mother's cunt."

I shot him. The rifle slammed into my shoulder, the report scattered birds and hurt my ears. The bullet hit him in the neck and sent him tumbling over the edge of the cliff.

"You kidding me?" Bartley asked.

"Well I wasn't going to torture the kid, and he didn't want to talk nice."

Bartley shook her head. "Now we've got to go find him, you know," she said. "Search his body."

"Maybe he'll have some tea."

We eventually found the wreckage of the man at the base of the cliff, his ribs sprouting from his chest. The noon sun and I both kept watch over the forest while Bartley combed over the body.

"Help me lift him," Bartley said.

I got my hands under what was left of the bandit's armpits and lifted. His insides dripped down my leg.

"I'm getting too old for this. The new world is getting too old for this." I said it, because it was what people were supposed to think, but I didn't really feel it. Peace didn't work for me. Battle is a thing that gets into my gut, makes me desperate to live. Love is a thing that gets into my gut, makes me wish I were dead.

Bartley went through his pockets. She pulled out a pack of cheap naked-lady cards, threw them off into the forest. In another pocket, she found a topo map. Last, she pulled out a radio. She clicked it off.

"Hell," I said. "They heard all of that."

"Hell indeed."

"What's the map tell us?" I asked.

"Nothing's marked on it, but it's pretty zoomed-in, doesn't cover more than about thirty-five square kilometers. Since the In-Between isn't in the center of it, I figure their camp might be. Puts it halfway between here and the tunnel."

"They know where we are," I said, "but we don't know where they are."

"They might hit us tonight."

"I bet the fire was just to flush us out," I said. "They set this kid here to see how we organized our defense."

"What's the plan?"

"You know I'd hate for you to go out alone..."

"But maybe I've got to go out alone," Bartley said.

"I'll go warn everyone, set patrols, get children to shelter."

"And I'll make it back up here into range to call it in once I've figured out where they are."

We started down the hill. The sun was halfway to the horizon; it was cutting into my eyes and baking that kid's blood into my clothes. We stepped out from the trees and scrambled down to the railroad tracks about a kilometer east of the In-Between. Bartley came with me the half a kilometer or so our paths overlapped.

"I always liked walking tracks," Bartley said.

"Yeah?" I asked. I wasn't really curious but I preferred to listen to her speak than listen to my heart beat arrhythmically like it always did after I shot somebody. Doc says it's just jitters, what some of the old books call "generalized anxiety." I say it's me getting off light, karmically speaking.

"Roads are hell," Bartley said, "because they're easy. It's easy to make a road, right? You just get a bunch of people to walk somewhere a lot, that'll make a road. You walk a road, it's easy, lulls you to sleep, and there's some asshole hiding with a gun and you don't even notice because you're lost in your head. Roads are hell."

"Sounds like me and Khalil. We fell into habit. Made a road."

"Railroads, though, railroads are great," Bartley went on. "They're hard to make. They're hard to walk. They're so *specialized*, and the best part is that they're specialized for something that doesn't exist anymore. These things weren't made for our cow-drawn boxcars or our little rail-bikes, they were made for kilometer-long chains of cars pulled by the sheer strength of coal. When you're using something specialized, and you're using it wrong, that's the beauty in this life."

"I thought you were grumpy," I said.

"I *was* grumpy," Bartley said. "But now I'm walking on railroad tracks."

◆

We'd built the In-Between in the narrow valley below the pass. The Green River guarded our north, the mountains our south. A road from the west met its end at the door to the lodge, and a railroad ran through the whole of our land. We were unwalled.

We were unwalled for a thousand reasons. We were unwalled because we were peaceful. We were unwalled because, though increasingly rare, mortars and grenades and rockets were still a part of this world. Even some helicopters had survived the electromagnetic waves that had wiped so much technology from the earth, as I'd heard it, and such vehicles have no respect for walls. We were unwalled because a stone wall blinds the defender as much as the attacker. We'd gated the road and the railway, but those gates remained open during daylight.

Khalil was waiting by the gate for me when I got back. He had that pick in his short afro, the one the trader had told me was tortoiseshell, and who was I to say it wasn't. The one Khalil had told me was lucky, and who was I to say it wasn't.

He saw me coming, and a smile split across his beard. The smile got bigger the closer I got, until I was in his arms.

"We heard a shot," he said. "Hours ago."

"I shot somebody," I said. I was so small in his embrace. He was one of the only people in the world who was large enough to make me small.

He kissed my forehead, and I tilted my neck up and looked into those black-brown eyes behind his glasses, those eyes the same color as mine, and I kissed him on the mouth.

"You all right?" he asked at last.

"I'm all right."

"It took hours. I've been waiting for you for hours."

I pulled away, set my rifle down at the guard post. The crows stood sentinel on the gate.

"I can't handle you worrying about me," I said.

It was the right thing to say, because it was true.

It was the wrong thing to say, because I loved him.

He lifted his glasses, rubbed at his eyes. "I know," he said. He walked away.

My eyes lingered on his back, and I still felt small. The wind wailed across the fields of tea.

I got the children and the infirm into the bomb shelter—a hundred-year-old relic of a paranoid generation that had been right about the apocalypse, just wrong about its timing—then set out organizing an all-hands watch. Fifteen people were on at all times, no able-bodied adults exempted from taking a shift. No one liked it, but no one complained. I don't tell the cooks what to feed us and I don't tell Doc how to sew us up and I don't tell Khalil or the other horticulturalists when to conscript us into the fields for a harvest.

It was late enough in spring that the sun lingered, low in the sky, and I found myself cleaning rifles and counting bullets. Which left me nothing to do with my brain but to run my conversation with Khalil over and over in my mind like I was locked in the computer room in the basement with a video running on an endless loop—I could turn my head away, but I could still hear everything. Watching a video, though, I could wait until the sun went down and the solar stopped and the computer died. There wasn't such an easy way out of my head.

◆

There's a certain kind of peace on a farm, and the tea leaves were emeralds in the moonlight. The night birds sang in the forest, the trees stood like crows on the horizon.

There's a certain kind of peace in holding a rifle, as well. It shares the same simplicity, the same honesty. With that rifle, in those fields, my intentions were bare—we worked the earth, we defended the fruits of our labor.

I walked our eastern perimeter, through the rows of tea and through the burned scar where so much of our tea had been. Ahead, at the gatehouse, electric lights spit a flood of red out across the tracks and into the hills. We used red to save our night vision. We used lights at all because they made a good distraction—made any potential attacker believe our attention was focused on the railroad.

I'd learned every bit I knew about tactics the hard way. There were more bodies buried in our fields than there were people living in the lodge.

But that night, while I clutched a radio in one hand and waited to hear from Bartley, they didn't come for us from the trees. They didn't come for us from the tracks, or over the Green River, or from the mountains or the roads. They came for us with artillery.

It took three seconds for two shots to destroy the lodge. I saw them, those meteors, as they arced through the sky on a low trajectory and reduced my home to rubble. They were tracer shells, marked to help their gunner aim, and they burned phosphorous through the sky. They'd come from the east. They'd come from Stampede Pass.

I'd leveled trees older than my grandparents to help build the lodge. I'd pedaled rebar eighty kilometers up the tracks from the ruins of Tacoma to re-enforce the stone and mortar construction, and I'd killed two people—a woman and a man—who'd tried to rob me on the way. I liked to think I knew the difference between the evil and the desperate, and those two had just been desperate. I'd left their bones in the forest.

Three seconds, two shots, and all our work was gone.

With adrenaline in me, I don't consciously process sound or scent or touch. Everything is visual, everything is slow motion. I ran through the green fields toward the shattered lodge as people streamed out. People were shouting. I might have been shouting.

I saw Khalil walk across the road, carrying someone toward the bomb shelter. That man existed to help people, to carry people, to nurse green shoots up out of the soil and into the light. I existed for other purposes. I gave up on returning to the lodge—they could rebuild without me, and Khalil was alive, and what good would I do, and I was their guard and I'd failed and I couldn't face Khalil—and I ran for the gate.

I set a rail cart onto the tracks, settled into the saddle, put my feet on the pedals, then gave a last look at the lodge. Khalil was watching me, hands on his hips. His chest heaved, he turned his head, and he walked away. His gait told me more than any words ever had. It was the gait of a man who'd given up.

I pedaled east with my rifle held across my lap. I pedaled until the adrenaline cleared and the evening's fog rose thicker and thicker and I had the chance to realize what a mess I'd just thrown myself into alone, which was better than acknowledging the mess from which I'd just fled.

It didn't make sense to destroy the lodge. It didn't make sense to destroy the fields. It made sense to *capture* our holdings. Whomever I was running off to try to shoot, I didn't understand them. If you know your enemy and you know yourself, you need not fear one hundred battles. If you know yourself and not your enemy, you will lose as often as you win. If you know neither yourself nor your enemy, you will never know victory.

◆

I'd pedaled those tracks hundreds of times. The Cascade Range was my home, I'd grown up in its shadow. But fear creeps into your system and renders the familiar into something alien. The fog was milk-thick, as thick as it had ever been. My eyes tracked movement I knew better than to register—the shifting of moonlight through wind-blown branches, the glint of light on the steel of the rails.

I passed a rusted junction box, still painted with pre-collapse graffiti, which meant the tunnel was only a few hundred meters out. I stopped pedaling, set the brake so the cart wouldn't roll back downhill, then dismounted as quietly as I could.

It's hard to disguise the sound of heels on gravel. I heard my own, but there was another footfall, fainter, right behind me. A hand clamped down on my shoulder. I whirled, went for the knife on my belt.

Bartley.

She had one finger to her lips, her eyes betraying sleepless exhaustion. We scrambled up the embankment, pausing where we could just see the tracks at the edge of our vision. My hands were on the bark of a poplar pine, its scent was in my head, and I was grounded.

"They're in the tunnel," she said. She was murmuring low into my ear. "They've got military ordinance. Two big guns on two rail cars, plus a whole train of weaponry stretching into the tunnel."

"Who are they?"

"Don't know. I've seen about twenty of them. Most of them are camped inside the tunnel, alongside the ordinance. Looks like they've been there a few days."

"Uniforms?" I asked.

"Nope."

"Motive?"

"No idea," Bartley said. "They fired a couple artillery shells. What'd they hit?"

"They took out the lodge."

I'd never known Bartley to wear her heart on her sleeve, but she took a breath at that. Then another.

"Casualties?" she asked.

"I didn't stop to count."

"We should kill them all." She wasn't judging their character, she was addressing a strategic concern.

"How?"

"I mined the tunnel, a couple of years back."

"What?" I asked that too loud, switching for a moment into whisper instead of murmur.

"I didn't tell anyone, because I thought people might get mad. And I figured our general assembly wouldn't go for it."

"How close do you have to get to set it off?" I asked.

"Close," Bartley said. "Real close. Ten feet inside the front of the tunnel, against the south side wall, there's a rotted hunk of plywood. Behind it, a cheap old breaker box I put in. Switch the first three and the last three breakers, then we've got two minutes to get clear."

"Will that set off the ordinance on the train?"

"Probably not."

"How do we get there?"

"I've got an idea."

"I'm not going to like it, am I?" I asked.

"Nope."

◆

"I'm here to negotiate our surrender."

The words were foreign in my throat and hung strangely in the air. They weren't my words. They weren't words I really knew how to say, but I said them loud and attracted the ire of a number of armed women and men. Women and men I hoped wouldn't object too immediately and violently to the rifle I still bore slung across my back.

The fog was thinner at the base of the tunnel, and it calmed me down to see the silhouette spires of the trees and the faint glow of stars above me.

Two flatbed rail cars extended out from the tunnel, each with an old-world gun larger than some houses. Inside the tunnel, a string of boxcars stretched farther than I could see.

A half-dozen people approached me, most no older than the kid I'd shot on the cliffside. I liked to think I knew the difference between the evil and the desperate, and these people weren't desperate, not on the face of things. Each had a rifle trained on me, each watched me with some mixture of indifference and malice. Evil isn't something we do to one another, it's the way in which we do it, it's why we do it.

There were two clear authorities—a man about ten years my senior, with gray flecked into his red hair, and a woman with at least twenty years on him. The two conversed briefly, and the man approached.

"General Samuel John," he said. He didn't offer his hand.

"Aiden Jackson," I said. I didn't offer my hand.

"Our terms are simple," the general said. "Anyone who leaves between now and noon tomorrow will not be hunted down and shot."

"Who are you?" I asked. "General of what army?"

"The New Republic of Washington," he said.

Another warlord.

"What's your claim on our land?" I asked.

I knew his answer before he said it. I grew more confident that I knew him, that I could outwit or outshoot him.

"Small holdings like yours and the rest of the 'new world' are a relic of an era we aim to put behind us," he said, on script. "Washington has suffered too long without central authority."

Lying to people is fun. It's kind of dangerous how fun it is. "You're right," I said.

"We will drive this train to the end of the line, laying waste to everything in our path, and raise forth our savior from the coastal waters."

That was a pretty different script.

"We'll raise new cities," the general said. His eyes rolled back, he held his palms face-up in front of him. "Pure cities, built of light and manna, and we will live in His grace."

"Until the zombies," the older woman added.

"Until the zombies come and devour those of us who remain in the cities."

I looked around, from bandit to bandit. Grins were painted on every face.

"You're screwing with me."

"Of course we're screwing with you," the general said. "We're not on some moral or religious quest. We've got artillery and we want the pass so that we can tax caravans, and if you try to stop us we'll kill you. That's the world now, that's always been the world. It's a good world for people like me and mine, and that's the only metric I judge by."

"We were going to just tax you, you know," the woman said. "A little bit of fire, a little show of force, then we'd tax you. But I heard you shoot my grandson."

All eyes and all guns were on me, which I wanted—within a certain, very limited, understanding of the word "want." I'd lured them away from the mouth of the tunnel. Behind the trumped-up highwaymen, in the thin fog, Bartley lizard-crawled toward the breaker box.

I didn't feel like lying anymore.

"You'll get yours," I said. "There've always been those who want power over others, there've always been people who don't. The whole of our history is the history of people like you killing people like me, of people like me killing people like you. You'll live a miserable shit life, distrustful and afraid, and you'll get yours. I'll get mine in the end, the same as you, but I'll have lived a life in a society of equals, among people I love. I'll have loved them."

"Hey!" One of the bandits, a young man, turned in time to see Bartley crawling into the tunnel. He raised his rifle and fired at my friend.

I turned and ran uphill, perpendicular to the mouth of the tunnel. Always run uphill—people don't like chasing uphill.

I made it behind a thick stump twenty meters up the embankment, and bullets lodged into the decades-dead tree flesh. I unslung and unsafetied my rifle, returning fire.

Bartley made it to cover herself, on the far side of the train from the bandits.

They could keep me pinned down and outflank me, put a bullet into me, then turn their attention to Bartley. I had two spare magazines, one friend, and no hope for backup. I had no hope at all.

I shouldn't have been cruel to Khalil. The man had left his family, left the safety and stability of Bainbridge Island, to follow me into the mountains and to the edge of the new world. He'd followed his dreams.

We'd met in the winter. Every winter since the first one, we'd walked out along the Green River to its source. We made a week of it, sixty kilometers round trip, and we'd held hands and stared at the breadth of the sky and camped in the snow and walked out along the ice. We'd never get the chance again.

He worried about me. He was right to worry. I was about to die.

Bartley caught my attention, then started banging on the steel of the car with the butt of her rifle. This drew all eyes, and they were out from cover, moving to flank me. I squatted up, aimed, and picked off the general with a round through his cheek. His head spun, his neck snapped, and his legs gave out.

The bandits turned away from Bartley, and she stood and shot the older woman—the second-in-command, perhaps, or maybe just the general's mother. Either way, she collapsed with a hole in her sternum.

A bullet grazed me then. It burned across my shoulder; blood welled up.

"Stay and guard the train!" one of the remaining women shouted into the tunnel. The four remaining gunners returned to cover, crouching by the wheels of the train.

Bartley ran, past the train and for the trees. She drew fire, but not from every rifle. I took two quick, deep breaths, let the oxygen fill me up, then rolled from cover. I'd learned long ago not to let myself listen for individual shots once I was committed. Fear is the antithesis of action.

I heard a scream, a woman's scream, and I ran down the embankment and into the dark of the tunnel. There was the plywood. Behind it, the breaker box. It was too dark to see, but I found the breakers by touch and tried not to focus on the muzzle flashes coming from outside and inside the tunnel alike.

Bullets are dangerous. I know that intimately. But most bullets aren't aimed, not really, and unaimed bullets are like lightning in a field. If you stay low, you'll survive, more likely than not.

I hit the six breakers.

Two of the gunners from outside had crossed the tracks, and I saw their boots as they worked their way down the other side of the train. I'd be flanked.

I rolled under the train and took shots at the boots. Hit one, was rewarded with a man falling prone, and I shot him in the temple.

I crawled, my forearms on the ties and gravel, the wound in my shoulder beginning to protest.

I shot another woman in the foot, and the remaining two bandits outside fell without me firing—Bartley was alive.

I was almost to the mouth of the tunnel when the charges blew, and only the behemoth of steel above me saved me from the cascade of rock that followed. It was no good to think about the lives that were about to end, suffocating in the darkness behind me. It was no good to question whether or not I was evil.

In the dust and fog, I crawled forward, toward the faint moonlight.

◆

Bartley had a hole in her leg where muscle and fat and skin had been, and I got her onto the rail cart with a tourniquet on her thigh. People say you can't use a tourniquet for more than a few minutes, but I'd learned the bloody way that you could get away with one longer if you needed.

"Hey, do me a favor," she said, as I started to pedal.

"What's that?"

"Don't let me die," she said.

"That's all?" I asked.

"That's all. Don't let me die."

"You're not dying."

"Okay, I've got another favor."

"What's that?"

"Don't let me die. I really don't want to die."

I pedaled harder. It was downhill, easy going, and we went in and out of fog banks, and Bartley went in and out of being in a mood to talk, went in and out of looking like she was going to make it. All I could think about was Khalil. About how sure I'd been I was going to die, about how sure I'd been I'd never see him again. It was a long half hour before we reached the ruins of the In-Between.

Three people met us at the gate, including the woman who'd come for the harvest, the one who'd danced with Khalil. She helped me carry Bartley to the makeshift infirmary set up on the road, any awkwardness between us lost to more pressing matters. Doc told Bartley that she'd live.

I gave a quick report, and that report spread quickly.

Khalil wasn't around, and a fear came over me, a fear worse than firefights. He was okay. I'd seen him escape the lodge, I knew he was okay. But he wasn't okay with me.

I first met him when we'd both been visiting Tacoma, during the death days, when neither of us thought we'd live to see twenty. I'd loved him half my life, the half that mattered.

I went down the concrete steps into the bomb shelter. It was full of people, and they were hurt and scared and they wanted to talk to me but they all had the distinct disadvantage of not being Khalil.

I went to the lodge, what remained of the hall we'd built. There were people who weren't Khalil picking through the smoking rubble, shoring up the surviving walls, digging for survivors and corpses.

I went to the remnants of the bridge that had once, in the old world, crossed the Green River. But there was no one there to kiss me in the shadows of the ruins, no one wading in the river with his hand on the small of my back, no one singing in sweet, low tones. I thought about walking into the river anyway, until the water took me. The river in spring is as cold as snow.

I went to the fields, and I found him at the northeast corner—the corner we'd seen from our poster bed. His hands swept across leaves. He sang wordless serenades to the tea.

"Khalil."

He heard me, because his body tensed and he paused his song, but he didn't turn around.

"Khalil, I'm sorry."

"For what?" He was far enough away that I could scarcely hear his voice.

"For a lot of things."

"You do what you do."

A breeze came across the fields from the river, whispering against the tears on my cheeks, and I fought harder to keep my voice level than I'd fought to stay alive an hour prior.

"I don't want to just do what I do," I said.

He turned toward me and he was crying harder than I was. He always cries harder than I do.

"It's okay if you worry about me," I said.

"You ran away tonight," he said. He didn't try to disguise the pain in his voice. "You went alone. Maybe it's too much for me, that you're not here when I need you, that you're never safe. That you take stupid risks."

I halved the distance between us, and he was just out of arm's reach.

"I was going to die tonight," I said. I sat down, hugged my knees. "I was going to die and I was never going to see you again, and now I've survived but what if I never get to be with you again?"

He sat down across from me, mirrored my pose.

"You never talk to me," he said.

"I know."

"Why don't you talk to me?"

"I'm afraid," I said. But I said it too quiet.

"What?"

"I'm afraid," I said, louder. "I'm afraid. I'm afraid of you and I'm afraid of us and I'm afraid of this new world we've built, that one day soon it'll be no place for me and everything I've done and everything I am. I'm afraid of everything that isn't winter and I'm afraid of everything but dying."

My eyes were closed, and I couldn't see him, and I couldn't hear him, and all I heard was my heart beating out of sync. For a minute at least, it was all I heard.

I didn't see him move, but his arms wrapped all the way around me, around my knees and my back. He held me. I let myself go. He kissed the top of my head, and I nuzzled into his neck.

"You do what you do," he said, "and I love you for it."

"You love me? All stupid? All covered in blood?"

"I love you," he said.

His hand went into my hair, and he held me like he used to. He held me like he wanted me. I took him by the beard and pulled his face against mine, felt his lips against mine, open-mouthed. His hands went to my hips, my fingers dug into his chest.

Smoke drifted up from the ruins of our home, and love was something in my gut and it made me want to live.

INTO THE GRAY

I only led the worst of men down to the Waking Waters and death, down to my love in the pool below the falls. I only led the foul men with filth on their tongues, the rich men who contrived to rule other men. I only led the men with hatred in their hearts and iron in their hands. I spurred them on with tales of hidden silver or the sight of my girlish thigh, down out from the mountain town of Scilla, down to the hills and the pines and the ruttish perfume of wildflowers.

All so that the Lady of the Waters might love me.

Well, that and so I could rob their corpses.

The morning sun sat low in the western sky, and the streets were empty near the edge of town. The man with me that day was handsome. He was twenty-five years my senior, with three teeth of silver, a gold-hilted sword and dagger, and a string of badges he'd won by gambling his life for the king's glory in a foreign land. A town like Scilla saw men like him only once a year, only for the night market.

He'd found me walking with a basket of flowers. I caught his eye and smiled him over and yet he seemed to think *he* was the one propositioning *me*.

For a moment, I considered laying with him anyways, without taking part in his death, maybe just taking a few of his things while he slept. For all his pomp and arrogance, I liked the shape of his jaw and the fervor in his eyes.

We walked arm in arm away from the market, the daisies under my arm.

"And you swear you're not a working girl?"

There was no good answer to a question like that. The answer was no: I don't exchange labor for coin, I murder and rob. Of course I couldn't tell him that, nor could I in good conscience distance myself from those among my friends who work more honestly.

I giggled instead. Men seem to like when I giggle at them. I don't understand how they don't see through it.

He jangled his full purse, laughing his horrid laugh. "Too many people think only about coin." As if it would be strange for those of us without to be concerned about acquiring what we need to feed ourselves, clothe ourselves, house ourselves. "It's weakness, pure and simple, and what people don't understand is that weakness is our enemy. We must kill the weakest parts of ourselves as surely as we put down our weakest foes before they gather strength."

He must have done terrible things to win awards like those pinned to his chest. If I focused on that, I could excuse the terrible things I planned to do.

"I know a better place than your room at the inn," I said.

"If you're not a working girl, there's no shame to be seen with you."

"I know a place, a better place, where the wind runs cool off the water. Where I can rinse, where you can rinse, where we'd taste our best for one another while only the deer of the forest look on."

"You've done this before," he said. He was hungry at my words, at the thought of watching me bathe.

I had. Twice before. He would be my third.

"So have you," I said.

"What do I call you?" he asked.

"Laria."

"A harlot's name."

"Fitting, then," I said, starting out for the edge of town with him in my wake. I didn't ask his name, because I didn't care to know it and because no one would ever call him it or anything else again.

He followed me along the long road that wound down from Scilla. I promised him it wasn't far, and I wasn't lying. We skirted off from the road into the pines and followed the sound of the water. We went downhill and downhill, to the tall and tranquil Waking Waters falls, then downhill to the pool at their base.

There are more impressive waterfalls in this world, but the Waking Waters has a beauty of the sort that has no need to be spectacular. On midsummer evenings, like that one, the sun sets behind the top of the falls and makes it glow while the shadows turn darker everywhere else.

My quarry's eyes flit across the woods around us, as though suddenly aware I might be leading him to ambush, but he was looking in the wrong place.

"After you," he said, gesturing at the water. He didn't trust me. He was a terrible man, but not an entirely stupid one.

I slipped off my shift with a smile, first at the man and then at the world around me. Wind carried a bit of mist and the scents of summer off of the water, and I strode toward and into the pool.

With each step, the water lapped at my skin. With each step, the water washed away the filth of poverty and the filth of the town and the filth of work—honest work, illicit work, it's all work.

He watched me, of course. I would have watched me too. I was beautiful.

The Lady found me when I was waist-deep, running her human hand along my thigh. I dove. She swam alongside me, pressing her body to mine, with her bare breasts and her fish-tail.

We kissed, there, underwater, and I ran my tongue along her sharp fish teeth until just a drop of blood found its way into her mouth. I liked to tease her. I liked when she was hungry.

We emerged. The man on the bank, now stripped down to muscle, watched with wide, incredulous eyes.

"The Lady of the Waking Waters," I said, by way of introduction.

I needn't say more. I'd never needed say more.

She's never told me a more proper name. I call her the Lady because I must call her something. For her own purposes, she has no need of a name.

A mermaid has her own magic, stronger than that of any creature born with legs, and even though she smiled and her teeth were white, thin razors, her eyes were bright and hazel. Her hair changed color as the sun, the wind, and the mist played off of it. Her skin was a perfect medium-brown. She could enchant any man alive.

He walked into the water, willingly, and I stepped out onto land.

He didn't scream, because she removed most of his throat in the first bite. The rust-red, blood-red water slipped away over the rocks to feed the forest.

It's always beautiful to watch someone perform their life's work. The man we'd murdered, perhaps he'd been beautiful at war. He might have been beautiful on top of me, inside me. But the Lady, she was beautiful as she stripped flesh from bone.

Only the worst of men. I had honor as a thief, so damned if I wouldn't have honor as a murderer.

I went to his belt, found his purse, and took those coins he'd rattled. The sun was hot on me as I worked my way through his clothes, unraveling the gold wire woven into his hems, unraveling the gold wire he'd wrapped around the hilt of his dagger to announce his wealth. I'd have to find someone to melt down the medals.

At last, I turned my attention from my work and back to the pool. The Lady was sunbathing on the rocks on the far side, and the water ran clear once more. She smiled, and I strode back into the water, back out to the Lady, my lover.

I put my mouth on hers, and she was gentle with me, kinder than anyone with two legs had ever been. When a mermaid's lips are against your skin, time slows. The white noise of the waterfall became a low and quiet roar and I saw every sweet drop of water as it cascaded down the mountainside.

She pleased me with her hands and mouth while my feet dangled in the cold pool, and she had me breathing fast and easy, fast and hard, fast and easy, fast and hard, while the world crawled by around me.

For a moment, with the last of the sun on me, I had coin enough, and I had love enough.

◆

"Can I just stay here with you?" I asked. The moon had risen, a crescent scythe in the field of stars. I hadn't told her of my plans. In truth, I was afraid she'd dissuade me.

She was in the water to her neck, and I laid on my side on a rock with my face near hers. The roar of the waterfall cut out the sounds of the night, yet I could hear my heart hammering in my chest.

"Of course not," she said. "I live in the water, and it would be the death of you by drowning to join me."

"I don't care if it kills me," I said, weeping.

"I do," she said. "I want you to still bring me men every few years when your hair has gone white and your skin hangs loose on your frame."

"You only want to see me every few years," I said.

"We're not the same," she told me. "It's not possible for us to lead the same life."

"What if it was possible, though? What if I changed? What if I found magic enough?"

"I love you as you are, Laria," the Lady said. She brushed the wet hair, plastered to my face, away from my eyes. "I love the way things are between us." She was sad, and smiling.

"You're using me," I said.

"That might be true, but I also love you."

The world was blurry, through the haze of my tears. She kissed my cheeks, awkwardly, like a boy just learning what romance tastes like. Time slowed again, and I realized no matter how fast she'd killed that man with her teeth, he'd had all the time in the world to experience death.

I envied him, a short moment, for losing his life to the Lady's teeth. Why are death and love and sex and change all tied up together in our heads?

But as her fingers ran down my neck, I grew calm. I was as happy as I ever was. She climbed out of the water, her tail transformed to legs. I laid on my bare back, and she straddled my hips, and we let time run slow once more.

◆

The night was full-dark, with clouds obscuring the moon, when I made it back to Scilla. The sun had gone to rest, but the town had not. Vendors from all over the island were setting up under eaves and on the cobbles. Fifty weeks a year, my home was a dry husk of a town. Two, it drew the finest wares and wanderers in the country.

There was good work to be had at the night market. All kinds of work, legal and not. But with the weight of gold in my purse, I had no need. I wasn't there for work. I was there for the witch.

A heavily-scarred cheesemonger cut into a wheel of something pungent and rich, and my stomach informed me I hadn't eaten since the sun was at its peak.

"He's sleeping off wine, that's what I figure," I heard. Next to the cheesemonger, two men-at-arms sat on a bench eating fried lamb, their polearms resting in the nooks of their arms. They spoke in the way of men who aren't used to manners, of men who don't care who hears them.

"The King's Fifty are not the sort to abandon their posts," the other man said, his voice full of gravel.

I'd killed one of the King's Fifty. Pride and terror fought for control of my emotions.

"He's probably fucking or drunk or just fucking drunk," the first man laughed. "He'll get here."

I hurried away into the crowd, lest they somehow see the heft of my purse and the medals within. I had to be careful. There likely wasn't a moneychanger disreputable enough to trust with my gold, not even the wire. As rumors raced through the market—a knight has been slain—my caution escalated to fear, and the physical sensation coursed through my body.

If I couldn't trust a moneychanger, then better to trust the witch.

I found her tent set between a child selling counterfeit treasure maps and a cooper as old as the moon. Such was the night market.

Henrietta the Haggard, people call her, though it said Henrietta the Honored on the tapestry hanging on the side of her tent. I couldn't read it, but once I saw a gentry-girl read it aloud to her father. I used to think it was funny, how Henrietta the Haggard had the wrong name written on her tent. Now it's not so funny. I know what it's like to need to advertise to the world what you are, so that people don't just assume you are what they think you are.

◆

"I have the coin to pay you," I told Henrietta.

The thick canvas walls blocked the light from the street, and only the red ember glow from a dying brazier lit either of us at all. Thick incense, of a scent too exotic to place, tickled my nose.

Weary lines were etched into the witch's dry skin, and she looked as old as the town, as old as the kingdom. Henrietta had as much magic as anyone on the island; she could look however she wanted. She chose to look decrepit. I liked that about her.

"You wish to become a creature of the lakes and rivers and the sea?" she asked.

I nodded.

Henrietta frowned. "Better to just let me read your palm and go."

I pulled the coins and the coiled gold wire out from my purse and placed them on the table. They gleamed, even in the scarce light of the embers.

"A spell like that would leave me drained a fortnight, at least. I'd lose all my other work. That's quite a wealth of gold you have, child, and it could buy most anything in the market. It cannot buy Henrietta for a fortnight."

I nodded. I'd expected that. I went back into my bag and pulled out the medals.

Her eyes grew wild, with surprise, greed, or suspicion.

"Tell me more specifically," she said. "What do you desire to become?"

"A mermaid."

"I can give you the tail of a fish and gills on your throat. I can point your teeth and give you a gullet built for blood. I will not work the dark magic required to make you immortal. I can't grant you magic of your own, and you won't be able to shift your tail to legs to move on land. You will be a creature of the water, and of the water only."

I'd figured that was likely.

"Tell me, child," Henrietta said, "have you been talking to the Lady of the Waking Waters?"

I thought no one knew of her but me. If Henrietta recognized the medals, she would know what happened to the soldier. She'd know my culpability in his death, sure, I'd counted on that—but she'd know the Lady's involvement as well.

"Breathe, child," Henrietta said. "Your eyes are wide and wild with guilt and it won't do to be seen that way. I'm in the business of revealing the truth of the future and the past, but I'm not in the business of informing on my customers."

She stood up—an imposing figure, like a stooped giantess—and went to close the flap of her tent. No light, no sound came in through that canvas. The incense seemed thicker, the air hazier.

"Why?" she asked.

"Does it matter?"

"Yes."

It took me a moment to collect my thoughts. "Because I'm in love," I said.

"Is that a reason to give up your life on land and your body?"

"What life?" I asked. "Selling flowers for copper? Risking everything, constantly, to steal gold? This is the third town I've lived in in five years."

"How will you run from your troubles, without legs?"

"I'll have the whole of the ocean!"

"All right," Henrietta said. "Stand up then, let's have a look at you."

I stood.

"You're a boy under all of that?" she asked. There was no judgment in her voice. Ever since I'd taken a woman's name and worn women's clothes, people quickly sorted themselves into three categories: those who wanted to fuck me, those who were repulsed by me, and those who simply didn't care. Henrietta didn't care.

"More or less," I said. It was hard to think of myself as a boy at all.

"Won't matter soon enough," she said. "Soon enough you'll be a fish. Come on then, let's get down to the water. I know a cove that should work."

"Right now?" I asked.

"You sounded like you were sure before."

"Shouldn't we wait until tomorrow? So I can, I don't know, get my affairs in order?"

"I thought there was nothing for you on land?"

Nothing suddenly felt like an exaggeration. There was Nettle and Fitch, the two girls I shared a room with in the loft over the stables. Would they be able to make copper enough for the landlord without me? And Fitch, the way she looked at me. I was in love with the Lady, that was as certain as the sun, but I liked the way Fitch looked at me too.

"I'll meet you down there," I said. "Give me, I don't know, an hour."

"I will cast the spell as the first light of dawn breaks over the water."

I started to collect my gold from the table.

"Leave that here," Henrietta said.

"What?"

"Leave that here so I know you're serious, so I know this isn't a prank, a waste of Henrietta the Honored's time. I will destroy some not-inexpensive things in preparation for this working, and I won't be cheated."

"Where's the cove?" I asked.

"Where the Waking Water feeds into the ocean. Don't be late, child. A spell works on its schedule, not yours. If I prepare the spell, it will be cast at dawn regardless of what any of us desire."

I nodded, and stood. The incense had me dizzy, and I stumbled out of the tent, back into the noise of crowded humanity.

◆

At least a dozen men-at-arms crowded together near the front gate, strapping on coat-of-plates and brigandine. Each of the men towered over me, and the heads of halberds and pikes towered over them in turn. I shied back. Menace was in the air, and my head was still fogged with the incense and magic from Henrietta's tent.

"Saw him leave with a girl," one man, a hostler in town for the market, said.

I flipped up my hood, hiding my feminine hair, and took a half step back into the gathered and gathering crowd.

"You tell me when they left, how tall this girl was, and I'll track Holann down sure as your mother's milk." The man who said that was a gray-haired old ranger, stocky and short with a glint of malice in his remaining eye.

Holann. The man I killed had been named Holann. Didn't matter.

"What," another soldier asked, "so we can catch him with another whore in the woods? Just let him sleep it off, we'll see him in the morning."

"You ever known him to abandon his post?" the ranger asked.

They argued for a while after that. The crowd lost interest and dispersed, and I found the shadow of a glassblower's stall to hide in.

They were going to find the Lady.

They would follow my tracks down the hills and through the trees and to the water, and they would find the Lady, and all the magic she could bring to bear wouldn't be enough to stop a company of the king's own men. Not if she didn't know they were coming.

Henrietta could wait. My transformation could wait. I ran.

◆

If I'd had time, I could have misled the tracker. I'm not sure how. I could have thought of something. There wasn't time.

I walked out of the town gate, through the crowd of arrivals, with my hood still obscuring my face. I made it to the tree line, stepped through, and went back to running.

There was no direct path, just a series of gullies and deer trails, and darkness obscured the forest. I didn't get lost. I'd gone that way a hundred times. I skinned my knee, deep, on the rocks when I slipped near the end, but I scarcely registered the pain. My love was in danger.

I stumbled out of the trees and waded into the pool at the base of the falls. I would have shouted her name, had she a name, had I not been afraid of calling attention to our location.

The night had grown cold, and the water sapped at my strength if not my resolve. I plunged through the falls and into the alcove behind. Phosphorescent moss cast faint light that glistened on wet stone.

I saw her sleeping on the shelf, with legs. It was so easy to imagine she slept with legs because she wanted to sleep next to me. It was so easy to imagine that land was her first home, that water was simply another realm she could travel within.

It wasn't fair, that she could walk and swim and I had to choose forever between one or the other. It wasn't fair that I should be the one who would sacrifice for us to be together, when it would be so much easier for her.

She was beautiful. In the usual ways, yes, but she was also beautiful in the ways that anyone might become, when you get to know the secret language of their body and their lives. She'd been alive so long, seen so much, developed so much beauty. The longer I might know her, the more of her hidden beauty I might unearth.

"My Lady," I whispered. I couldn't hear my own words over the roar of the water.

"My Lady!" I shouted.

She woke, twitching, thrashing like a fish, and for a moment she wasn't human. She was never human.

"You're back," she said, as she came to her senses. "So soon."

"They're coming," I said.

"Prey?"

"Too many," I said. "Men-at-arms. Friends of the man you...we... killed."

She nodded.

A crueler person—maybe any human—would have blamed me.

"Have you come to die for me? With me?" she asked. There was no fear in her voice, nor even grim determination. She asked it like she might ask my thoughts on the weather. No, she asked it like she asked before she kissed me, before she touched me. She was asking for my consent.

For a moment, I wanted to die alongside her as fiercely as I wanted to kiss her. My life had been brief, to be sure, but many lives are, and length alone is no grounds on which to judge.

"I've come to warn you," I said, as the urge passed, "and I've no intention of dying. We have to make for the ocean."

"I chose this pool a hundred years ago, as a yearling. It is my home," she said.

"You'll find another."

"Is that what you do? Go from place to place, rootless?"

"Every time they come after me," I agreed.

"I can't live like you. I wouldn't survive, any more than you'd survive drowning."

"I want a home," I said. "I want *you* to be home. I don't care where it is, as long as you're there."

"I can't live like you."

Tears fought their way down my cheeks and I was glad for the cold spray of the falls that disguised them.

"Can you do it this once?" I asked. "Leave your home?"

"No," she said. "It would be nicer to stay here, don't you think? Nicer to enjoy one another, then fight and die?" She kissed me then, and I had endless time to consider it.

She might have kissed me longer than I thought, because when my mouth broke from hers, I heard a distant crashing that likely couldn't be anything but an armored man sliding down a slope.

I took her by the hand. I had no weapons but a knife, and no training in combat. If I stayed, it would be purely symbolic. There was no reason not to run, not to save myself. Still, I didn't let go.

"I see them!" someone shouted. "There, in the pool!"

"Just a couple of girls!" another man's voice called back. He kept speaking, too, after that, but I couldn't make out the words.

I couldn't see them. They were hidden by the trees.

I tried to lead the Lady away, but she resisted.

"We can't fight them all," I said.

"Yes we can," she said. "We might not be able to stop them all, but we can certainly fight them."

Then they came out of the woods as fog began to rise, and they were terrible. The white-painted armor of the King lent them a ghostly look, made worse by the rising fog and the starlight. Their pikes were death, their swords were death, and contrary to every song ever sung, death is the opposite of love.

I wanted love.

My body was numb with adrenaline and cold water, and I was up to my waist in the pool. I got my knife into my hand.

They approached with their pikes and shouted their words that insisted on surrender but I don't know that I heard them or anything at all.

A spear reached for me, and the Lady took it by the haft and pulled its wielder off balance, and another spear sliced her shoulder while she did and her dark blood ran into the water. More spears were coming.

Something broke in her as her skin split apart. "You're right," she said. "I'll make for the ocean."

We dove under, swam until the pool grew too shallow, then ran along the creek.

As I vaulted a fallen log, I rested my left hand on the trunk of a nearby tree for balance. A crossbow bolt shot through my palm, pinning me.

The Lady broke the shaft of the quarrel and I pulled free my hand. Another bolt cut through my cape.

Every obstacle we crossed increased our lead, because a thief and a fey can move faster through the woods than those who are armed and armored. Soon they gave up on shooting at us entirely. Soon after, we couldn't hear them.

"They know we're following the creek," I said. "If we break from it, we can lose them in the fog."

"If I can't be in my pool, I need to be in the ocean. You can hide in the fog. I can make my way alone."

"No," I whispered, and kept going, my wounded hand wrapped in my cloak.

We reached the top of another waterfall, one that sent the creek cascading down to the beach. I looked down into the dark gray nothing of the morning. Somewhere down there was the ocean, and presumably Henrietta on the beach nearby. It wasn't too late for the spell.

It would be a hell of a climb to get down there, however.

The Lady turned to me, looked me in the eyes. She was searching, trying to understand me.

"There's a witch," I said, as I held her by the waist, "meeting me at the beach. She said she can transform me."

"Into a creature of the sea?" the Lady asked.

"Yeah."

"Is that what you want?"

"I want to be with you," I said. "However I can."

"Then do it," she said. Her eyes were still searching my face. "Be with me."

Was there no passion in her voice because I didn't know how to listen for it? Was there no passion in her voice because there was none in her heart? Or was there passion, deep passion, and my terror kept me from hearing it?

Without another word, the Lady knelt down and climbed over the edge of the cliff. I'd have to climb down after, with my left hand useless.

Nothing to do but to do it. I knelt down, looking for a ledge.

A crossbow bolt found my leg and I pitched forward, down into the fog, down into the gray.

◆

The ocean has its own kind of cold, a rough and salty cold that will kill you as sure as the snowmelt cold of mountain rivers. I hit that cold and it cracked me into consciousness, but my leg wouldn't respond to my commands and my hand was warm with blood.

There was no surface in sight.

I'd tried. No one could say I hadn't tried.

Most people would say I'd gotten what I deserved, and maybe they'd be talking about me being a thief and murderer, but more than a few would say it because I was a monster and I'd always been a monster.

Nettle and Fitch would miss me, and Fitch might miss me for more than my share of the rent. But mourning isn't always just a hardship, it's part of the beauty of life. My death might lend them beauty.

I'd also saved my love.

Who, to be honest, I shouldn't have loved.

Water made its way into my lungs. Cold water shouldn't feel like fire. It did.

She loved me, in her way. I loved her, in mine. We could have had that love slowly. I could have not become obsessed. I could have fed her men and those men's coins could have fed me.

Instead, I was drowning.

I closed my eyes because I couldn't see anything anyway, and there was that fire in my chest. Better to sleep than to burn.

I slept.

I woke on shore with her mouth on mine and the fire was out of my chest, in every way, all at once. I wasn't drowning anymore. That was her magic. I wasn't obsessed anymore. That was mine.

Behind her, a stooped giantess of a witch held aloft a raw crystal the size of a boulder. The mist seemed to shrink away from it and her, leaving us in a bubble of clarity in an obscured world.

"Good morning, child," Henrietta said, with an uncharacteristic giggle in her voice. "I'm glad you could make it."

"Laria," the Lady said. Even then, even as I stood on the precipice of death, her face was without emotion.

"I'm fine," I said, because I wasn't dead and I probably wasn't even dying, and by that standard, everything was fine. I struggled to my knees. Gentle waves lapped against me, and the sand was cool beneath me.

"The spell is cast," Henrietta said. "The dawn will break in a moment, and the first ray will strike this crystal and all you must do is stand in its light if you choose. The Sea Mother will take you for her own."

"Wait," I said.

"I cannot."

"Stand down!" a man's voice shouted, louder than the waves, echoing against the cliffside.

He approached, a silhouette with a crossbow drawn. The Lady ran at him. He shot once, missed.

He stepped out of the mist and into the circle, dropping his crossbow and drawing a short sword. It was the tracker. He must have come ahead of the rest of the men, being the only one capable of climbing down the cliff.

"Stand down!" he shouted again.

The Lady lunged for his sword hand, but he was too fast. He swung at her and missed.

They danced, both too experienced to easily defeat the other. Since he had friends coming, however, time was on his side.

He cut the Lady, shallow across the other shoulder as she'd been cut before, and her blood ran red. I could see the color this time. It was almost dawn.

"I killed him!" I said, standing, shouting. "I killed that man whose name I don't care to know; I stole every copper he's ever taken from a corpse in war."

It worked. The man turned his attention to me. I limped closer, until I was just outside the range of his blade.

"I am going to live my life on land so that I can kill a thousand like him, starting with you."

"You won't kill me, bædling," the tracker said. "You'll hang by sundown."

Dawn broke, the crystal caught the first ray, and it shot toward me. I dove at the tracker. He swung, reflexively, but missed. My body slammed into his legs. He fell over me into the light, into the spell.

Incoherent red rage consumed his body and he blistered and he screamed. His legs fused and grew scales, his neck split open into bloody gills, and he screamed. His teeth fell into the sand and fangs grew in their stead, and he screamed.

The lady took the sword from his hand, held it to his throat.

"Should we gut him?" she asked.

"Help him into the water," I answered. "Let the Sea Mother take him."

The Lady and I rolled him across the wet sand and into the waves. He stopped screaming. Soon he was gone, cursed to the depths.

"What now?" the Lady asked.

I had to leave town. The rest of the men would be after me. Maybe Nettle and Finch would come with me, maybe not. I'd make it work. I had before, I would again.

"We'll go our ways," I said. Dawn brought clarity the way it's supposed to. "I'll grow old, and I'll bring you men once every few years."

"That will be enough for you?"

"It will."

THE BONES OF CHILDREN

To most of society, I am a monster. Oh, I don't have tentacles, or horns, or goat's feet, or anything of the sort. Nevertheless, the first entry in *Liber Monstrorum*, the oldest known Western book of monsters, is a man who dresses as a woman. Sure, I'm a woman who dresses like a woman, but most of society doesn't believe me about that because trans women are still seen as deceivers. That book was written sometime in the seventh or eighth century, and I'm not entirely certain I can say that much has changed.

It's strange, then, that I should wind up hunting after monsters. It's strange that I should be referring to ancient tomes—both real and fictional—as potential sources of truth. It's strange that I should come to take Lovecraft's work far too seriously, especially considering what I assume he would make of me. It's strange that I should be searching in attics for portals into unknown and unknowable dimensions.

Okay, that last bit would be strange for anyone.

I mean to say only that I was a reluctant scholar of the occult—as though any claims I might make of my inherent skepticism will make what I have to relate any more believable.

I want to be clear that I understand H.P. Lovecraft to be a writer of fiction. I don't think he believed any of what he wrote to be true. His work is fanciful, and while his prose was outdated even for the time, I enjoy his ability to weave stories and touch at the horror hidden inside the human mind.

What I've come to believe, however, and what I expect to fail to convince you of, is that H.P. Lovecraft worked from sources—sometimes near to plagiaristicly—that were not nearly so fictional.

◆

It started for me with dreams. I've always been a deep sleeper, never bothered much by dreams. No dreams so beautiful that waking life cannot compare; no dreams so horrid I wake screaming. I've always had mundane, forgettable dreams. Until two years ago, in my fifth decade of life.

I moved in with a partner, a woman named E——, two years ago. Along with a small group of miscreants and queers, we'd bought a derelict farm in western Massachusetts. Everyone else wanted to build their own houses on the property, so E—— and I moved into the old farmhouse. Things were fine for the first six months, when we lived in the library on the ground floor, but as soon as we finished renovations on the master bedroom and moved upstairs, the dreams started.

Most of the dreams, though bizarre, were non-egregious. I had dreams about washing blades and washing bones in a skyscraper overlooking a dead city. The city was always the same, full of brutalist structures shorter than the tower. The tasks I was engaged in changed from dream to dream, but they were always mundane and generally contained enough traces of what I'd done that day to convince me that nothing untoward was happening to my mind as I slept.

At midwinter, I dreamt of carving a living child into quarters. As I dreamt of piercing his skin, my hands shook. The visceral feel of it made me want to retch, or cry, or stop, but I did none of those things. As I pulled bones from sockets, my whole body shook so hard that I woke.

I wanted E—— to hold me, but she slept every night with the help of pills—haunted by her own nightmares, as she had been since her youth—so I held her instead and cried into her hair.

Only in the morning did I notice the dried blood beneath my fingernails.

It was E—— who told me that my dream reminded her of a Lovecraft story, "The Dreams in the Witch House," and set me on the terrible path I walk today.

I listened to an audio production of the story the next day while I worked in the garden. Then I devoured book after book after story after poem by H.P. Lovecraft. Every word he'd put to paper felt like it hit some discordant note in my soul—okay, I don't believe in souls, so let's say brain. Everything he'd written was so close to, yet so far from, some truth. I knew it in my heart. And by heart, I still mean brain.

In the story, the city of the Elder Things is lit by three stars: one red, one yellow, one blue. In my dreams, that dead, brutalist city had three yellow suns and it had buildings suited for people, not winged demon barrels. So close, yet so far away.

A few weeks later I had another dream, about another human sacrifice. I still didn't believe the dreams, but I assure you I went over every inch of that bedroom with tape measure to prove the Euclidian nature of its geometry. In the end, I started sharing E—'s medication and the dreams subsided, thank the Lord. And by Lord, I mean pharmacology.

None of my landmates, and least of all my partner, wanted to discuss the matter with me. E— herself had lost a child to SIDS, and I knew better than to push the issue of dead children.

I did what any girl would do in the same situation. I joined a support group for the Lovecraft-obsessed. A few friends from Boston had been into all this occult shit, so I hit them up and started going to meetings, driving the couple of hours every week. They didn't call them support group meetings, and if there had been twelve steps, they would have been the twelve steps for summoning Yog-Sothoth or something, not the steps for ridding oneself of eldritch nightmares. I still used it as a support group. Everyone had stories about occurrences and observations of the uncanny and arcane. I didn't believe any of them, and I eventually realized I thought they were idiots for believing me. Still, attending seemed to quiet the growing, nagging sensation in the back of my throat and the back of my mind. It stopped, for a few blissful hours, the ever-present sensation I had under my fingernails of rending and tearing. It stopped the chanting, the demonic mantras, that broke into my consciousness as intrusive thoughts.

A man named Y— was at almost every meeting. He was a young, attractive, light-skinned Black man with old-fashioned spectacles perched perilously at the end of his nose. He always had a different book sticking out of his coat pocket, and he always kept his eye on the door of wherever we met—often a bookstore's basement or some DIY show space that would never pass fire code. For months, he never said a word. Along with the other women and people of color who came, we shared a sort of illicit bond—we were the sorts that Lovecraft reviled, and that brought us together. At least, I assumed it did. Maybe that was just me, as a white girl, projecting.

One night, in early May, at least fifteen of us crowded into the back room of a punk-owned pizza joint after close. We'd just heard from another woman with dreams of child sacrifice frighteningly similar to my own, though hers took place in a birch forest, when Y— walked to the center of the room to speak.

"I'm going to find the witch-house," he said. "That's what Lovecraft called it, right? The witch-house? A boarding house with the bones of children in the walls, with a person-faced rat and a timeless witch? A house with an attic room you can't measure right? It's real. I'm going to find it."

The room got so quiet we heard a bicycle pass on the street.

"Most of you don't know me well enough to know that I'm a cat burglar by trade, but I am. It pays well enough that I don't have to work more than once or twice a year, and I'm good enough at my job that even if you ratted me out to the cops, they wouldn't be able to pin anything on me, I don't think." He looked around the room as he talked. Gone was the quiet, shy man I'd seen for months. In his place was a man who was charismatic, outgoing, with a sort of infectious enthusiasm. "I started coming here to this group because of a book I found robbing a place last year in—let's just say a different city. A real far north city. I'd gotten a tip about a rare book collector who didn't treat people very well, and I like sleeping at night so I like robbing people like that. I got in the front door, because people think having their locks and alarms and cameras wired into the internet is a good idea, made my way to the library, and took my fill.

"I sold off the esoteric pornography and the overpriced occultist books easily enough, but some of what looked interesting to me was much harder to find buyers for. A few things were so rare I couldn't safely move them without going through so many middlemen that I wouldn't make shit, and a few were just so... so *weird* that I couldn't figure out how and where to list them, let alone figure out how to advertise them as worth anything."

He walked back over to his chair, picked up his book bag, and pulled out a stack of pamphlets in plastic sleeves. He held up one. Yellow aged its tattered cover, but in blackletter font I could see the title: "Ruminations On Non-Secular Matters." He held up another: "The Church of Christ the Weeping Man." A third: "Underneath the Dreams of Men." A final: "Inside the Stars of Gods."

I looked around the room. All of us were almost hungry with desire for those books, whatever they held. That was the sort of obsession this group fostered, that I was participating in.

"All of these works are anonymous. All of them can be dated to the turn of the twentieth century. None of them exists on the internet, even as references or in library catalogs. They're written in fairly different styles. If I had to guess, I'd say that 'Dreams of Men' and 'Stars of Gods' have one author, and the other two were written by two other people. And if I'll cut right to it, the thing is: I am convinced that Lovecraft read these and maybe others in this series. I'm also convinced that these are works of journalism."

I gasped. I was kind of embarrassed by the gesture and put my hand over my mouth, but there it was.

"Why didn't you say anything?" one of the more cumbersome of our group asked. That was G——. I think there were three types of people in attendance. The curious, who came for entertainment. The cursed, like myself, who came to find answers. Then there were the true believers, who just wanted something to be interesting in this world and had attached themselves to Lovecraft for whatever reason. G—— was a true believer. I should be kinder to the true believers, but they grated on me. G—— was the worst of them.

"Like Lovecraft, I assumed they were fiction. But after hearing everyone's stories during the past months, I found myself doubting. One of these, in particular," with this he held up "Underneath the Dreams of Men," "is so startlingly similar... not to Lovecraft's 'Dreams in the Witch House,' but to some of the stories I've heard you all tell. I got sort of obsessed."

Everyone turned to look at me and the other woman with the sacrificial dreams.

"In 'The Dreams of Men,' our journalist author relates the story of an old man he meets, known only as X——. He's ebony black, and he describes himself as a free man, the son of a free woman, the daughter of a slave. When he was younger, before the war, X—— took up residence in a boarding house in upstate New York. He's subject to a fair amount of racial abuse at the hands of the matron of the house, some of the white guests, and even from another Black guest with lighter skin. To get away from everyone, he ends up taking the worst room, the attic room. Things aren't right up there, and he hears things. He sees things. He can't make sense of it. He starts dreaming, and in his dreams he's sacrificing children in a strange city. He wakes up every morning with bones at the foot of his bed, and every morning he packs them into the walls and goes a little bit crazier. One day he wakes up with a statue, about a foot high, of a satyr or a devil, made out of some metal he can't figure out, with writing across the bottom in letters he doesn't recognize."

"Then what happens?" I asked. I'd never woken up to bones, but it still felt like I was asking about my own future.

"That's about the sum of it," Y— said. "X— moves out after a year, when he can't handle it anymore, and settles in Maine. Becomes a lobster fisherman, because lobsters don't have bones and fishermen don't have to deal with people much. Throws the statue into the ocean after a couple years of staring at it. The journalist relates his story, adds a couple notes about failing to find any of the people or places he's referenced, plus some nineteenth-century theories about dreams and their meaning, and that's it.

"I've got a lot of free time, what with my generous work schedule. I never found out the author of the text, but I've been trying to track down the subject of the story. Two weeks ago, I found him. He was real. Xavier Day. Thank God his name started with an X, or I probably never would have found him. But a black-as-night lobster fisherman was... let's go with 'something of a rarity' in nineteenth-century Maine, so that helped. He lived in a town near Lubec. He's buried in an overgrown cemetery on private land—near as I can tell, the town was too racist to bury him in the churchyard, or maybe they considered him a witch. Here's a photo of his stone."

Y— passed around his phone. The stone was hard to read and completely unadorned.

"This says he lived from 1812 until 1925," I said. "That can't be right."

"I looked into that," Y— said. "It's what he claimed, and no one had evidence otherwise. He told people he figured he was immortal."

"How'd he die?" I asked.

"Drowned."

"What's this in the lower left of the photo?" I asked. There was a blur of yellowish white, a pile of something on his grave.

"Go to the next photo," Y— said.

I did.

They were bones.

"Bones," Y— said. "The bones of children."

For a long moment, no one said a word. I passed the phone on, and everyone stared in disbelief.

Then, theatrically, Y— reached into his bag and pulled out a statuette and placed it on the table.

"I did some diving," Y— said. "I found this." It was a devil, in that Christian style of a man with Caucasian features and the legs of a goat. A band of Norse runes encircled the base.

"What does that say?" G— asked.

Y— and I answered at the same time. "Nyarlathotep."

◆

At our insistence, Y— read each of the four pamphlets to us. We stayed so late that night that we only left when an employee came to open the restaurant in the morning.

For the curious, this was the best entertainment they'd had in ages. For the true believers, it was vindication. For us cursed... well, I didn't know what to believe or what to think. I still don't.

Over the next week, we tracked down the boarding house in New York. It's one of the only parts of this whole thing I can take any credit for. My family is from upstate, and one of my aunts studies regional folklore and another studies regional history. There was a town where kids in the nineteenth century had died young and the old had all seemed to live past one hundred. No one told ghost stories about the place. Every other town in New York had ghost stories about them but this one. It was so conspicuously un-haunted that it was clearly haunted. It wasn't a town anymore, but a few buildings remained, most of them on the state's historic registry.

That's how I found myself in the company of a gentleman thief as we scaled the outside wall of a witch-house under the light of the full moon.

"Old-fashioned security means old-fashioned method of entry," Y— told me as he opened the storm shutters of the attic window with a crowbar. I'd wanted to take a tour during the day and slip away from the guide, but Y— had insisted what we needed to do required the dead of night.

The attic room was wrong, that much was obvious. It was unnameably wrong, though, indescribably so. Like that feeling when you're trying to put on fishnets and they're tangled in more than direction at once and you somehow have to unroll them in both directions at the same time, that's what it felt like looking at the room. There were four walls and a vaulted ceiling, but sometimes it felt like there were five walls, and when I stood I got a trace of vertigo. Like I was high in the air. Like I was in that skyscraper, looking out over that city, sharpening knives.

I wanted to leave.

"We've got to pry open the walls, carefully," Y— said.

"Let me try."

He handed me the crowbar.

I smashed it into the nearest wall, putting my hip into it like swinging a bat in Little League. Again. Again. There was no "carefully" left in my body. I needed answers.

Bones came pouring out as the wall fell down. The bones of children.

◆

After that night, I spent a month trying to convince E— and the rest of my friends to sell the land and move somewhere else, anywhere else. It became clear, however, that she didn't believe me and that she wouldn't come with me. So I left her.

The dreams haven't come back, not since I left that place. Instead, I dream of E—, and I miss her.

I live with Y— now, and a few of the other cursed ones from the group. I think investigating this shit is driving me as crazy as the dreams had, but I don't know what else to do. I can't get it out of my brain. I can't forgive myself for the monster I was, in my sleep, in some alien city across the cosmos. I understand, now, that I was sacrificing real children to a devil I don't believe in.

Now, whenever I cut anything, even vegetables, I think about human flesh. Whenever I see the concrete of a city, I think about the three suns. Whenever I imagine the respite of death, I think about who or what will leave mementos of horror on my grave.

Worst of all, when I see children, I think of their bones.

MARY MARROW

Mary Marrow lives in a casket about eight miles up Deer Run Creek. Grownups tell you she's dead, because she doesn't move and she doesn't breathe, but they know that's not true. They just don't want you to be scared. If she was dead, then why doesn't she rot?

She's not dead. I saw her drown, but she's not dead.

Grownups don't want you afraid of her, but the truth is that you *should* be afraid of her. You should stay clear of her body, sure enough, but you should also never drink from Deer Run when it runs red, and you should never eat the red berries that grow along the bank, and you should never make anyone in town here cross. You never know which of us do her bidding.

I used to do her bidding.

I was once young like you are. Most old women tell you that not for your sake, but for their own sake. They're reminding themselves that, as impossible as it seems, they used to be young. I'm telling you for your sake. I don't want to remember being young.

When I was maybe fourteen, I was beautiful, and that I'm telling you for my own sake. All the boys and some of the girls knew it, and sometimes I'd let them bring me favors: a loaf of bread, a jar of jam, a pretty rock, a pilfered bracelet, things of that nature. Mary Marrow, she was just Mary Olgden then, she brought me berries. Those red berries, the ones that grow on the bank that feed crows and squirrels.

"Don't eat them," she said, after the first time she offered me a handful, "or you'll fall in love with me." She ate one herself and she smiled and the purple juice stained her lips as sure as lipstick.

"I will not fall in love with you, Mary Olgden," I told her. I ate two of the berries. They're sour but still good, like beer or old love.

"Now you're going to fall for me," she said, laughing.

I didn't believe her, though, because I had my eyes on another girl, on Lora Haroldson. Lora only liked boys, sometimes the same boys I liked, and I didn't know better yet than to fall for a girl who only liked boys.

Two years came and went, fast as rain. I left school at sixteen to work in the factory. Another two years went by like a passing storm. The summer I turned eighteen, Lora Haroldson moved away to the city for school. Those bright, long days of summer, I was as sad as the depths of snow.

That summer, Mary Olgden became an orphan. Her parents were found hanging, apparent suicide—no one thinks that now, but it's what we thought then. Mary said Olgden was a family name, and she didn't have a family, she didn't want a family, so she changed her name to Mary Marrow.

We didn't see her much. She was off in the woods more days and nights than not, skipping shifts at the factory as often as not. The Olgden's house fell into the sorry state you know it to be today. The lawn grew up as high as the fence, brambles tore the pickets asunder, and a murder of crows took up residence in the apple tree.

That house is safe, by the way. Some tame things look terrifying. You can even eat the apples, though an untended tree doesn't make for good fruit.

People whispered words like "magic" and "witchcraft" when Mary wasn't around. By the time I was eighteen, people began to whisper those words when she *was* around. Soon thereafter, people stopped bothering to keep their voices at a whisper.

I barely noticed any of this. I barely thought about the young Ms. Marrow. A few times more, she'd brought me presents, but she knew she was not high on my list of suitors and never tried hard to woo me.

I determined not to wed anyone. I let many of those suitors go home happy and they left me happy, but I didn't want to marry anyone. I had a reputation, of course, but I didn't care. No one who matters cares about that sort of thing.

Still, I pined for Lora.

I took to walking in the woods that summer, after every early morning shift. I'd learned most of its paths and glades and ruins on this or that tryst and I started going further and farther afield. I never got lost, because at the end of every day, when the sun dipped low enough to touch the peak of Grayhill Mountain, I walked east or west as needed to find Deer Run Creek and followed it home.

I was walking home on the day of the equinox, with plenty far to go and little hope of reaching town before dark, when I saw a red glow on the water ahead of me. There was a man—if you could call him that—as thin as needle, as thin as a lie, and where his nude skin touched the water, the water glowed red. His hair was long and feminine, but I could see nothing of his face at that distance. Like a baptist, or a husband carrying his bride across the threshold, he held Mary Marrow in all her Sunday clothes.

She looked at me, and she grinned a wild grin, and the man—the devil or angel or some beast in between—put Mary Marrow beneath the cold water and drowned her. I stood still, on the bank twenty yards upstream, and watched.

I should have run to her, I know that. I carried a large enough knife when I walked those woods; I should have put it between that creature's ribs. I didn't. I stood as still as a deer in the moonlight, as still as a rock in the water.

I'm not sure I took a single breath, all that time Mary's lungs filled with water.

The man lifted her up and carried her to shore. He set her body in an open casket, then walked into the woods and disappeared. I've never seen him again.

I ran to her.

Her lips were stained purple, with the blood of those berries. Just like her lips are still, if you walk those eight miles upstream to see her, which you should not.

She wasn't breathing. Her eyes were open and hazel, shining bright enough to retain their color even as color fled the rest of everything with the coming of night.

I laid down at the foot of her casket, right down on my back on the rocks. I couldn't tell you why I did it. I wasn't in my right head. As the last of the light left the world, I fell asleep.

I woke up with the moon above me. I couldn't move. I couldn't speak.

Mary Marrow climbed out of her casket and stood over me, watching me. She smiled, a soft smile, a beautiful smile.

I'd never noticed how beautiful she was.

"You have come to love me," she said. It wasn't a question. As she watched me unwavering, I slowly, fearfully, fell back to sleep.

In the morning, she was once more lying in that pine box. I had not dreamt her drowning, but I had certainly dreamt her rising to speak. I was certain of it.

I was also certain, however, that I loved her.

Not one day, in the fifty years that have passed from then to now, have I lingered on thoughts of Lora Haroldson. The candle I'd held for her was blown out by a vile wind, a witchwind.

I went home, changed for work, and didn't go back upstream for some time after that. I didn't tell anyone what I'd seen, either, and no one reported Mary missing because no one missed her. More shifts for the rest of us.

I kept at my habits, though I took my suitors downstream instead of upstream. Then, with the last echoes of summer fading out, so did my fancy for casual affairs. After my shifts in the factory, I took to staying inside with books.

On Samhain, I worked a double and only got out after the land was lit by a waning crescent of a moon. I was restless. I didn't even change out of my work clothes, I just walked up Deer Run a few hours to see my love.

She wasn't alone. Three others lay on rocks, each asleep on their backs. One was a drifter I'd seen in town. Another was a child, a stranger. The third... the third was Lora Haroldson. To this day, I don't know if Mary had ensorcelled her so that I could see her again, to take vengeance on me for having once loved another, or by happenstance.

I found space between the tramp and the woman who had once been my heart's desire and I slept.

Once more, I woke to starlight and to paralysis and to Mary Marrow, standing over me, watching me.

"There are sixteen men on the old road tomorrow," she said. "They will come alone or in groups of two and three. I want seven of them here and alive, eight of them dead, and one to believe he has escaped our wrath."

I fell back asleep.

I woke with the sun on my face. I was late for work, but I didn't care. I didn't go to work.

With my new fellows, I made my way to the old road, which is what we used to call the hiking trail that runs from the town to the peak of Grayhill and out to mountains beyond. It was popular with tourists. It's still there, though the paving stones have sunk deep into the earth and few dare to walk it.

We found a place where the trees crowded in close and we waited.

We killed eight men on the path, with rocks and knives. Bashing and breaking and carving and carving and carving. We captured seven men, who kicked and bit and screamed. We let one man escape.

The seven, we led back to Mary. We tied them to trees, each so he faced the creek, each so he could watch.

We drowned the men, one after the other. Myself and Lora held each one underwater while they thrashed like fish. We never cut them, but the river glowed red around our skin as their sorrows and their joys and their dreams and their memories died. Some of that red drifted downstream.

The next day, the berries along the bank were ripe and red and beautiful.

We ate them, joyous. I'd never been so content and calm, surrounded by my new family, sitting at the feet of our love Mary.

I did the witch's dark work for a decade. Followers came and went—Lora was with us a year only before she returned to her studies, released from service. Others, like the drifter and the child, eventually died at the hands of those we destroyed. Myself, I drowned men and I cut men and I ate the flesh of men. I set fire to barns and I set fire to fields and I set fire to houses full of people. I also led the chosen to meet their new master.

I'd never known love like the love of Mary Marrow. Every meal I ate was richer, every dream I had more beautiful, every woman and man I knew more passionate, while I served her.

A decade was a long time to me back then, and I wanted more from life. I prayed to Mary, like I'd never prayed to Christ, to release me. She did.

For another ten years, I wandered these hills, living off of ramps and rabbits. I was afraid of being found for my crimes, and more than that I was afraid of seeing the woman I had loved, with her purple lips, her hazel eyes, unbreathing. I was afraid of the power she held over me. I was afraid of that thing that may or may not have been love. So I just wandered.

A decade was still a long time to me back then, and I came home. The factory is always hiring. The factory doesn't care to know where you've been and what you've done.

I don't do her work, not anymore. Now I tell children, like you, to stay away. To not be curious. To live simple lives, to work at the factory, to let magic be feared. You must not stain your lips by eating berries, and you must never drink the water when it runs red.

I tell children like you to absolutely, whatever you do, not go eight miles upstream and visit Mary Marrow where she rests on the east bank of the river, to not sleep at the foot of her casket and let her into your dreams and into your hearts. Never join her loving family.

You must never do that.

BEYOND SAPPHIRE GLASS

Sometimes at night, with Kevin curled up against me, I think about you. I think about you and I can't sleep but all I want to do is sleep. All I want to do is sleep because sleep resets my emotions and I don't want to think about you.

I remember when you first came to us, a pilgrim. You reached the top of the steps on your twentieth birthday and I saw you spinning around the mountaintop, looking out at the whole world, out to every horizon. It was a clear day, a summer day. You have a summer birthday. I don't think that matters anymore, but I can't make myself forget.

We told you what we told every pilgrim: if your health wasn't bad, you had to stay with us a year before we'd lead you into the depths, before an angel would show you to the sapphire gate. Before we'd let you upload your mind, before we'd incinerate your body. One year with us so we knew that you knew that you were certain. A lot of people call the wait "purgatory." You didn't and I don't.

We caught one another staring so many times we made a game of it, laughing and turning our eyes from one another for just a second before staring again. Then one day it escalated to tag, and we chased each other like we were children, and you tackled me and I skinned my arm on the rocks and you pinned me down and I don't remember which one of us broke the awkward silence first but I remember that one of us asked and we kissed. You'd never kissed a girl. I'd never kissed a pilgrim. And the air smelled of clover.

I was Janna and you were Hannah, and for the whole of the year you made everyone pronounce your name like it rhymed with mine. Janna and Hannah.

One day you asked me to come with you. I can't get that day out of my head. It was springtime, and we were at the foot of the mountain loading our bags for the long hike home. You said it simple. "Come with me."

And I agreed, because I'd misunderstood.

"Where?" I asked. "We'd have to go far. I don't know what the others would do if they saw me again. We sign up for life."

"Come with me into the machine," you said. "Live forever with me."

I got that vacant look on my face. You never saw it much. Kevin sees it a lot. He hates it.

"I can't," I told you.

"You upload when you're old anyway, don't you?" you asked.

"I'm not an angel," I said.

You waited for me to explain.

"Every guardian stands watch over eternity," I said. "Some of us think we watch over heaven. They call themselves angels."

"What is it you do, if you're not watching over heaven?"

"I guard machines full of the programmed echoes of personalities. I guard eleven billion programs that think they're people. They're not in heaven. There is no heaven, least of all in a computer."

"You think I'm killing myself," you said.

"I do," I told you.

"If it's as awful as all that, why do you do it? Why be a guardian?"

"Sometimes I think that the kindest thing I could do would be to cut the wires," I told you. I was being cold to you. I'm fairly sure it was the only time I ever was. I'm fairly sure because sometimes I think about everything we did together and everything I ever said to you, as if that could help me make sense of what happened. "But I won't break the machines, and I'd kill anyone who tries, because what I think about it doesn't really matter. Those people put copies of themselves there in limbo, and we agreed to guard them. I maintain the machines because by doing so, I guarantee they're the only machines of any kind in the world. Everyone who wanted computers and clocks and industry uploaded themselves and left the rest of us a scorched and sacred paradise. If we shut down the machines, then people who want those things will build them on Earth again, where they don't belong."

"People like me," you said.

"People like you," I agreed.

And that probably should have been the end of us, there at the base of the mountain, with the spring's chill in the air between us, but we stared at one another sadly until our fingers intertwined and we never talked about it again. I blame pheromones and first love. And we climbed back up the six thousand stairs and we reveled in our bodies when they ached from the climb and we reveled in our bodies when we touched that night under the thick wool covers in my quarters. And I never understood why you went to the sapphire gate and you'll never understand why I didn't come with you.

I talk to what's left of you sometimes, but it wouldn't be fair to tell you any of this. After all, I'm going to grow old and die, and you're already dead and you're going to live forever.

And Kevin snores and he doesn't know what to do with my body, and I think I love him, but every time summer comes around I catch the scent of clover and it's like you're over me, your lips poised just above me. The thought of you washes over me and I'm drowning and I get so desperate that I storm down the grand staircase to the server room and I call your name and you always make time for me, but I don't tell you what's on my mind because you don't want to hear it and it wouldn't do either of us any good.

You're dead and I can never bury you.

I think that's love.

THE NORTHERN HOST

For all its lingering horror and misery, the wake of a war is rich terrain for a folklorist like myself—more people report more supernatural experiences during times of war than times of peace. Some of my peers have argued the stress and shock of battle leaves our brains more susceptible to mass delusion. Others claim that the veil between worlds remains thin when so many are passing from life to death.

The second American civil war has been no exception.

Most famously, of course, soldiers from each of the three armies present at the Fifteen Day Siege of St. Louis reported a wailing man who walked among the wounded, healing some and ending the lives of others. On the Cascadian front, Rebel forces spoke of black bears who in effect stood sentry for their guerrilla positions. During the White Army's occupation of Washington, D.C., civilians and soldiers alike reported apparitions pouring out of the Pentagon crater every new moon.

Of all the various myths and legends to spring up in the wake of the recent conflict, however, I find myself most strongly drawn to the stories of the Northern Host. Never have I heard a myth recounted in such detail by such a wide variety of people.

My favorite telling comes from Pvt. Sarah Daher and the battle of Asheville. This interview was recorded in the spring of 2035 and lightly edited for clarity with permission of the subject. Note that the subject refers to the White Army by pejoratives throughout—these have been left intact for the historical record.

◆

Could you introduce yourself and tell me what you saw?

My name is Sarah Daher. I'm thirty-one years old. I live in Asheville in the Appalachian region of the United States of America on stolen Cherokee land. My US military rank was Private. They made us all privates when they incorporated the irregulars into the Army, but

I only served in the Union to fight the White Army. A year later, and I'm one of those crazy radicals who doesn't think the Reconfiguration goes far enough.

I'd never fired a gun in my life before the irregulars, and I hope I'll never fire another one again. By temperament, I'm neither a lover or a fighter. I'm just your average transgirl who likes cats and hates Nazis.

I fought in three engagements: in Weaverville, Leicester, and Asheville. I think I killed two people. One of them, I know I killed him. I saw him bleed out and I saw him taken away in a black bag. The other person was a man I shot in the thigh during the battle of Asheville. I didn't know you can die from a bullet in the thigh, but I've spent a lot of time looking at casualty records and someone who fit that man's general description died in that battle from a bullet to the thigh.

Does that bother you?

Yes? No? I don't know. I don't lose sleep over it. But I think about it a lot. I looked at the dox on both of them. The first guy was a true believer, a real blood and soil type. It doesn't bother me that I mingled those two things for him. The second man though, I'm not so sure. He signed up because his son signed up. I don't have any kids myself, but I could see myself doing that. His son survived the war.

Have you been in contact with his son?

No, fuck that guy. That kid is a fucking Nazi and I don't know how he talked his way out of the tribunals.

Can you tell me what you saw at the Battle of Asheville?

This was during the Fash's spring offensive last year. You know, Hitler's birthday, April 20th. By that point, the White Army was pretty much done, but they weren't about to go down without doing some major symbolic damage.

So there were about forty of us, all irregulars, with our own commanders. No Army oversight. Morale was down, we felt pretty abandoned. Common sentiment in the South. I was on the street out in front of the library walking rounds. Downtown was half rubble at that point. Only the library was standing, because symbols matter and all that bullshit, so that's where we were making a stand.

Neither side had artillery really by that point. The brass had just commandeered even our RPGs for the "real" fight. Air support wasn't coming, not for them and not for us. Really, the Battle of Asheville was like nothing to the rest of the world, and we knew it.

So I was doing rounds, thinking about my shit luck, thinking maybe I was gonna die and how so many people had died that what's another dead girl to add to the pile. I was thinking about how at least *this* dead girl was going to die surrounded by or in defense of books. Then I heard dogs, from around the side of the building. One barked loud and near, the other sort of distant and echoey.

I went to check it out, turned the corner, and there was this naked guy. He was pale as hell, tall, tattooed and scarred and, like I said, he was as naked as the sun. I stared at him. He stared at me. I got so distracted trying to figure him out that it took me a moment to realize there were nine others behind him, or maybe they weren't there at first, I don't know. Most of them were men, mostly of the tall Norse-looking variety, but there was a Middle Eastern man and a three women, including one who by my read was Latinx.

No dogs anywhere that I could see.

The man closest to me, he asked me something in some language I didn't know. I just kind of stared. He asked me another question, in another language.

"What?" I asked. "Who are you?"

"Who are we fighting?" he asked. His accent was thick, and I couldn't place it for the life of me. I mean, I know *now*, but I sure as shit didn't know then.

"We?" I asked. "What?" I was due back out front because I was a sentry doing the rounds and this sure needed reporting, but what the hell was I going to tell people?

"Who are we fighting? Where are we?"

"You're in Asheville," I said. "Who are you?"

"Ah, the American conflict," the man said. Behind him, others nodded. Their movements were sloppy, dreamlike. They were drunk, I later realized. One of them had dried blood running down from her lip and onto her not-insubstantial belly.

"You're fighting the nationalists," the first one said. "We're here to help you."

"Who are you?" I asked. This third time, he actually answered.

"My name is Belgr. We are the dead. We are the Einherjar, from Valhalla. Every day, we are sent to a battle to fight and we die."

The others, behind him, nodded. Definitely drunk.

Now, I know there were good folks on our side who were into

European paganism, but you have to understand that a lot more of the fash were into that shit than anyone else. If they hadn't been naked and drunk, I might have mistaken them for the enemy and shot them.

"Valhalla," I said, reciting the tiny bit I knew, "that's where Vikings go if they die in battle. Feast every day and fight every night in Odin's hall. Until the end of the world, when you fight and die also, but like, a wolf eats the sun or something."

"Close enough," Belgr said. "I mean, Odin only gets half the battle dead. And Viking isn't a good name for us. But sure."

"And you're here because..."

"We are to take arms alongside you, fight your enemies, and die today."

"Am I going to die today, too?"

"Only the seers and the gods know that."

I'd been calling myself a witch half my life, but honestly that was mostly because I liked tarot and astrology and pentagrams and shit. I've never been someone who took the supernatural all that seriously. But nothing in the world made sense like it used to. Fascists had just been driven out of DC, Cascadia had not only seceded but was in a civil war of its own now, Mexico was gone and replaced by self-governing states of almost every stripe in the political rainbow, China had backed white supremacists and other nationalist types in an American civil war, and anti-government leftists were fighting alongside weirdos like me in the damn US Army. I can't say those things are as weird as naked dead don't-call-us-Vikings talking to me on the street, but somehow all of that was just comparably bizarre.

"Come, let us arm ourselves and fight together, you and I," Belgr said.

So that's how I met the Northern Host. Most people don't believe me, assume it was just some drunk wingnuts, maybe some irregulars I'd never met before. But I saw what I saw and I believe it. The rest of us who survived, they saw it too.

How did it go?

Pardon?

The battle. How did it go?

We got the Einhenjar into irregulars garb and armed them. There were plenty of guns at that point, in that forgotten hellhole of a front. Bullets, not so much, but plenty of guns. They were all comfortable with firearms, though one fellow groused about what he wouldn't do for an axe and shield and another said what we had was fine but monofilament web guns were better than any combat shotgun.

To hear them tell it—oh, fuck it, why am I pretending like I don't believe them? I believe them with every bit of my soul, and damn what people think of me for it. The Northern Host fights every night, and every night they are in a different time and place. Most battles in human history were in the past, they said, which sounds optimistic doesn't it, but they said they've fought in every century up to the twenty-fourth. Nothing happens after the twenty-fourth century. Ragnarök, most likely. The end of the world, wolves eating the sun and the moon, all of that.

They stood guard with me out front. Around midday, we got hit with an EMP. We knew that was coming, it didn't screw us up much. We had a hardened phone in the basement, and all our weapons operated just as well in dumb mode as smart mode. Including our own EMPs. The White Army showed up, maybe a hundred men. All men. That's their whole schtick. They came in on motorcycles and ATVs and horses. More schtick. Look how fucking folksy they are. We hit them with EMPs anyway, level the field, and took out the ATVs. The bikes were retrofitted no-electric and a horse... you can't EMP a horse. I don't know if there was a skirmish in that war that didn't start with both sides ritually knocking the other one back to basically the twentieth century. I think the tactical EMP is the reason there's anything left of this country.

We took a few potshots while they were still at range, but we didn't have the ammo to waste on anything else. Don't think we did any damage. They took up position further up the hill, in the ruins of the old Basilica.

Then we waited.

We should have mined the church. That old thing was blown half to shit already, it wouldn't have made the world any worse if we'd either leveled it or hidden explosives throughout. But, you know, ethical war or whatever. Don't mine churches. The other side leveled every mosque, synagogue, and "heretic" church they got their hands on, not to mention libraries and universities and even the goddammed Statue of Liberty because they hate immigrants, but we were supposed to fighting "ethical war." Those two words don't got nothing to do with one another and everyone knows it.

So they holed up in the Basilica and we pulled back into the library and we had one of those good old fashioned standoffs where people slowly die from sniper fire and everything is awful.

That's when Laura got shot, right in the head, because we missed a spot when we bulletproofed the facade. She's dead. She had natural red hair but she always dyed it redder, and her favorite show was *Buffy the Vampire Slayer*, and she liked to drink water out of long-stemmed glasses. She was... I think she was thirty-seven. Way past drafting age. She volunteered. It was her first engagement. She was only there because she loved books.

Had plenty of time to avoid looking at her corpse, while she was in there with us dead.

Dwight was another one of my friends in the unit, one of my favorite people hands down. Total weirdo, and he was all obsessed with that Viking shit and the dark ages in general. Both his parents had come over from Sweden, though his dad was originally from Nigeria. Dwight had one degree in medieval studies and another in African history, and I can't tell you how many times during basic he'd run down the details of this or that ancient battle, whether in Europe or Africa. If there were guns involved, he didn't care about it. But if there were swords and armor, or spears and shields, he was all in.

He started talking to the Vikings first thing. He was the first person to believe them—to really believe them—and his faith was contagious. While we were pinned down, he asked them everything. Mostly, they were quiet, even taciturn. But there was one thing they were very insistent on, that I overheard them talking about.

"Nazis don't go to Valhalla."

"But why not?" Dwight asked.

"It takes two things to go to Valhalla," the spokesperson said. "You have to die in battle, and you have to venerate Odin."

"A bunch of those fuckers are Odinists," he said.

"No they aren't. They're nationalists, fascists, racial separatists, they're all kinds of things, but they don't venerate Odin, whatever they think."

"What do you mean?"

"They only know one half of Odin. They know the masculine side, the heterosexual side. The Christian side. They worship a bastardization of our god, a bastardization first created by a nationalist Christian eight hundred years ago that's only gotten further afield since.

Our Odin practices women's magic, the magic of the... the sexually penetrated. We also worship female gods of war and male gods of the hearth and gods who change gender when they're bored. Nazis don't understand that, any of it. In life, we raided sometimes. Traded other times. We also did all sorts of things that won't fit your modern sensibilities. Things that, were I alive, you might kill me for. But we're not Nazis, and people who worship a Christian version of our god most certainly do not go to Valhalla."

It was as if the man had used up every word allotted to him for the day, because I don't believe a one of them spoke again before the battle began in earnest.

How long was that?

Another hour, maybe? The sun was still right overhead when the White Army rushed us.

It was a bullshit move, rushing us. One part overconfidence and one part desperation, if you can imagine that. They knew they were losing the war, at that point, but they had us more than two-to-one, and we all know the KKKommanders don't give two shits about the lives of their men.

That's when I put a bullet in man's leg. While he was in the street, running. It was a good shot. He was running, and I led the target and everything. I'd been aiming for center body mass, but still. At least a hundred yards against a moving target. I was proud of that shot at the time, on a technical level, even if I'm not sure I'm proud of it anymore now that I know the man's name.

We expected the charge. What we didn't expect was the ordinance that knocked the reinforced front door off its hinges, but that happened, and almost all the fighting happened right there on the first floor, among the empty shelves. The whole thing felt like it lasted a half hour. I've looked it up since. From the time of the first blast to the time the last shot was fired, we're talking about three minutes and twelve seconds.

We thought they were going to pour in through the door after they blew it the fuck off, so James got in there with our one functioning automatic and he took at least ten of the fash down with him before someone got him in the neck.

It was a feint, and they blew a hole in the side of the building while that was going on and that's where they got in. Close-quarters combat is a whole different beast. A worse one, maybe. Maybe a better one. I go back and forth about that, sometimes, instead of sleeping. I think about the pros and cons of various types of absolute horror. Is it better to see your death coming, or get picked off without knowing it?

I would have thought the Vikings would expend themselves right off. I mean... Vikings. They were starting to sober up by that point, but still, they'd been drinking. And they were already dead. And they were doomed to die. But they were smarter than that, never risked themselves unnecessarily.

Your next assumption, of a comrade you know is doomed, is that they'd sacrifice themselves to save others. None of that, either. They knew they were the best trained soldiers on the field, and that in order for us to win, they had to be in the fight as long as they could. They were smart like that. Assholes like that.

I stationed myself in the back. I fancy myself more a sniper than the assault sort, so I watched the whole thing go down. I also only hit three targets out of a hundred and seventeen bullets I fired, but that's another story.

I watched us win. We took casualties of fifty percent—half of those were KIA—but we defeated a force twice our strength. I watched the Einherjar bayonet men and shoot them, and I saw one of the Viking women break a man's face apart with her fists. Soon after, a bullet found her heart and she collapsed with a smile on her lips. She disappeared. Like, literally, she phased out of existence, beam me up Scotty.

We pushed them back out onto the pavement—when I say "we" I'm honestly not being fair, because I didn't do much of it myself. We had them scattered and running. Most of them.

Dwight was out there, waving a pistol in one hand and swinging a wooden-stock rifle like a club in the other. A Viking with a shotgun stood beside him.

I think the same fashy little shit killed them both, maybe in the same three round burst.

I tagged the fashy in his belly, and his friends helped him get away, and the remaining Nazis ran. He survived his wound. Why do we have so much information about the war? Does it do me any good to know who I killed who and I didn't?

And Dwight?

Dwight lay alone on the concrete. Face down. There wasn't much blood, but he was dead.

Two ravens sat atop him, one on each shoulder. I've never seen a raven in Asheville in my life. Not before, not since. There were two of them. As big as people say those things are.

They barked, and they sounded like dogs. One was loud, like it was right where it was. The other one was distant, echoing. Then they flew away, directly up and towards the sun and I tried to watch to see where they went but you can't look directly at the sun like that. I looked back down, and Dwight was gone. Okay so his body was still there but there was *something* about him that was gone and I don't know how to tell you what it was.

That was that. We won. Sort of. They didn't storm the library, which I guess means we won, but sometimes I think I'd burn every single book in that place if it would bring back Laura or Dwight or any of the rest of my friends. The war was over, at that point, even if we didn't know it yet. So what did they die for? I guess for symbols. Maybe symbols matter that much, I don't know.

I deserted after that. Half the survivors of the Battle of Asheville died less than a week later up in Pittsburgh, and I suppose I'd be dead if I'd gone and it probably makes me a coward that I didn't. It's not that I was afraid of dying. It was that I was afraid of dying in battle.

Because I believe in Odin now. It's hard not to believe in a god without venerating him. I don't want to go to Valhalla. I don't want to fight ever again, let alone every night. I don't want to serve with the Einherjar at the twilight of the gods sometime in the twenty-fifth century. If I don't want to do that, then I don't want to die in battle.

Dwight, though, I expect he's happy. I expect he dies every day with a smile on his lips and mead in his belly.

He won't have to fight alongside the monsters of the human race, either. Because as I learned in Asheville, Nazis don't go to Valhalla.

MALEDICTION

A night like any night, my bare mattress on the floor, old window glass between me and the street outside. A few bottles on the floor, one filled with piss in the corner—the toilet was three stories down and if there'd ever been a railing, there certainly wasn't one now and I'd rather piss into a bottle than break my neck drunk in the dark.

Eduard had come and gone and he'd taken the best of me with him in his mouth and I was spent. I might have even been happy. I'd asked him to stay of course. I always asked him to stay.

"These houses freak me out," he'd said, pulling on his pants both legs at a time with his fat beautiful ass on the edge of my bed.

"Door like mine, cops can't get in," I'd told him. "Not without us hearing."

There was a back way out, too. A window, out onto the neighbor's roof. You could get across a whole city block on rooftops in the right parts of Baltimore.

"Angels can get into this shit," Eduard had told me, and then he'd left. The bar had fallen back down across the door and woken the mice in the walls and cupboards. Eduard spoke street American with a middling-thick German accent and his words had a way of staying in the room after he was gone.

He liked everything about me that I didn't like about myself. He thinks I'm all hardened and shit.

I don't see myself as a graverobber. It's not like that.

◆

She'd died in spring like everyone else. Everyone does it in the springtime. Blood makes the flowers bloom and it melts the snow and it wakes the world from winter. She'd hanged herself, which is kind of classy, isn't it, and there used to be like 600,000 people in this city and now there's less than half of that, but the flowers know how to bloom.

Death is really simple for the dead but it's really complicated for everyone else. Ten years now of suicide spring and I'll tell you one thing: the unemployment rate's gone down. Plenty of work for anyone who wants it—it's just that I don't want it.

So I cut her down, that's kind of like work I guess, and I buried her in Druid Hill with the rest of everyone else, and that was definitely work because if you want a free house you'd better at least put in the work to bury its tenants. And I had to put in that door to keep out criminals and cops, but I got friends who helped with that because maybe we're a morbid bunch but at least we help one another out.

It's not graverobbing though. I didn't sell much of her stuff. Nothing that looked personal. I left that stuff in case family ever comes, which it never will. That old lady's gold jewelry haunts me, though, since there's a *compro oro* place just down the street next to the beer and wine store—I think one guy owns both places, it's hard to tell—and I have to see that gold any time I go into her bedroom, which is basically never. That jewelry haunts me almost as much as she does.

No one knows what it is, but all of a sudden, ten years back, about one in seven of us is going to cut themselves or eat glass or jump off of something they shouldn't. Well, some people say they know what it is. Eduard says he knows what it is. Says his mother told him. She knows it from the old country. I think maybe the old country is Brazil, but maybe it's Germany. Eduard does a lot of things really well but talking about himself isn't one of those things.

There are seven angels returned to the world in anger and vengeance, and they fall prey on everyone in the night and they breathe their curses into our lungs. They fight over every soul. They fight over which of us gets what curse.

But I don't have a soul and neither does anyone I've ever met because the world is full of horror but it's not angelic horror, it's just regular horror, the kind you don't need gods or souls or angels to drum up. Like the look on that woman's face when I cut her down. That's the horror in this world, something that was in her eyes and in her mind that's gone now because she's gone, gone to rot, gone to dust and shadows.

◆

A night like any night, my solar LED lamp spitting out its cum-colored glow on the water-damaged fake wood floor. Some books I'd never read were sitting in a milk crate and the two or three books I read again and again were stacked up near my couch-cushion pillow.

If I got drunk enough, I wouldn't dream about her.

I wouldn't see that face swinging back and forth with the wind of a summer storm coming in through her open window. I wouldn't hear those voices, the conspiratorial whispers, quiet like whispers and mice. I wouldn't hear the rustle of bird wings and or catch the glint of feathers and flesh just past as far as I could see in the dark.

I reached for a bottle. It was empty.

I reached for another. It was empty.

I could stay up till dawn, I decided. But I was at the wrong stage of drunk for that to be true.

You're not supposed to sell beer after midnight in Maryland, but the liquor control board has been hit just as hard by this whole "everyone's dead so no one's working" bit as everywhere else and I was pretty sure the white guy who owned the *compro oro* was going to sell to me, or at least the guys he exploited who would be working at that hour might.

I scrambled for my phone and checked my balance. My bank account was as empty as the bottles around me.

I'm not a graverobber but I didn't want to see that lady while I was sleeping so I got up and crept down to the second floor, one hand on the wall because I'm not one-in-seven and I didn't have the slightest desire to teeter off the side of those stairs and land on the floor thirty feet down.

The door to her bedroom was ajar because it was always ajar. If I left it closed the mice would scratch their claws into the wood and by consequence into my eardrums and I didn't like that, so better to just grant them free passage. Most of them live in her bedroom. I think they go out to hunt. I don't want to know what they hunt, but I honestly think its cats. Which is almost too fucked up to think about, a swarm of those little mice getting some stray cornered in the alley, driving it back, one brave mouse leading the charge and ending up dead but its comrades marching on, pouring over the concrete to sink their teeth into mangy flesh. Brave little shits, those mice.

I had my LED lantern in hand. You can't hold it in front of you like a flashlight, you have to hold it back behind your field of vision like a torch.

The mice scattered before I could see them as more than just a writhing mat on the floor, and I found her dresser. I just took a pair of earrings. That's all, just a pair of earrings. She didn't need them, she was dead. I needed them, because I didn't want to see her while I was sleeping.

I locked up behind me, three keys for three locks and then hit the app on my phone that dropped the bar inside. You can't be too careful—gotta mix hi-tech and low-tech if you want to stay safe. The only light on the street was the blue glow of the cop camera. "We're still here," it's like it was saying. "Everyone you care about is dead and this city is a shell but don't worry, the police are still here. We might help you and we might kill you and you'll never know which it is. But we're here and we can see you."

Some nights I'd talk back to the thing, answer its wordless taunts with wild strings of obscenities. No one can string together obscenities like a street punk faggot, you've got to understand. To half the world, I was an obscenity myself.

But no invectives came to me so I just flashed the cops my cock and kept walking. The *compro oro* was closed and the beer and wine was closed. I was going to keep going, but the thing about flashing a snitch-ass blue light lamppost is that it snitched on me and the cops were coming and I ran the whole way home and got that big beautiful door slammed shut before the cops decided it wasn't even worth leaving their cruiser.

I climbed the stairs by the light of my phone. Even put the earrings back.

◆

Eduard says there are seven angels and they've each got a curse. They can look like anything they want, which usually means they look like anything *we* want, he says. You grow up in America, you're probably going to see them as angels with wings and all that shit. It's what most of us want, I guess. It's like, the American Dream of cursed seraphim.

Eduard said his moms got kissed by the Angel of Longing and she's never been the same and never will be, that for the rest of her life she's going to be missing her sister. But of course she's going to be missing her sister. Her sister is dead now six years, cut up by thugs in the countryside. That wasn't a curse; that was just the shit luck of life.

His grandpa got kissed by the Angel of Sorrow, he says, and the old man spends half his day weeping. There's an Angel of Passion who lets your heart consume itself in the fire of feeling until you've got nothing left and there's an Angel of Harm who obviously got to the lady I buried in the park. There's four others besides, but I'd stopped listening because you can only hear so much of that shit before it starts to get at you.

◆

A night like any night and I lay awake growing more sober by the minute. "Go to sleep," I kept saying, but that's kind of a fuck off bad way to make yourself fall asleep, so it didn't work. I watched headlights drive their way across my wall in big waves of light that crashed into the corners and disappeared faster than they'd come on. There was a lot of traffic at night and sometimes I wondered who was driving and where were they going so late and maybe I wondered what angel had gotten to them or was going to.

Was there an angel of car accidents? It seemed like a lot of people went down in car accidents. But maybe that had always been the case.

There must have been an angel of "you basically won't ever manage to fall asleep after you sober up" because that one had kissed me a long time ago. But there were only seven. Eduard was certain. And if there were only seven angels, their curses were probably a bit less specific or at least a bit more dramatic. I mean, I cut that lady down. She'd hanged herself by the neck and her hands had just been in the pockets of her dress like there was nothing the matter in the world. Like she was out for a Sunday stroll, just walking on air.

Me, if I was hanging from an exposed ceiling beam I'd be clutching and ripping at the rope until my hands were a mess of blood. Maybe that's just me though.

That's how I fell asleep, too, thinking about that lady. Fucking sobriety.

◆

She didn't come into my dreams. Oh, how I wish it'd been her who'd come into my dreams.

He looked something like Eduard. Husky, hairy. He was a bear of an angel. No wings. I guess I believe in sexy men more than I believe in some heavenly host.

I heard him come in and I knew he was there. By the door. Just standing there at my door, watching me. I couldn't see him, not at first. Then a car started past, then it stopped on my street, and in the headlights through my window I could see his thick black beard and the sunken pits that served as his eyes. He was nude, his flaccid cock uncut. He took a step toward me, watching me.

He craned his head to the side like a dog might. He was curious.

Then he smiled, and my body locked up under the power of his gaze.

He walked toward me, his head still cocked. Three purposeful strides and he loomed into the whole of my field of vision. I heard a car door somewhere. The light stayed on my angel.

"Which one are you?" I asked. I couldn't look away, and he straddled my chest. His head shot to attention and I could just barely see his white-blue eyes deep and buried in the darkness cast by his brow.

"No matter where you go," he said, in my voice, "they or someone else will be after you." He leaned down and kissed me, full on the mouth, his tongue caressing my teeth, blood running down from his gums, into my throat.

Then he was gone and I was awake and a police battering ram hit the door. My wondrous door.

I'd bitten deep into my lip and I sat up and wiped blood from my maw. I stared dumbfounded at where he'd been, all the while the battering ram beat out a failed rhythm like some shitty drummer.

I spent a couple breaths pretending like I didn't believe what he'd told me. I mean, it was a dream. I'd been asleep. Real things don't happen when you're asleep, except like pissing your bed or something. But by the time I heard them crash through the door and into the front hall, I knew he'd been telling the truth. They were going to come for me, always.

I scrambled around my room to pack my shit, because I was going to escape, because the only thing worse than running is getting caught. Toothbrush, phone, pants, a book I'd like to say I've read. That's all you need in this world.

I kept a length of rebar by the door to my room. Not in case cops come in. As much as you might want to, you can't hit cops in the face with rebar. I kept it just for, you know, people. In case people came in. I kind of lost some time standing around with that rebar in my hand, trying to figure out if I should take it.

I heard them on the steps. I threw my backpack on and looked in the corner of my room, saw those pee bottles. They were capped. I hoped one of those cops was going to drink my piss. I hoped one of them was going to be like, "Fuck, he got away, let's search his shit."

Then his buddy would say, "Well he's got a couple 40s of Steel—you want one?" and they would toast and drink that shit. And they'd probably spit it out, right, but what if they didn't?

You've gotta hold onto hope that good things are going to happen in this world.

Instead of finding me gone, though, they found me still there, daydreaming about them drinking my piss. One cop came in, she had a fucking SWAT shield, and then her buddy came in looking like he owned the place. None of us owned the place.

Then the Angel of Persecution came in behind them, just as naked as he'd been in my dream, and he pointed at me, and he said in my own fucking voice, "There he is."

And that's just not fair, if you ask me, because I was awake.

So I grabbed that rebar and I smashed in that angel's face—or tried to. I got his mouth even bloodier than he'd gotten mine, and I looked again and it wasn't my angel, it was just a uniformed cop. I didn't suppose I'd be able to explain that I hadn't meant to break part of his face with a length of steel rod. I ran.

"Get him!" he yelled, in his own voice, which wasn't anything like my voice. I've got a nice voice. To be fair, he might have had a nice voice before I'd staved in his teeth.

I got a taser barb in my back for my troubles but only one of them so it didn't complete the circuit and I just kept running and it ripped out of me, I think, and then I was out the window, on the neighbor's roof. I turned around just in time to see a gloved hand on the sill. I brought my bare foot down on it, but that didn't do any good, so I slammed the window shut. That did some good.

People say you can run to fend off panic but it turns out that's not true when you're running across rooftops with three cops behind you firing their handguns—thank fucking God they were mediocre shots or I'd be dead. When I hit the end of the block I failed at some parkour shit I'd seen on YouTube, and it's a good thing no one's picked up the trash in a year because otherwise I'd also be dead. Instead, I broke some ribs and the garbage bags broke my fall.

The cops fired a few rounds into the sea of rats and rot around me before they gave up and fucked off. A clean getaway. Nothing to worry about.

Except fingerprints and DNA and that fucking monographed pillow that Eduard had made me back when we were first courting and did nice shit like that for each other. The cops were going to know who I was. That was something to worry about, something I was never going to stop worrying about. Cops are like elephants—they never forget a grudge. Or maybe that's crows.

Cops are worse than crows because they're everywhere, even still.

◆

People say you can run to fend off panic but it's not true when you never stop running.

I see that face everywhere. I've seen him driving a commercial van, and he turned to look at me and waved. He rang me up at the deli once. He's in the background of my selfies, indistinct and leering. He's at shows and bars and he's out of the corner of my eye and sometimes he just straight up attacks me in alleys or shows up with cops and tries to bust me, and he laughs my laugh when I run in fear. It's been two years and I'll never be the same again and I'll never trust anyone because anyone might be him.

I hear him every time I speak. It's no longer him who talks in my voice, it's me who talks in his.

I wish I had guts like that old lady did, but I don't, because here I am on the end of my proverbial rope and I'm scrabbling and ripping at it and my hands are bloody and raw and I'm still breathing.

I'm still breathing, but I'm not sure why.

INVISIBLE PEOPLE

The last light of the sun came down through the broken windows, all pretty and shit, catching on that big jagged shard of glass and then pouring out into the room over my bed. Over Marcellus. He snored in that way he always did, endearing and soft.

I hurried to dress in the last of the daylight, but once I was done, I lingered. I paced, I ran my fingers through my beard, I watched the twilit horizon and counted the silhouette bones of the buildings Portland calls its skyline.

Anything but go to work.

It had been a lot easier, stealing from rich people, back before the anxiety had hit. I miss those days, when my biggest problems were external. It's easier to steer clear of cops than it is to get away from whole chunks of my brain.

I can't get on the net, either. I mean, I can still get in... the people in the office next door haven't updated their wifi encryption since 2019. I just can't bring myself to sign on. Not even the Darknet. It may not be corporate, but it's still the net. There's just too much data in the feed. Too much shit to worry about. Every day, someone's sick. Some friend of a friend's got cancer or your ex-boyfriend—the one you haven't seen since high school—is in for surgery. Someone you met at a party six months ago got caught doing something and needs bail. The awful shit tragedies of two thousand "friends" pile up worse than the latest mass shooting or another pandemic scare. And those are bad enough. I can't get on the net. I won't.

But I've got to eat.

The room went dark and I stumbled my way through the warehouse. Five paces out of the room, I turned the corner. A window let in enough street light and, there, past the accumulated junk of fifteen squatters, I could see the door at the bottom of the stairs. I pressed my body into the bar and I was outside. The squat's chemical smell was gone, leaving only that sickly shit stink that comes in off the Willamette, dampened a bit by the endless winter rain.

I pulled out a phone—who still uses handheld phones?—and I told it to call Ramirez.

"I'm sorry," my phone said. "I couldn't understand your request."

Fucking thing still didn't like my accent.

"Ramirez," I told it. "There're only six numbers in my phone. Only one of them starts with R. Fucking call Ramirez, Siri."

"Processing."

It said it was processing but I think it just said that to be nice. I'm glad my phone is nice to me.

"I'm sorry," it said. "I couldn't understand your request."

"Call R-A-M-I-R-E-Z."

No processing delay. It rang and she answered.

"What do you want, Vasyl?"

I could never read her tone of voice. Maybe I'd caught her at a bad time. Maybe she was still mad at me about May Day. Maybe she was tired. People who aren't me seem to just kind of pick up information like that when they talk to people. I don't think they even second-guess themselves. It seems like magic to me.

"I'm looking for work," I said.

"Of course you are," she replied.

There's some irony to that. Work was the last thing I wanted. But I was walking east, away from the water and the dead bastions of industry. I was walking towards work.

"I'll meet you," she told me, and hung up.

A random helicopter went overhead and my eyes grew wide and wild. There was a dumpster, I could throw the phone in there. Not secure enough. It was two blocks to the river, I could sprint, probably get the worst evidence into the water before I surrendered. But no searchlight lit me up from the dark heavens and the sounds of the rotors faded from the world before the adrenaline cleared my system.

I picked up the pace.

I got to the corner of Grand and Belmont, went under an awning. I took out my phone, called no one, and put it to my ear, started pacing. Fake phone call—you need a reason why you're just standing around on a street corner or you'll deal with cops. Cops and I didn't get along, and I had the warrants to prove it.

Ramirez's car rolled up, black and glossy in the rain, picking up the dull blue of the streetlights. I climbed in the passenger door. No

Ramirez. No driver at all. Typical. It probably wasn't a slight; it was just efficiency. I closed the door and the car took off up Grand, heading north up past Rosa Parks, then wove into a neighborhood and stopped in front of a house I'd never seen before.

Kids were playing on the block, chasing a glowie, laughing as the ball darted between them with a mind of its own. They laughed harder when one kid tackled the thing on the pavement and another three dog-piled up.

Most of the houses on the street were burned out, and not one of them had a light on in the window. Those kids weren't from the block, or else they were squatters. Either way, they seemed happy enough.

The house in front of me was blacked out, I realized. The windows were too dark to just be unlit. It was three stories, painted the color of sand, and had an overgrown garden full of lavender and those creepy fucking passionflowers with their alien little stamen or what-ever-the-fuck those antennae things are. The whole place was a paint-peeled reminder of the rise and fall of the Portland middle class.

A camera over the door saw my scowling mug and decided to let me in.

"You've got face-rec on your fucking door?" I called, when the door closed behind me.

"Good to see you too," I heard her say.

The house was an empty shell, a dusty showroom. Ramirez was sitting lotus in the dining room, her yoga mat spread out on the hardwood floor.

In the corner, discreet against the moulding, was a matte black box no bigger than my fist. Hair-thin cabling ran out its top and into the ground of a three-prong outlet nearby. If it worked right, that little wire kept the modem from overheating its core and spitting fire-hot bullshit all over the room.

It didn't even have an indicator light. The best tech doesn't anymore. The best tech doesn't want you to even know it's there.

"Sit down," she said, indicating the room as a whole. She made eye contact. Or maybe it's better just to say she looked my direction. I couldn't see her eyes behind those Readpro FOV contacts and their bright blue glow. And she probably hadn't bothered to look past the screen that filled her vision.

I sat.

"What kind of work?" she asked.

"Anything," I said. Then I thought it over. "Anything that's not on Lightnet or Darknet. Anything I can do direct."

"You're still not over it?" she asked.

I could have hit her.

"No," I told her instead. "I'm still not over it."

"Maybe you should see somebody," she told me. "If your anxiety's so bad it's keeping you offline, maybe you should do something about it."

A million answers poured into my head unheeded. I took a few breaths, then picked the only one that hurt to say: "I am."

Even squatters needed therapy, and mine came from a woman named Helga. She'd worked as a cognitive therapist for three decades before she got laid off and her husband took her savings on a one-way trip to Florida. Motherfucker had got his comeuppance, though, in one of those nightmare storms, and her cash and his corpse had washed out to sea. She moved into a squat a few months later, and we all did what we could to help one another out. Me, I fixed things. Helga, she fixed people.

"Well," Ramirez said, from her tech-zen holier-than-thou fucking yoga mat on the floor of a stolen house, "let's get to work."

She meant well. She was probably even my friend. But people don't open up in person anymore. Were we really friends if I never read her status updates? If our profiles weren't linked?

I took out my laptop. It was encrypted to nine hells with layered volumes, but I think what kept it safe is that no one even used the fucking things anymore. No one under thirty remembered how they worked and sure as hell no one of any age spent their time trying to fig-ure out how to break into them—the damn thing still had a CD drive. I couldn't just move my eyes across the screen to shift its focus, I had to drag a little icon of an arrow around the screen and I had to press buttons on the keyboard. It was tactile. It did non-tactile things, but I could still touch it. I could close it. I could look away from it.

"There's an exec in Rackman Ltd who's been leaving a trail of meta that leads right offshore," Ramirez told me.

Ramirez was a fixer, not a hacker. She kept track of information, things like who needed robbing and where they kept their shit. But she couldn't get in the proverbial door.

"How much?" I asked.

She answered. Not an insubstantial sum.

It was a simple job. Break into Jonathan Albrecht's files and then his offshore bank account. Take out two percent. Any more than that and he might decide hiring a hit squad was worth the financial and legal liabilities. If we were lucky, we'd find some blackmail while we were in there, wire it up on a deadman switch so if I stopped breathing, his wife would find out about his affair or, if nothing else, the IRS would find out about his tax dodge. And I'd walk away with $5k for a night's work. Simple.

Took me all night.

Ramirez did yoga for a while, murmuring instructions to her contact lens computer while in downward dog and a thousand other poses. She said the names aloud—revolved triangle, pigeon, camel—and presumably got some kind of biofeedback telling her if she was doing them right. The rest of her jabbering was pure business though—checking up on clients and projects and whatever the hell it was she did besides find me yuppies to rob.

I live in a world where some people feel it's more efficient if they multitask their relaxation with their work.

Ramirez was a squatter because it was cool. She was a criminal because it was fun. Honestly, with her skills and drive and education and upbringing—but minus her criminal record, perhaps—she could have *been* the mark we were about to rob. She could have had his job and his life and his underlings and his investments. But as she told me once, stealing felt a lot more honest when it was illegal.

I was still going hard at Albrecht's vapor drive when she checked in with me at 2am. Simple jobs aren't always simple. Ramirez stretched out on the yoga mat and fell asleep.

By 3am I'd gotten his biometrics from the pizza delivery system and was leveraging them against his drive's encryption. The privacy arms race is amusing. Lock things up with your biometrics, sure. It's a bad idea, but you'll do it anyway. Make it so your thumbprint opens your phone. But then one day you want to get into your phone when it's in the other room, and all you've got's your friend's computer. So keep your thumbprint online somewhere. What do you lock that up with? Another thirty-character passcode? Or maybe your retinal scan? Great. Now where do you keep *that*? For a hacker, it's a logic puzzle—once you get one clue, you leverage it against the rest.

By 4am I had everything I needed to convince his bank I was him. I set his account to make a series of payments to thirty different bank accounts, each transaction pre-approved. Random timed intervals between the transactions kept them from tripping the bank's security. Work isn't so bad.

It was 4:30am when the battering ram slammed against the front door, a bass thud that dropped me into my body from where I'd been lost in the screen.

"Pigs!" Ramirez shouted, going from sleeping to standing as fast as I'd managed to look up from my computer.

We'd lose it all if Albrecht—which is to say, I—didn't authorize the bizarre series of transactions at the end. I hate it the fucking worst when I want to fucking panic but I can't. I wanted to cut and run, but if I cut I lost it all and if I ran, well, there wasn't really anywhere to go.

"Time left?" Ramirez asked.

"Twelve minutes thirty-four," I said.

The ram hit the door again, and the frame cracked but didn't buckle. Ramirez must have done more for security than the face-rec camera.

Fuck, the camera.

"What's the face-rec hooked up to?" I asked.

"Kind of busy right now," she answered. She was typing away on the bare kitchen counter, pressing keys on an illusory keyboard only she could see.

"Is it fucking hooked up to Lightnet?" I asked.

"Yeah it's fucking hooked up to Lightnet. You think I got a face-rec database in my pocket?"

The battering ram slammed again, and this time I heard cussing from other side. They'd move to breaching rounds soon, and me without my gas mask.

"You know I'm tagged!" I shouted. 11:36 left.

"There're here for *you*?" she answered, still typing away.

"There're from the bank," I said. "Not the bank we're robbing, the bank that owns the house. I'm tagged for B&E."

A shotgun racked outside and I lost it, triggered into memory.

◆

It was May Day, five years back, and we were all lined up, arm-in-arm—undocumented migrants and squatters' rights activists, all of us riffraff who just refused to disappear or die. I felt powerful, more powerful than I'd ever felt in my life. I felt more powerful in that company than I'd ever been while digging through the personal files of the most powerful men in the world, because that day I was part of something greater than myself.

The police weren't having it, and they did their best to corral us. But there we were, in unvanquishable number, flooding the downtown streets of Portland, disrupting the easy flow of capital. At least that day, the invisible were visible.

But the police attacked a few hundred of us at the base of the Burnside Bridge.

I knew what their plan had been, at least from up high, at least officially. I leaked it a few days later. They were supposed to leave us an exit, disperse us with gas and force as necessary.

But they didn't leave us an exit. The news crews dutifully departed rather than face arrest, and the cops came in with bludgeons and pepper spray. They'd tried a few new toys out on us that day, dazzlers and sticky guns and a goddam make-you-puke cannon, but at the end of it all, nothing beats the raw force of sticks and airborne poison.

And we had our arms linked together, us brave people, and we were nonviolent back then, most of us. A lot can change in five years. People can learn a lot about the nature of power.

Ramirez had been next to me, our elbows locked. On my other side, a woman I'd never met. Fifty years old I'd say. We stared the police down.

A cop came out from the police wall in front of us, took three steps towards me, looked me in the eyes, and raised the barrel of a shotgun, racking it. And I let go. I unlocked my arms and turned my face in fear.

They took the old woman off in handcuffs, and they took me off in handcuffs, and I've forgotten that cop's face but I'll never forget the barrel of his gun. And maybe I'm lucky Ramirez still works with me, still trusts me at all. I know I don't trust myself.

◆

The shotgun blast brought me back to the present day, but the door held. Ramirez had done her homework.

Ten minutes, forty-three seconds left on the clock. I went into child pose. I'd never needed child pose as a child. Panic came over me in waves like fever, burning everything from my brain except the thought "I am not okay."

"I'm sorry about the camera," Ramirez said, in the bizarre quiet. Whatever she'd been doing, she'd done it, and we didn't have much to do but wait to see what the fates had in store.

"It happens," I said.

We waited out the clock in silence. I needed to quit, I decided, during short bouts of lucidity. No more hacking and no more breaking and entering. If I got out of there, I'd never be back. I'd just keep my head down.

I wasn't okay.

Better to just eat trash—trash was free. Sure, there were too many squatters around Southeast Portland, so I'd have to leave town. Go somewhere where I couldn't have a community. Maybe Marcellus would come with me. He said he loved me, and he might even mean it, and that might even be enough.

I'd never be okay.

Or the forest. The fires were worse every year, but I wasn't afraid of death and I wasn't afraid of fire. I was afraid of police and I was afraid of cages. Trapped in a barricaded house with bank cops outside, I kept myself as calm as I could by thinking about pleasant things, like burning alive in a forest fire.

I wasn't okay.

The clock ran out. The transactions were complete, and Albrecht signed off on them. Ramirez gave me my cut within seconds. It did nothing to change my situation.

The cops shot at the windows next, their rounds leaving cracks in the first layer of bulletproof plexi. More cursing. Ramirez was sweating—literally sweating. I thought I'd experienced every symptom of fear, but I was wrong. I didn't sweat. That was a pleasant thought in the morass of my brain.

Then I heard the air-raid siren. A hand-cranked thing, coming closer. And the cops outside started cussing in earnest.

"Darknet?" I asked. It took me a long time to formulate words.

Ramirez nodded. "I put out the call as soon as I saw them."

I uncurled my left arm from its place around my knees and set the door camera up on my screen. There were lights outside—squatters gathered at the closest street corner. The cops turned their backs to us, pistols and tasers drawn.

There'd be too many of us out there for them to start shooting. That was the idea, at least. And every squatter on the street was wearing a camera broadcasting to Darknet. And for every camera there was someone at home who would rather be asleep, hitting the big fat censor button on a console or tablet or field-of-vision device every time something on screen might incriminate anyone but the police. Was it fair? Hardly. But the other side had been doing it for decades.

Just knowing they were out there, the burning waves of fear lost the worst of their power over me. But they remained.

I heard the crack of a grenade launcher and saw a muzzle flash, lasting so much longer on my screen thanks to the wonders of a low frames-per-second camera. The police were shooting teargas, I'd guess.

Ramirez was looking at me, saying something, but it was just white noise to me. All I could hear was the ruckus outside and the cold sound of my slow-beating heart. I really shouldn't have gone to work. I should have stayed in bed. I wasn't okay.

"We gotta go!" Ramirez was shouting. She didn't need to shout—words that promised a chance of escape cut through every frequency.

She had her yoga mat rolled up under her arm, the modem in her hand, and her teeth gritted. Whatever she saw on the Darknet, it must have been more promising than the haze I saw on my screen. I slammed the laptop shut.

She threw open the door and dove into a cloud of pink smoke—cover, provided by our side.

I ran, choking my way into a maelstrom of shouts and smoke and pepper spray. The cop silhouettes were the ones bulky with gear and belts and guns. My friends' silhouettes were the thin ones and the fat ones unencumbered by armor or by much weaponry. They were the ones that kept on the move, playing mouse to the police's cat.

The police were outnumbered but unafraid, backed by an empire's worth of legitimacy. They had jails and judges and healthcare and rich patrons and immunity. We had whatever we could make or steal or whatever minimum wage could buy.

Ferocity was enough that night. A cop grabbed at Ramirez as she sprinted past—they always go for the smallest target—but backed off when a heavyset woman stepped closer with a ski mask and a bat.

No one got hurt, no one got arrested. Thirty squatters—most of them strangers, some of them kids—had turned out for the alarm and the cops beat a retreat once we were past their line.

Invisible people take care of one another.

If the bank would budget for it, the cops would be back during the day, combing the house for the clues they weren't going to find. Worst case, Ramirez was going to get tagged the same as me as a person of note and she'd have to be more careful around cameras in hot neighborhoods. But more likely than anything else, the bank would drop it. We won, and they weren't going to want to draw attention to that. We won, but I didn't feel much like a winner.

I was on edge the whole ride back to my neighborhood. Every time I saw another car on the street, I got a little spike of adrenaline. In the dark, every set of headlights was Schrödinger's cop car.

Ramirez rode with me back to my neighborhood and I had her drop me off a few blocks from home. I wouldn't let her self-driving car take me closer. I don't trust the things. One day, I'm going to get into some friend's car and the car itself is gonna just drive us both to jail. I know better than most people that machines will take orders from anyone with good enough code.

"Thanks for the work," I told her when I got out in the soft twilight of morning.

She laughed. Not the condescending, haughty laughter I keep thinking she'll belt out, but a childish giggle that reminded me why I trusted her. "We'd make so much money together," she said.

"I'll call you when I'm starving," I told her. And she drove off.

It wasn't her fault. She lived like she'd never been hurt, like she'd never been broken, so I kept her at arm's length. Her strength reminded me of my weakness.

There's something I tell myself, a kind of mantra I mutter on long nights when the far-off sirens keep me wired or when I'm walking home through the fog and trying desperately not to jump at my own shadow as I pass from the light of one streetlight to another and my own silhouette suddenly appears in front of me. And that mantra is: beauty lies on the far side of fear.

Everything I've done in my life that I'm proud of has terrified me. I'd earned enough that night to keep a whole warehouse of people eating well for the next three months, and that wasn't nothing. It might just be worth it.

◆

Marcellus was lying on his back and snoring in earnest when I crept back into the room. He'd wrapped himself up in the comforter and I had to pry him free to get my naked body into the bed with him. But he murmured in joy when my hand found his chest, and I held him tight and cried with relief and fear in equal parts.

I was home, I had Marcellus. But my house was stolen and my partner was a felon, so both were things that the state could take away.

"How was it?" he asked, half-awake.

"It was work," I said.

"Fucking work," he mumbled. His eyes closed and he snored in that way he always did, endearing and soft.

WE WHO WILL DESTROY THE FUTURE

"You know how most people break out of prison in this century?" Maya asked Yannick. The Flats of Cleveland spread out below their rooftop vantage, an endless mess of dead warehouses and deserted streets lit up by the hot summer sun.

"I don't think most people break out of prison," Yannick said.

"Helicopter. Something like half the jailbreaks. Usually it's their wife who's flying, sometimes their friends. Land in the yard with a hostage, fly the hell out of there."

"You need to get a wife," Yannick said.

Maya toed a loose brick, and it tumbled over the edge of the warehouse, thudding into the plastic lid of a dumpster forty feet below.

"Little late for that," she said.

"Little early," Yannick said.

"You fucking *like* it here," Maya said.

"I mean, it could be worse."

"You like shitty 2010s video games and shitty 2010s pre-Hennesian punk rock and I bet you even like shitty 2010s fashion."

"The fashion's going to get better in what, like fifteen years, if even that?" Yannick said.

"In fifteen years I'm going to be *so fucking old*," Maya said. "I'm not waiting around *five* fucking years. I'm getting out before I turn thirty. You know why they dump us here? You know why I think the twenty-first century is the prison century?"

"Because the Corrective Council abolished the death penalty and couldn't send any more people to Stalinist Russia without someone noticing?"

"I bet they calculated that twenty-first century America was the worst placetime to live with the longest life expectancy. Highest rates of anxiety in recorded history, but they're gonna cure cancer soon enough that we'll have plenty of time to suffer." Maya tried to toe another brick off the edge, but it wouldn't budge. She pulled back to kick it, changed her mind, stomped on the silver tar paper roof.

"There's some good stuff here too though," Yannick said.

"Yeah? Like what?"

"I don't know. Hip-hop? Mechanical bicycles? Taco Bell?"

"Hip-hop is good," Maya admitted.

"Look, there're really two kinds of time-convicts, right? There the people who accept it, integrate themselves—"

"Get a shitty job, get stuck in some monogamous marriage—"

"And there're wackjobs who tell everyone the truth for so long and get told they're crazy for so long that they just give up and actually *go* crazy."

"What do you want from me?" Maya asked. "I'm wearing high-waisted short shorts and I'm wearing shoes and I say things like 'GTFO' and I don't talk about my background in post-temporal string inoculation. I pretend like I think Žižek is hard-to-follow yet innovative."

Maya paced. The warehouse had been abandoned for decades, since labor had gone overseas. Corporate globalization was one of those weird stupid quirks of human history, like when medieval peasants would all get infected with dance mania and thousands of them danced erratically until they fell unconscious or died.

But there she was, standing on the skeletal remains of a building gutted by a quirk of history.

"Help me with this," she said. She staggered back over to Yannick, an air-conditioning window unit in her arms. "Some asshole actually parked a BMW in this neighborhood. I want to drop this on it."

Yannick did that thing he always did where he shrugged with his eyebrows, then he stood to his full six-foot-six and helped her. He was a good friend. A good cell-mate.

"We gotta swing it back and forth for momentum, like one-two-three-go, if we're going to get that car," Maya said.

"All right."

They launched the air conditioner over the wall of the warehouse. It soared fifteen feet laterally, then fell fast and scraped down the passenger side of their target, scratching up the paint.

"Fuck," Maya said. "What the hell else can we throw?"

"Come on," Yannick said. "It was close enough."

"It wasn't!" Maya jumped up on the loose brick wall, spun on one heel to face her friend. "You're not thinking big. You can't just let shit happen to you. You can't just scrape the side of the BMW, you gotta smash in the windshield. You can't just get used to time exile—you've got to *make a fucking jailbreak*."

◆

"You know the other way people do it?" Maya asked. The dark came in the window of their apartment, the only lighting the glow of a romantic comedy playing on the laptop on the coffee table.

"Do what?" Yannick asked.

"They take a guard hostage," Maya said. "Improvise a weapon, get it up on the guard's throat, pistol from their holster. And boom."

"Boom what?"

"Boom, you're out of there. 'Don't mess with me or I'll waste this bozo.'"

"I don't think anyone says 'waste this bozo' though. You've got the slang all wrong."

"Least of anyone's worries. You can say it however you want when you've got a shiv up to some guy's throat. That's what power is."

On the screen, the characters were walking through a park, cute and earnest.

"Movies were the worst form of mass entertainment ever produced," Maya announced.

"I like movies," Yannick said.

"They're flat. None of the expression of theatre, the depth of prose, the immersion of good AR or even VR. A hundred and fifty years of entertainment dark ages."

On the screen, the characters were sitting in a pretty little New York City cafe.

"Don't they all get caught afterwards, the people who break out?" Yannick asked.

Maya pulled her bare feet up to sit cross-legged on the couch. "Yeah," she said. "Usually in a few days. They go home to their families, or go see their friends. Cops are waiting for them. Happens every time. I won't do that."

"If you can't go see your family or your friends, what's the point of a jailbreak?"

"This movie is moronic. Why would the protagonist pick between these guys? They both like her, she likes both of them. Date them both. There, movie's over. I solved it."

"Maya Havel, the woman who single-handedly destroyed a genre."

Maya stood up, slammed the laptop shut. "It's just not *right*. Fuck what's fair or unfair, but it's not *right*. This isn't how it happens. I'm *not supposed to be here*. I've *got to fix it*."

"You can't fix it."

"*I refuse to accept that!*"

◆

Maya's text tone sounded in the middle of the night. Eight months into her exile and she still hadn't gotten used to the idea that people had to communicate via text messages. Worse, her phone didn't even know when it was okay to bother her and when it wasn't.

She stared at her ceiling fan as it beat against the air. Her phone chirped again. There was no such thing as an innocuous text tone—since humans naturally tie their electronics into their limbic systems, every noise her phone could possibly make had the power to set her on edge. She nudged Yannick off the crook of her arm, then reached for the nightstand to grab the devil machine.

"People say that living well is the best revenge, but they're wrong," it read. An unknown number, local area code.

Then the second message: "I can think of a lot of better ways to get revenge than eating organic food and doing yoga. I bet you could too."

She tapped on Yannick's bare chest, woke him up.

"What?" he asked. She handed him the phone.

While she read the message again over his shoulder, another appeared: "If you want to help me destroy the future, meet me at night passing the earth to day."

"All right," Yannick typed. He pressed send.

"Hey, why would you do that?" Maya asked, grabbing her phone.

"You were going to say yes anyway, weren't you?" Yannick asked.

"What, to some riddle sent by some stranger in the middle of the night?"

"It's hardly a riddle."

"Well I don't know it," Maya said.

"Oh, whatever. Get up, get dressed. I'll show you where you're going. I'm guessing you're supposed to be there by sunrise."

◆

The pre-dawn streets were empty but for the people who regularly slept outside, and most of them were sleeping. Street lights turned red and green for no one, and Maya and Yannick blew through intersections on their bicycles without a sideways glance.

At MLK and Euclid, Yannick stopped.

"What, we're here?" Maya asked.

"Turn right on Euclid, head into Wade Lagoon. There's a statue there. 'Night Passing the Earth to Day.'"

"How do you know that? Why aren't you coming?"

"Because I like parks. Because your mysterious friend texted you, not me. Hit me up when you're done."

"You're going to bail on me like that?"

"Yeah," Yannick said. "I'm going to go find a cafe or something. Somewhere's got to open soon. You need anything, let me know."

"What if I need you to come with me?" Maya asked.

"You don't need me to go with you," Yannick said. He nudged his foot back into the toe clips and rode off.

There was nothing good to kick in easy reach. Maya rode against the sparse traffic, forcing the two cars she passed to honk and swerve, and the light of dawn encroached upon the city.

Along the steps down into the manicured park, overlooking the reflecting pool, two bronze-casted women struggled with the weight of the world. The inscription on the pedestal said that they were transferring the huge metal orb from one to another, but to Maya it looked more like they were working together to one-two-three-go the Earth into the water.

Leaning against the statue, smoking a cigarette, was a thin white man Maya's age. He wore a backwards red baseball cap, a woman's suit jacket, wide-legged pants, and antique running shoes. Clearly, he was fresh from the future, where they gave you whatever clothes they thought vaguely fit the century of your exile.

Maya stopped five paces away.

"Maya?" The man's eyes were bright and blue, his face open and welcoming.

"You are?" Without planning, she closed the distance between them.

"My name's Naro." He offered his left hand.

"You shake with your right. You might want to change your name. Try Norman—it's the contemporary variant of Naro."

"Norman." The man offered his right hand.

"How and why'd you find me?" Maya asked, instead of shaking.

"They gave me a dossier on everyone here when I signed up as a timer."

Maya stepped back, then scanned the park for other enemies.

"Relax," Norman said. "I'm going rogue. Just took the timeguard deal because they offered it. Gives me a better chance for revenge."

"That's fucked up. Or clever." Maya didn't let down her guard.

"I found you because I read up on everyone. I read about Mr. Morrison, who's taken work as a butcher. Fitting enough, with what he did to those kids. Dr. Ramnath, a murderess three times over. Mr. Kruger defrauded the bank. You know he's paying it back, indentured as a timer?"

"I didn't know," Maya said. Roughly one in ten convicts were indentured as undercovers, feigning true exile and keeping tabs on the rest of them.

"He's got less than a year left. You know they give us software, lets us track phones, eavesdrop? I won't use it."

"Why me?" Maya asked.

"In Cleveland 2016, you've got a whole mess of murderers and grand larcenists. Then there's you. Sentenced to more than eight hundred years for sedition."

"I didn't even do it, I didn't even write that thing."

"*The Nine Guides and their Inevitable Deaths*? That was a masterwork. I'd own up to that if I were you. Cult hit. Kind of preachy, drags in the middle, but I'll tell you what, it's widely regarded as the best augment of 2834. Even if everyone was too afraid to put it up for award consideration."

"Is that it? You're coming back here to get me to confess? Get me to brag about *Their Inevitable Deaths* and clear up the case?"

Norman sat down on the steps and set his elbows on his knees, resting his chin on a fist. "I'm here to *recruit* you. Whether or not you wrote it."

Maya tossed that around in her head. The morning birds were singing in the distance.

"You know who the timeguards are," she said. "We'll take one hostage, get out of here."

"It won't work," Norman said. "Timers are indentured. We aren't worth anything."

Maya paced.

"Is Yannick a timer?" she asked.

"What? No. He was your co-defendant, wasn't he?"

"Why didn't you text him too, then?"

"I got the feeling, the media got the feeling, that he was just kind of dragged into it all by you," Norman said. "Just your boyfriend. That's not the kind of guy I'm looking for."

"He's not really my boyfriend," Maya said, then wished she hadn't. She stopped pacing, looked up at the bare-chested women Night and Day.

"There's something better than getting home," Norman said. "There's revenge."

"Destroy the future?"

"Destroy the future," he agreed.

◆

"No way is this a good idea," Yannick said. "He *admitted* he's a timer. How can this be a good idea?"

A dead fish stink came off the lake as they walked along the concrete pier, the water likely too toxic for swimming. Another quirk of history—humanity treating the Earth like its own personal piss pot. That's what Venus was for.

"What're they going to do? Exile me? They've got no reason to set me up."

"You just think he's handsome."

"So would you."

"Meaningless," Yannick said. "I think everyone is handsome. You're the picky one."

"I'm not going to do anything. I'm just going along with it so far as to see what he's planning," Maya said.

"Would you have taken a timeguard deal? If they'd offered you one?"

"God no," Maya said.

"You ever heard of anyone getting a timeguard deal without snitching?"

"No."

They reached the end of the pier. Lake Erie stretched out to the horizon.

"I can't handle this," Maya said. "I don't know if he's right, but I've got to see what he's thinking. I can't handle waking up at five to serve coffee. I can't handle how much my coworkers *care* about coffee. I can't handle everyone running around like their political choices have merit when I know the economy is going to collapse in less than a century. I can't stand pretending like I don't know things. I can't stand waiting in line and taking busses and how people treat animals like pets and I can't stand all the shit and piss fucking tragedies of the era. There's nothing for me here. Nothing."

Yannick climbed up the short chain link fence, perching on it like a gargoyle. "I'm here," he said.

"I know," Maya said. "It's not enough. I'm sorry, but it's not."

Yannick turned his face away from her, stared out over the water.

"You just think he's handsome."

◆

He looked up from his coffee as she approached. Since the morning, he'd changed into a black t-shirt and tight black pants—he looked like any other twenty-something in the cafe. His eyes met hers and she fought down the desire to return his smile. There was a cup of tea waiting in front of her seat, still warm.

"Wasn't sure you'd come," he said.

"Bullshit," Maya replied.

Two men at the next table over were lost in a loud religious argument, and Maya found herself leaning in toward Norman to catch his words.

"It's not bullshit," he said. "I wasn't sure you'd trust a timer."

"What's your plan?" she asked. "I've been running it over in my head all day. There's nothing we can do in the twenty-first century to fuck up the twenty-ninth. Not *our* twenty-ninth. Anything we do—"

"Anything we do that affects the course of history *between now and our future* will necessarily mean we'll be affecting a parallel spacetime, not our own."

"Exactly," Maya said.

"What year were you convicted? 2835?"

"Yeah."

"I was convicted in 2843."

"Ha, I'm older than you," Maya said.

"Anything we do that affects the course of history between now and our future will affect a parallel spacetime instead of our own. But we're going to set a slowfuse on a full-bore crackoid, let it burrow into the earth. The day after they shunted me off to this century? It goes boom. No more future."

"That would literally blow the entire planet apart," Maya said.

"Yeah," Norman said.

"A full-bore crackoid on that slow a fuse would destroy the future that exiled us and every other parallel that branches out from now."

"Yeah," Norman said.

"You're crazy."

"I need your help," Norman said. "I know how to build a slowfuse, but I'm not sure I could put together the crackoid. Post-temporal string bombs are mostly beyond me."

Maya took the teabag out of her cup and placed it on a saucer, then blew over the tea.

"Why would you do it?" she asked, after an uncomfortable pause.

"Because I don't know what else to do," Norman said. He was pleading with her. Every bit of him told her that she had power, that he needed her. "I can't stand feeling helpless. I can't stand living here, but I can't stand the idea of going home. A world run by the Nine Guides is no world to live in—you know that."

"I know that. But the whole planet?"

"Just one sliver of spacetime," Norman said. "Just *our* future. The ones born from *this* shit society. A trillion million earths will still be there, just not the ones ruled by the Nine."

"What did you do?" Maya asked.

"What?"

"Sorry, I'm the queen of non-sequitur. It's how my brain works. What got you exiled, and what got you a timeguard deal?"

"Mass murder. I helped blow up a good chunk of parliament."

"Like in *Their Inevitable Deaths*," Maya said.

"We didn't get any Guides. Killed a lot of bureaucrats, no Guides."

"And they let you take a deal?"

"I just built the bomb," he said. "At twenty-four, I was barely old enough to stand trial. Mostly, though, they let me cut a deal because I agreed to rat out the mastermind. I ratted out my dad."

"Your dad."

"He was a monster. The only good thing he ever did was bomb parliament. I didn't rat him out to save my skin—I ratted him out to hurt him."

"How the hell is this going to help me trust you?" Maya asked.

"It's not, probably. But I'm not lying to you. Whatever else you want to say about me, I don't lie."

"There's no way I could build a crackoid without access to modern equipment. And it's not my specialty."

"I've got the pieces in my apartment," Norman said. "I smuggled them across. But I'm not sure I could reconstruct it if I tried. I need you."

If he'd smiled or batted his eyes or laid on his obvious charm, Maya would have stood up, walked away, and never spoken to him again. Instead, he just looked at her, earnest, hopeful, almost in love.

"You think I wrote *Their Inevitable Deaths*," Maya said.

"Yeah."

"You're so big into honesty, but you think I lied to you about that."

"I don't hold other people to the same code I hold myself," he said.

"You're sincerely the most fucked up, confusing person I've ever met."

Norman opened his wallet, pulled out two old-fashioned paper tickets. "I've always loved millennial-era plays. Can I take you to the theatre?"

◆

His apartment was in a better part of town, closer to the water. They'd been drunk on gin and tonic during the play, but Maya made sure she was sober by the time they made it into the building. She made better decisions sober.

"Damn, they set you up nice," Maya said, as they reached the third floor landing.

"This is nice?" Norman asked.

"My place, you've got to go around the backyard of this ugly over-sized house, get up some rickety stairs."

Norman opened the door and Maya stepped into a studio apartment with big windows and no furniture. A built-in countertop split the living space from the kitchen. A cot was shoved into one corner, a black duffel in another.

Maya's phone chirped. She pulled it out, saw a text from Yannick: "Where are you?" She turned off the ringer.

"Let's see it," Maya said. "Let's see what you've got of this bomb."

"I can't get you anything to drink or something?"

"You've already recruited me. You can lay off the charm."

Norman went to the bag, unzipped it. The scent of oil and metal fell into the room, and he took out a pistol, set it on the windowsill.

"They gave you a period weapon?"

"In case anyone tries what you wanted to try." He pulled out a clip, then popped out the first bullet and handed it to Maya. "Take the bullet out of its casing."

Maya did. Instead of gunpowder—she was pretty sure period weapons were fired with gunpowder—the shell held six grains of hyper-compressed. "Can I use that counter?" she asked.

"Right now?"

Maya caught Norman looking over at his cot in the corner.

"It won't take me more than an hour, if everything's here," Maya said. "Let's get this started before I lose my nerve."

"Okay," Norman said. He shoved aside some liquor bottles on the counter, then took a swig of gin from one. He offered it to Maya, his big handsome eyes imploring. She faked a drink and held onto the bottle.

Sensing his discomfort, she put a hand on the small of his back, smiled. The tension dropped out of his body, at least a little, and she turned to her work. Each hyper-compressed was a sphere the size of a coarse grain of sand. One by one, she placed them on the counter, then smacked them hard with the base of the bottle of gin. Each cracked open, each holding nearly a cubic foot of matter. She had everything she would need.

A crackoid is semi-organic, and Maya spent the next hour measuring cultures and proto-cultures. Done right, these cultures, incubated in a fast-forward chassis, would evolve—more or less instantly—into a short-lived creature that would send its roots through the earth and sunder the world. Usually, they were used for asteroid mining. Most famously, rogue scientists had used one to settle the debate once and for all if Pluto was a planet.

All the times humanity developed the power to destroy itself utterly, and it never had. Or, more likely, it had done it a hundred million times in a hundred million ways in alternate spacetimes, but of course Maya could not have been born into a world that did not exist.

The slowfuse, in contrast to its payload, was purely mechanical. Its twin purposes were to drill deep into the earth and to tell the chassis when to begin its work.

Across the counter, Norman worked methodically, intently, even happily. They caught one another's eyes a few times as they worked. Maya missed that. The complexity of the work, the complexity of the work relationships. If only any of it made sense.

"Where are we going to put it?" she asked.

"Into the lake," Norman said. "The lake has never dried, it's never been developed. They'll never find it."

"You've put a lot of thought into this, haven't you?"

"I spent six months in solitary awaiting trial."

They went back to their work.

In the end, it was no bigger than a pipe bomb. Norman held it aloft. "Little things matter," he said.

◆

After they were let out of the cab a few blocks from the pier, Maya checked her phone.

"Got Chinese. Didn't order you any, since I haven't heard from you," Yannick had sent. An hour later, he'd sent, "Hope you're all right."

She put the phone away.

The pair walked in silence. The crackoid was heavy in her purse. The streetlights on the pier were broken, and everything was dark.

They reached the water.

"Should we do it?" Norman asked.

"Yeah." Maya handed him the crackoid.

"Together?" Norman asked.

"You do it." She took a step back.

He pitched it with all the strength in his young body, and it sailed through the dark sky, then fell into the dark water. Norman pulled himself up the waist-high fence to look for the ripples.

Maya held up the gun in a two-handed grip. "One-two-three-go," she said, under her breath. The shot rang out over the water, and Norman turned to her when the bullet hit his back. She emptied the clip into his body, afraid of aiming for his handsome eyes.

When he was dead, she pushed him over the fence and watched his body hit the lake. His punctured lungs took on water, and he began to sink.

"Fuck off," Maya said, at what she could see of his corpse. "You can't just blow up a fucking planet with people on it."

She threw the gun as far as she could. It sailed through the dark sky, then fell into the dark water.

◆

She was walking down the street to her apartment, headed for the fence, headed for home and sleep and a presumably grumpy Yannick, when a BMW drove at her and stopped only a few feet away.

Mr. Kruger, short and thin with short and thin black hair, got out from the driver door.

"Maya Havel."

She was too tired to run. She raised her hands in surrender.

The passenger door opened, and a Guide's Prosecutor stepped out. She was easily distinguished, wearing a medium, matte gray that ate the light and radiated darkness.

"Put your hands down, girl. This ain't a stickup." Her attempt at contemporary slang would have been comical, were she not a frightening vision and an agent of vengeance.

"I followed you," Mr. Kruger said. "I'm sorry. It's my job."

"We found your crackoid," the Guideswoman said. "It was nonfunctional. You did that on purpose."

"I did," Maya said.

"You're a hero," the Guideswoman said. "Beyond what I'm equipped to express."

"Yeah, well." Maya put down her hands, started walking toward her house.

"They're offering you a full pardon," Kruger said.

Maya stopped and turned back toward the car. The paint was scratched along the passenger-side door. "Are you serious?"

"We are," the gray angel said.

"Eat shit." Maya walked through the yard of her apartment, toward the backyard, toward the rickety stairs and her crappy apartment. Norman had been right about a lot of things, and a world ruled by the Nine Guides was no world for Maya.

They called after her, but she kept walking.

Yannick was sleeping—or feigning sleep—on the couch when she came in. He sat up and rubbed at his eyes.

"Where were you?"

Maya poured herself a drink, downed it. Poured another, nursed it. The twenty-first century had decent booze and it had hip-hop and it had her boyfriend.

"I shot some guy who thought I wrote your book."

MEN OF THE ASHEN MORROW

The doe was near to dead before Sal got her knife up to its throat, but it still looked her in the eye as she drew the blade through its skin and severed its grasp on life. It took blood to call the end of summer; exactly how much blood was always the question. In her plain voice, in her human tongue, she sang:

A half a hundred legs has Hulokk
a half a thousand teeth has He.
A half a million men ate Hulokk
a half a billion moons is He.

The five hunters behind her breathed in deep, breathed in unison. They were close, their lips almost to her ears, and the wordless chant was heavy in the air. Four sets of lips belonged to men she cared not much for. The other belonged to Lelein, a woman who had breathed hard into her ear in other moments, passionate moments. The trees hung boughs high above the hunters, the moss of the ancient forest soft beneath their soft-heeled boots.

In and out, in and out, the six hunters took deep, violent gulps of air.

He would come. Not for the sacrifice—what's a deer to the god of all rivers and roots and everything on the ground and beneath it—but for the hunters. Hulokk would come when summoned by His people. As like as not, He'd take someone with Him.

Sal didn't want to die, and she assumed none of her companions did either. But Hulokk must freeze the earth to end the summer, and winter must come for the snows to settle onto the hills, and the snows must come to keep the creatures from the West at bay. Risk was necessary to life, always.

Deep breaths, violent breaths.

Ten summers prior, as a young woman, Sal had performed the ritual. Hulokk had come, she'd spoken with Him, and He'd departed with nothing more than the buck they'd slaughtered. It had been the first time in living memory that the summoners had convinced the god to spare them all. Sal was counting on that luck. She was counting on her own strength.

The doe's blood melted and burned the earth. The smell of old rot poured into the forest. The ground collapsed, pulling the saplings and ferns down into the underworld, and Sal and her company stepped back.

A single segmented leg, infinitely thin and long, crept out from the hole. First one, then another. Then another, another, another. Slower than the setting of the summer sun, His fat, round worm body of flesh and stone rose into the air. His belly was awash with eyes.

He looked at Sal, and Sal borrowed the breath of the other hunters. She spoke, in the tongue of the gods:

"I ask you, Hulokk, to bring an end to summer."

"I will not." Hulokk's voice was a thousand voices, across and below the audible.

"I ask you, Hulokk, to bring an end to summer."

"I will not." Ancient trees trembled and fell, and Sal felt her heart quiver in her chest from the physical force of the voice.

"I ask you, Hulokk, to bring an end to summer."

"I will."

Four legs shot out and wrapped around Lelein, and she screamed, hoarse and angry.

"I ask you, Hulokk," Sal started, but it took more magic than she could summon to keep her voice in the tongue of the gods. She finished her sentence meekly, in a human language. "To spare our lives."

The god dragged Sal's lover into the depths of the earth. At the last moment, the eldest among the hunters put a quarrel through Lelein's throat, silencing her forever.

As the world grew silent, Sal collapsed at the edge of the of sinkhole and clawed at the dirt in lieu of weeping.

Hulokk froze the earth, and autumn came, then winter.

◆

A lifetime later, Sal was gray-haired and tired, her skin aged by sun and time. No one had yet called for winter, and the summer had been five months too long already. Bright, monstrous creatures were stirring in the west, but Sal had done the work fifteen times herself; the burden of sacrifice should be shared by other collectives. She had other matters, simpler matters, to attend to.

The forest bison in front of her was near to dead, its breathing labored and slow, fluid likely having filled its lungs. It lay in a blade of sunlight that pierced the thick canopy above. Red and iron blood stained its gray and grizzled fur and the cold steel of crossbow bolts stuck from its hide like thorns.

Sal approached.

"I can do this," Reka said. She was the youngest of the six, her face still unlined. Too young to be hunting at all.

"Too dangerous," Sal said. One hand held the seax, the other held the rest of the collective at bay. She met the dying beast's eyes.

"Live free, die free," she whispered. "Life is struggle, death is not." She put all the magic in her body behind the words.

The massive eyes closed, and Sal drew her blade across the bison's throat.

Her hunting collective spent a long afternoon butchering and salting meat. They packed it into six barrels, each with the name of a town or city stenciled in black across its oaken staves. One each was addressed for the four towns of Laria, two for the city Laros itself.

She heard the hooves a few miles off, well before her younger and less-attuned companions. But the noise didn't seem to signal danger, so she said nothing.

Closer, birdsong cast music down from the trees, and the thick carpet of wildflowers sent up perfume almost strong enough to mask the scents of blood and marrow.

Sal sat on the cart, watching her companions work and the team of mules pick at the grass and flowers. It wasn't fair, of course, how often she took sentry. The hunters were a collective of equals, and by rights she should be doing the same hard labor. But she'd lived seventy-times-twelve moons, and she'd spent the whole of the day on the move, tracking their prey. She deserved the rest. Her crossbow was loaded, its stock balanced on the rail of the cart as she kept watch. There was no rest except death.

The rider was almost upon them before her companions noticed, but neither humans nor horses had been much of a threat to anyone in the valley for an endless succession of moons.

"Sal Everett and company?" the rider asked, his face obscured under a thick black beard, the style in the city.

"We're the Men of the Ashen Morrow, thank you," Sal corrected.

Not one of the Men were men, but Sal preferred tradition to semantic accuracy and the collective's name had gone unchanged for ninety times twelve moons.

"Sal Everett, I presume," the rider continued, addressing Sal directly and ignoring the frown that grew on her face.

"I'm Sal," she said.

"I've come directly from the great assembly," he said. "The summer is in its fifth moon and no one has come forward to summon its end. I've been empowered to ask you, on behalf of the whole of Laria, to do this. Summon the god Hulokk."

Sal spat, off to the side. "The reason no one's come forward is because everyone's hoping we'll do it."

"Will you?"

"No."

"Why not?"

"Someone else's turn."

The man considered her words for a moment while birdsong filled the silence.

"You know why people ask this of you," he said at last. His eyes darted from her to her companions, all of whom were armed, all of whom he'd prefer not to anger. "There's no one more capable."

"Summer after summer, we've done it. Summer after summer I've lost friends and..." She let her anger keep tears at bay. "No one else will ever get better at speaking with gods if no one else will risk it. Go back your great assembly," she said, "and tell them Sal Everett is an old woman who's lost too much already. Tell them they can send me students, if they wish, but no commands."

The man looked at her without sympathy. "All my life I'd heard stories of Sal Everett, and here you are a coward."

"Fuck off," Sal said. The rider didn't take her meaning clearly enough, so she fired a bolt into the bough above his head. A branch broke, and it fell with a crack, startling the horse.

The rider spun around and took off at a canter.

The birds were silent; the hunters were silent. The mules went on grazing.

Sal climbed down off the cart, started rooting through the duff for her crossbow bolt. She found it, still intact, and for a moment she remembered the bolt that had pierced Lelein—a broadhead, for hunting. A mercy.

Sal's life had been too full of all the wrong sorts of mercy.

◆

Their summer lodge was a sprawling stone house built in a liminal space between prairie and wood. The eaves hung low over the windows to fight off the summer sun, and the windows themselves were simple cloth screen. Nearby, Sal and the rest of the collective crouched in a circle under the shade of an ancient oak. By the looks on her companions' faces, no one was happy.

"You don't get to decide that," Hels said. She'd born two children; both were off with their father in the city. Silver and ash were creeping into her hair, and she was the next-oldest after Sal.

"We've done the work the last ten summers," Sal said. "It should rotate. The risk should be spread out across collectives."

"We've done the work because we're the best," Reka said. Her voice was low, her shoulders broad, and she was as proud of her power as she was of her youth—as though either were things she'd chosen. Every time Sal looked at her, she saw Lelein. Reka could have been Lelein's granddaughter, had Lelein lived to bear children.

"All the more reason we should leave it to someone else," Sal said. "The best should step aside, not end up indispensable. It's healthier for everybody."

More importantly, it was healthier for those five she saw as her children. She couldn't bear to lose another. Not to her own weakness.

"I'm not saying your decision is wrong," Hels said. "I'm saying it isn't your decision to make."

"*I'm* saying the decision is wrong," Reka said. Blood went to her cheeks and her fists clenched and released.

"Do you want to die?" Sal asked. "Do you? Because that's what happens when you summon a god and ask it a favor. Someone dies."

"Last summer—" Reka started.

"Last summer nothing," Sal interrupted. "Last summer we got lucky. The summer before that, we got lucky. Three summers ago? Five? Eight? Hunters died. I've summoned Hulokk fifteen times and I've lost nine friends to the effort." Eight friends and a lover.

The other collectives, she knew, had much worse tallies. For all their efforts, no other summoners had ever held strength in their voices long enough to demand Hulokk spare their lives. Every time anyone but Sal called the god, He took one in the six down with Him. When Sal did it, sometimes she failed and sometimes she managed.

"I'm tired of this shit. I'm tired of watching you all die."

I'm tired of surviving your deaths, she didn't need to say.

"I'm sorry," Sal said. "I shouldn't have spoken for us all so simply. I'm not in charge. But I refuse to participate, and we are six, and the ritual takes six. One 'no' is enough."

◆

The milky moon hung low over the western hills, lighting the last scraps of snow that capped them. The night air was sticky and thick, though the worst of the day's heat was fading, and Sal walked alone in the prairie. Her knees hurt, like they'd hurt for hundreds of moons.

It was Lelein who had taught Sal to love the prairie, to love the bright wash of wildflowers and the tide-like brush of wind against the tips of the grass. So many moons had come and gone and so many memories had blossomed and faded. But Lelein remained. She who was not forgotten was not yet dead.

In the distance, a buck lifted his great crowned head, a silhouette against the sky. A breeze swept across the land, bringing the smell of dead grass—the world needed the rains of autumn. What cruelty it was that only the magic and sacrifice of humans could cut the heat of the warming world.

In the distance, she heard the kitchen door shut and Hels making her way across the field. Sal knew her footsteps and soon smelled her heady scent. Most moonlit nights, she would have loved the younger woman's company for a walk across the land.

"You're not going to talk me into it," Sal said, quietly, while they were still far apart. Hels had enough magic of her own to make out the words at distance.

Hels came to her, took Sal by the arm. A few more deer walked out from the tree line and joined the buck in the field.

Hels pointed them out. "Why don't we keep animals for meat?" she asked.

"You're not going to convince me."

"We keep plants for grain and fruit, but we don't keep animals for meat. Two hundred summers ago, when the seasons were regular and the snow never melted in the hills, we kept animals. More than just horses and mules and dogs. We kept bison and deer, hogs and fowl. Why don't we keep them anymore?"

Sal ignored the question.

"Because the terror and hell—or the brute banality—of a life lived caged bleeds into the meat. We eat it, and it gets into us; it ruins us. Drains our magic. Living free is important; dying free is important."

"I don't see what you're getting at," Sal said.

"Are you afraid of dying?"

"No."

"Neither are we," Hels said. "We live free. We'll die free. You need to let us do that."

"Someone else should do it."

"Are you that stubborn?"

Clouds drifted in front of the moon, and much of the field turned to shadow. Only the lanterns by the lodge still cast light.

"Yes," Sal said.

Hels dropped Sal's arm. "You're greedy," she said, walking away. "We all lose people."

Sal stood alone in the field, feeling the absence of her friend's touch. Hels was right about one thing. Being open to death was the cost of living free.

The moon broke free of the clouds, and she saw the deer in the field. Traditionally, it took six casters to sacrifice an animal and call Hulokk. But Sal was the strongest magician in the valley. Maybe she could do it alone, even if just one final time.

◆

The buck stared at her with angry eyes, but Sal's words had crawled into its mind and stilled its dying body. Dragging the beast from field to forest, she made slow progress. The bolt's fletching caught on the low branches of the edge forest, and the buck caterwauled into the night.

It was a perverse thing to do, to cause an animal to suffer like that.

It needed doing.

She'd been late to the life of a hunter. Struck by wanderlust at twenty times twelve moons, she'd left her work as a cobbler in the city and been accepted on probationary terms to the Men of the Ashen Morrow—one of the hundreds of hunter collectives. Most of her new fellows were the children of hunters and farmers. But she was alive with magic, and magic flows unevenly through space and time; its practitioners do well to wander. Despite her upbringing, she'd become a hunter.

She dragged the animal by horns for hours. Her muscles were in agony, but she dared not stop for rest. She pushed on—exhaustion was an old friend. The buck was screaming in pain, but she hadn't the strength to lift it across her back.

By the time she reached the heart of the forest, near enough Hulokk's domain, she heard the rest of her collective searching the woods. Their footsteps were too soft, too careful to be any but those of hunters. Sal had to hurry. She spied a tangled thicket and made her way for the refuge of its densest depths. Low pines burst forth from brambles, failing to reach the sky. Ahead of the dawn, morning fog rose and lonely birds sang.

The buck had suffered, but it hadn't died. Sal laid it down heavily in the dirt, then paced around it, ducking under branches, pulling her wool trousers free from thorns. She circled it six times widdershins, then she stopped.

Her companions were closer. They'd found her trail. If they found her, they'd try to help her. If they found her, she'd lose another friend.

She got her knife up to the animal's throat, and it stared into the depths of her as she drew the blade through its skin. In her plain voice, ragged with exhaustion, she sang:

A half a hundred legs has Hulokk
a half a thousand teeth has He.
A half a million men ate Hulokk
a half a billion moons is He.

The song was older than the city, as old as the woods. She sang it in the language of the first of her people to settle the land.

The melody faded to nothing, and Sal breathed in quick, violent breaths. Staccato, ritual breathing.

The blood ran fast from the creature's neck; it ran hot into the earth, burning soil and stone as it mingled with the magic of Sal's breath.

The ground fell away, pulling the buck and the surrounding brambles down into the underworld. Sal shied back, still keeping complex rhythm with her lungs.

Hulokk arose, as he always had, tremendous and horrid and sheathed in dispassionate eyes.

Sal opened her mouth, and no voice came out. She couldn't find the power to speak. Always before, she'd had the breath of her fellows to draw upon.

She had the sky, though, and all the world's air. She focused her strength, in the core of her chest, and summoned the night's wind to fill her lungs.

"I ask you, Hulokk..." she began in the old tongue, but the air fled her chest faster than she could fill it. Her voice failed.

Hulokk stared at her, impassive.

Sal determined to take strength from the earth. The dirt beneath her feet hardened to stone and gave her a conduit to the core of the earth's magic.

"I ask you, Hulokk, to bring an end..." She collapsed to her knees, unable to finish. No other magic in the world was as strong as that of collective spirit.

"I'm sorry," she said, in the common tongue.

Hulokk's gaze swept over her, each eye moving together with its neighbors like grass blown by a winter wind.

"I've killed us all, haven't I?"

He towered above her, impassive. He'd likely end her life, but without the ritual words he wouldn't freeze the earth and it would be six moons at least before he'd appear when summoned. The snows would melt; the bright monsters would flood into the valley and kill her children.

"Oh vanity, I've killed us all."

One long leg crept toward her, stroked her cheek. The thought of death was no comfort, just then, unlike it so often had been. She would die a failure, lain low by pride. Worse, she would die having brought death to so many who'd relied upon her. She had to survive, at least long enough for the Men to find her. At least long enough to complete the casting and beseech Hulokk for winter.

She felt down into her gut, pulled forth what power she had, and shouted. Birds scattered from trees, and the Men heard her. They were running, now.

A second segmented leg wrapped around her waist, trying to pull her toward the pit and its master. She flung out her arms and called branches to her, lashing herself in place with magic.

She was off the ground, her body stretched between the trees and the god. Maybe her arms would rip free from her shoulders, maybe her torso from her legs.

More insectoid limbs lashed out, ripping at the foliage that held her, and Sal drained every bit of her strength to call the nearby brambles to dig their thorns into her body and hold her in place.

Through it all, Hulokk made no noise. Sal struggled, but Hulokk was no more angry at her resistance than Sal could be at the bowstring when she reloaded her crossbow.

Reka was the first to reach her, war axe held at her side but still in her nightclothes. Hels and the others were shortly behind. When they saw Hulokk, half of the hunters fell into breathing shallow and long, half of them fell into breathing fast and deep.

Young Reka spoke, in the tongue of the gods. "I ask you, Hulokk, to bring an end to summer."

"I will not." The thousand voices of god tore through the thicket.

"I ask you, Hulokk, to bring an end to summer."

"I will not."

"I ask you, Hulokk, to bring an end to summer."

"I will."

Sal released the vines and brambles that held her and dropped to the earth, near to unconsciousness, still cocooned in the long legs of the god. With the casting complete, the thought of her coming oblivion was warmer than the summer air.

But Hulokk let her go. Sal lay empty and exhausted upon the bloody soil. Her vision blurry from pain, she saw the thin legs embrace Reka.

"Take me," Sal whispered. But she spoke the common tongue.

Every eye on His belly focused on Reka, and Reka screamed wordless as Hulokk dragged her down, after the deer, into the underworld, severing her grasp on life.

◆

"She who is not forgotten is not yet dead," Hels said. The five Men held hands in a circle and wept for themselves, for their own loss, while the light of dawn cast soft shadows from the elder trees of the funeral grove.

Sal wept for Reka and she wept for Lelein, and she wept for her own bruised and torn old body and the wounds of loss that would never heal. She wept for all she'd sacrificed, and all the more she would in the future.

Because next year, she would volunteer. Every year until she was unable, by age or by death, she would call an end to the summer and spare others the torment of survival.

While the Men cried, the storm clouds of autumn gathered above them. Winter would come.

A REASONABLE PLACE IF YOU'RE CAREFUL

Review of Stony Fork Campground in the Jefferson National Forest
   Five out of Five

◆

It's only twelve dollars a night. The mountains are beautiful, the trees are beautiful. A handsome little creek runs right through the campground.

I used to look forward to dying, back before I'd met the dead. The thought of death had been a comforting one. Death had felt like sleep, like oblivion. Oblivion is the place where forgotten things go. I've long wanted to forget, so I've always wanted to be forgotten.

I used to envy the mayfly its fleeting, flitting life. I envied the mouse, consumed whole by the snake. I envied my mother, dead these long years.

But there's a certain type of pine that only grows at the base of these Appalachian hills, recognizable by its silver needles, black bark, and deep red shelf mushrooms that grow along it. A few grow along the creek in the campground. Its inner bark is neither poisonous nor edible, and, as other reviewers have recommended, I ate a sliver of it while I was here. Now I have nothing, no one, left to envy.

I've learned there's no escape in death, no rest, no sleep. There's no peaceful island on the far side of some river of fire, no boatman. No heavenly gates, no reincarnation. I saw the dead. They're pitiful spirits, transformed by trauma, who wander helpless and bored. They sit under trees and gaze up at Godless skies. They wade in creeks and streams, un-cleansed and un-cleanable.

Their features and faces bear the weight of entropy, and they go from recognizable to shapeless over the course of centuries. Some must have walked across or under oceans, because I saw a samurai without a sword or words or love. I saw soldiers and peasants and runaway slaves and I saw the best people and the worst people. They're all dead and they're all undying.

The vision passed by morning, but it's been months and I still can't shake what I saw. I know what awaits us and I'll never sleep well again. Please ignore the other reviews that encourage you to eat the inner bark of those trees.

It's not safe.

But the bathrooms are clean and there's hot water for the showers. All the living people were amiable enough. I recommend this campground to anyone passing through southwest Virginia.

THE NAME OF THE FOREST

The woods were shrubby and shitty and full of ticks. It was the kind of embarrassing midwest excuse for a forest that is both the result of clear-cutting and that makes me think a second clearcut would, just in this one case, be an improvement. The sun was on the back of my neck and I'd had my thumb outstretched for hours. The muscles in my face hurt from smiling at every single motherfucker who wouldn't pick me up.

I wanted to get out my slingshot and shoot every car that went by. Hopefully the drivers would swerve into one of the aforementioned piece of shit trees, and that would be two birds with one stone. Three, really, since I hate cars as much as I hate their drivers and scrawny midwestern trees.

If I think too hard about it, the fantasy falls apart. If the car doesn't have any empty seats, maybe I shouldn't murder its driver. If it's a woman driving alone, can I really blame her for not picking me up? I'm twenty, people think I'm thirty, and I look exactly like I smell—like I walked off the set of a post-apocalyptic film, one that couldn't afford armor. Really, I'd just come off a freight train. That isn't the furthest thing in the world from a post-apocalyptic film set.

But I shouldn't murder the drivers, because this isn't the post-apocalypse. And killing people is wrong. Even people who don't pick me up.

◆

Sometimes people do pick me up, even out there on a back highway in Illinois, even when dark is settling in, even when the person is a woman driving alone.

She pulled up in an old Ford station wagon, got out of the car, and shoved things aside in the back seat to make room for my pack. She didn't come across as a hippie or nothing. Just a fairly normal woman, maybe in her early thirties, ambiguously non-white.

"Where you going?" she asked me, when we were both standing outside her car.

"South."

"Yeah but where?"

Usually I'm supposed to ask her that, right off. That's the first rule of not getting murdered or almost-as-bad-as-murdered. (I've been almost-as-bad-as-murdered before and some people say it's worse than being murdered but I've got nothing to compare it to. I think it's subjective, at the end of the day.) First rule of hitchhiking is I ask where they're going. If they say they don't know, I don't get in the car.

Well, usually I do anyway when the sun is on my neck and those murder-faced ticks are staring at me from the tops of the shrubs, just shouting "Hey fucker, get closer, I want to make you sick."

"St. Louis." It was sort of true. I was going to St. Louis inasmuch as I'm ever going anywhere. Not all who wander are lost, sure, but at that point, I definitely was.

"I'll take you as far as Normal," she said.

Normal's a city in Illinois, a bit down the road. As the name implies, it's kind of a shit town.

"Thanks." I got in the car.

◆

"What's your name?" she asked, as we barreled down the road. She didn't drive slow.

"Jimmy."

"Suzie," she said. "What do you do?"

"You mean for money?"

"Sure. For money."

I told her the truth, which was kind of stupid.

"Mostly I steal books from Barnes & Noble and sell them on the internet."

"Really?"

"Mostly," I said.

"What else do you do?"

Sell handjobs to ugly old fuckers at truck stops, sell handjobs to handsome young fuckers at truck stops, pose nude for art students, pose nude for creeps, panhandle, strip copper from abandoned buildings, strip copper from houses under construction, pick moldy grapes for wine, trim weed, stand in weed fields with a shotgun and hope to fucking god I never have to shoot anyone.

"Mostly just steal books."

"You steal any good ones?" she asked. My gamble paid off. She was in on my crime. It's a short step from accomplice to friend.

"Almost always just textbooks, to be honest."

"You ever get caught?"

"Every state's got a felony limit. You never steal more than the limit, you're fine, within a certain understanding of the word 'fine.'"

"So you've been caught? "

"What do you do?"

"I teach pottery. At a summer camp, at the moment. At private schools, the rest of the year."

A potter. She'd flown right in under my hippie radar. Some people use hippie as a pejorative, but not me—I've spent enough time out in the world to know good hippies are basically the best people, even if bad hippies are basically the worst.

"You like it?" I asked.

"I love it. It's also driving me completely nuts."

"Why?"

"I've been staring at spinning clay for twenty years. You stare long enough into the clay, it starts to stare back at you."

"You live in Normal?" I asked.

"No, Alton, right outside St. Louis. I only told you I was going to Normal in case you were awful and I wanted to get rid of you sooner. You seem alright, though."

I smiled my winningest smile, with my crooked teeth and everything. But she didn't even look at me, because she was looking at the road, because she was going at least 90mph and she was a good hippie. She didn't want to get us both dead. Though to be real, I didn't really care one way or the other about that.

◆

Three days later I was still at her house. It's kind of a crustlord thing to do, to stay there that long, but she wanted me to stay as much as I didn't feel like leaving. I was hoping she'd let me stick around longer, to be honest. It was nice to have a roof and food, and I had a good time helping out around the house and yard. We weren't sexual, but I slept in her bed and we were kind of romantic. That's about half my best relationships, right there. Half my best friendships, too.

She'd picked me up on a Tuesday night, taken me home. Big old probably-not-haunted house, right up on a hill at the edge of the neighborhood that ignorant white people tell you not to go into, the kind of neighborhood I'd just tell you not to be an ignorant white person in.

Friday, she came home from work with groceries under her arm and her clothes covered in clay. I'd spent the day reading books and building her a raised planter in the yard and I was about halfway through making her a passive solar food dehydrator I didn't really know how to make.

"I saw your future," she said, heading into the kitchen with the food.

"Yeah?" I followed her, started putting food away.

"I heard it in the clay."

I've never given much credence to magic. Probably believed in it the same way I believed in yoga. Magic is a thing you can do to your mind to make your mind do what you want it to. So I didn't believe in fortunetelling or astrology any more than I believed in god, but my lack of belief has never stopped any of my friends. People got something out of all that bullshit, so who was I to call it bullshit to their faces?

"The clay hasn't spoken to me in months, and here you are and it's started again."

"It talks to you."

"People hear the spirits in every art. They just don't talk about it."

I had no idea if that was true. I couldn't say it wasn't. I didn't hear spirits when I wrote zines or built shacks but I've also never made much claim to being an artist.

"What's my future?" I asked.

"It's good," she said. "Your long, hard journey is coming to an end."

"All right," I said, because what the fuck else could I say. Most people, I would have guessed they were hitting on me, telling me to stick around and that I wasn't going to be lonely anymore. With Suzie, I just chalked it up to hippie nonsense.

"Do you want to go camping?" she asked.

I've never been known to say no to that.

"When? Now?"

"Tonight. Now."

That's always kind of a trick question. If I said no, and she wanted to go by herself, then I'd have to move on. So we loaded up her station wagon with food and we drove off into the sunset, towards something like nature. Because Suzie drives like a fucking maniac, we made it to a campground in Missouri not too late at night.

It was the kind of campground you have to pay for, but she paid the whole twenty bucks because I'm a scumfuck I guess and just let her pay for it. Honestly I was sort of expecting her to want to sleep with me and I was going to let her, even though I only half wanted to. Since I'm a pro sometimes, I guess that worked out into my head as my half of the money, even though that's not really how it works.

There was hardly anyone else at the campground, so we snagged the best spot—a massive oak overlooked its picnic table, which overlooked a spindly river. I cooked us up canned lentil soup with fresh garlic and onion while she told me about the stars. Older people who know a lot of shit are cool. Older people who don't are sort of doubly-disappointing. But Suzie wasn't even that much older than me, and she knew a ton of shit.

She told me about the stars in the Southern Hemisphere too, which made me kind of sad. For all my travels, I'd never left the country. Forty-eight states in five years, and I was pretty sure I could get myself into Mexico, maybe even legally, but the idea of heading off further seemed impossibly expensive. I'd read about riding in the wheel wells of airplanes, but mostly about people who died in the attempt.

Other friends of mine had hopped freight trains that got loaded up onto barges and shipped up to Alaska or down to Central America, but half of those friends of mine had been turned around by border guards when they got where they were trying to go. I guess there was that one friend who got murdered in Guatemala but that's neither here nor there, because my friends get murdered a lot of places and sometimes they do that murdering to themselves.

Suzie told me about the stars and I didn't tell her about any of my dead friends, because those two things aren't related and because I was happy just chopping onions and letting her think that's why I was crying.

While we ate, an old pickup rolled in and took the spot next to us. The man who got out looked like my future—grizzled and gray and alone—and he didn't bother setting up a tent, just laid down a tarp and put a sleeping bag on top. He waved at us, we waved back, and he sat down at his picnic table to read.

"What's in St. Louis?" Suzie asked, as I scrubbed the bowls.

"Fucking nothing," I said. "Some squats, some friends. Maybe I'll be there for a week."

"You don't have much of a sense of purpose in your life, do you?"

"I don't."

"I kind of want to die," she said. "Not an active thing, usually. Just sometimes hope I'll get lucky one day and die."

I'd felt that way for the whole of the past year. Grief hits you when you're traveling, and you don't really have a place to just let yourself shut down and ignore the world for a while. You gotta keep going, always, and that gets old.

"It gets lonely, being alive," she said. "It's like you're disconnected from the world. All those bits of you that should be in the earth, should be part of everything, are stuck in your body."

"How do you hope it'll happen?" I asked.

"Fire seems good."

"Fire?"

"People say fire hurts and maybe it does but the only time I've ever been burned, it was second-degree, all over my hand, and I'm pretty sure the fire just burned out my nerves because I didn't feel anything. Not for a half-an-hour at least. If I was burning, like dying, wouldn't it just burn my nerves away?"

"I don't think that's how it works." I looked back up at the stars. I've always liked Orion. I'm a city kid. Orion is the only constellation I know. He's got that bow and that sword and he's invulnerable.

"What about you?" she asked. "How do you hope you'll die?"

"Freezing to death." I didn't need to think about that.

"Really?"

"You just shut down, give up, and warmth comes over you and you take off your clothes and you die. That's how I want to go—naked and warm."

◆

After dinner, the moon was nearly full and Suzie threw on a backpack and took me hiking down the railroad tracks. We were in the woods, and they were real woods—thick old oaks interspersed with pine and fir, and a deep handsome creek ran alongside the tracks. The air was clear and sharp. The four-foot saplings in between railroad ties told me pretty quick that the railroad wasn't in use. Suzie knew her way, and we found our footing with the help of red LED headlamps.

"You've been here before," I said.

"Took my ex here a lot."

"I can see why."

"He wouldn't let me do what I need to do out here, though," Suzie said.

Maybe I shouldn't have gotten into the car with her on Tuesday.

"Let you do what?"

"There's something under these tracks, something that wants its way out into the air. It's starving."

One of those dead friends of mine, she'd been cut up in Arizona by a madman. Another took a beating from a cop in Wisconsin and died of complications a year later. A third got a bullet in the back of the head in some shitty southern town. He'd just been walking into his squat when this guy trying to get into a gang followed him through the door and bang there goes my friend. The fellow in Guatemala got mugged to death. Desert, hospital, shit town America, Latin American slum. Never anyone in the forest. I'd be the first, which is kind of special.

This is the kind of shit I think about. I wish it wasn't.

"This trapped something, you saw it in the clay?"

"It stopped talking to me months ago, started again today." She still sounded like the nice hippie who'd picked me up hitching.

I kept walking with her, because I've got more curiosity than sense and because in for a penny, in for setting a demon loose into the world, that's what I always say. Helped that I didn't believe in demons. Helped that I wasn't overly attached to being alive. We went about a mile down the tracks, over a sketchy, rusted out bridge, through fields of moonlight and summer flowers and back into the trees. She stopped about fifteen feet from a little trickle of a waterfall coming down over the rocks.

"Here," she said. She kicked the rail, and I looked down to inspect.

I know a lot about train tracks. I spend a lot of time walking on them and a lot my energy thinking about how I might get squished between them and train wheels when I catch on the fly.

There was a date nail driven into the railroad tie. A date nail isn't a spike, just a regular old nail with a number punched into its head. This one said 98.

"This tie is from 1898," I said. "Pretty much one of the oldest dated railroads in the country."

"That makes sense," Suzie said. "But look at the spikes."

I did. The railroad spikes, which are driven into the railroad ties to keep the baseplate and the rail stable, were adorned with numbers. Each one bore three sixes, in a triangle.

"Holy shit," I said. "That's cool."

"Yeah," Suzie said.

"Usually there are letters here, the brand of the manufacturer."

"These ones just show their purpose."

"How many of these are there?" I asked.

"Twenty-three of them."

"And you want to pull them up?"

"It'll take both of us ," she said. "I summon it, you pull up the spikes."

"Can I keep some of them?" I asked. I had some blacksmith friends who made knives from rail spikes, and these ones said 666 on the base.

"You don't believe me about any of this," she asked, "do you?"

"No."

"Months of silence, and it talked to me again just today."

"What happened to your ex?"

"It didn't work out." It wasn't hard to imagine him buried somewhere nearby.

"This why you picked me up hitchhiking?"

"It is."

When I was a kid, flying had scared the shit out of me. Last time I flew, though, was to a friend's funeral. Her mother had paid for my flight. I spent the whole trip thinking about the plane crashing, about free fall. Thinking about that had set me free, let me just marvel in the majesty of sunrise out through the window.

"All right," I said. "Fuck it."

She took a small crowbar from her bag, and I went at it. But a crowbar is actually a fuck-off bad way to get a spike out of a railroad tie, as it happens. I found a loose baseplate—a flat rectangle of steel—for a lever and got it up on a big chunk of gravel for a fulcrum, and jammed that under the lip of the first spike. I just jumped up and down on the damn thing, inching the spike out.

Suzie had a crescent wrench and banged a simple, steady beat on one of the tracks. The moon had gone behind the trees, and our headlamps cast a red glow over each other and the little pocket of the world we could see. It took hours, but I pulled out spikes, one at a time. There was the iron smell of rust, the clang of steel on steel, the sounds of night birds, and the trickle of water. Foxfire glowed in the distance. I got drunk, maybe spellbound, on darkness and strangeness and the ceaseless rhythm.

I jumped a final time, reached down, and pulled out the twenty-third spike. Suzie built to a crescendo, then stopped.

There, in our red light, was movement. It looked like black ashes coming up from fire, the way those tiny bugs came out from the ground and climbed into the sky. First like ashes, sparse and intermittent, but then like smoke, thick and black, spreading into the air, and like a spill of oil out along the ground.

We watched for ten minutes, and the flood of crawlers and fliers continued unabated. We walked back to the campground in the red light.

◆

I slept with Suzie that night. It wasn't to pay my half of the money, either. It was because I felt like we had power. I felt like we could do anything in the world. We did each other.

◆

I woke up with what felt like water in my ear. I jammed my finger in there and fished around, trying to equalize the pressure. I pulled something out. It was a tick, black and gray in the pre-dawn light.

That woke me up.

My memory worked its way backwards through the previous night's events, and I scrambled through the tent searching for a condom, for proof we'd used protection. I found it, tied shut. There were at least a dozen ticks crawling across the latex. We'd left the door to the tent partially unzipped.

That's when I remembered what came before the sex, and suddenly the condom seemed like a total non-issue. I stuck my head outside.

The world was a sea of chittering black. Everything—the tent, the trees, the picnic table, the shitty fire grill filled with shitty peoples' shitty trash—was carpeted with ticks. The sky was thick with swarms of arachnids or insects or whatever they were.

Our neighbor, the old man, was lying on his tarp, unmoving, as ticks drained his blood and locusts swarmed his face.

I zipped the tent shut and started ripping off my clothes looking for bugs.

"What's the matter?" Suzie asked. She was sleepy-eyed and smiling.

"The fucking world is being eaten by ticks and locusts."

"Calm down," she said. She closed her eyes again.

I only had about seven of the motherfuckers stuck on me, and I crushed their little faces with my multitool pliers and ripped them out. I scoured the tent, turning everything that moved into an eight-legged corpse.

"Hey," I said. "I need you to wake up."

Suzie opened her eyes.

"I'm freaking out."

"What about?" She sat up, put her arm around me, started stroking my neck and tracing her fingers along my face.

As a society, our sense of reality is built on a rough consensus. In order to keep the aberrations—hallucinations, psychosis, paranoia, all that—from taking over, we constantly double-check our assumptions with the people around us. Everything from "did you hear that?" to "is it a reasonable thing to murder someone because they didn't pick me up hitchhiking?" is something we run past other people to keep ourselves a bit more grounded.

But the ground outside was covered in billions of ticks and the only person around to compare notes with was Suzie.

"What did we free?" I asked. "What did we do?"

I saw a tick latched on to her collarbone, and started at it with pliers, but she pulled my arm down.

"It's a part of this place," she said. "Part of this forest and this river. Before the railroad, this forest wasn't a good place to live. It was only a good place to die. But dying here meant dying well, like fire, like freezing."

"Where are we?" I asked.

"It's got a name you can't pronounce with less than a million chitin bodies," she said.

I had nothing to say to that, so I didn't say anything.

In the silence, I heard it. I heard the demon's name, the name of the forest.

◆

Sometimes I hop freight trains, and I get up alongside a steel leviathan and jump onto a ladder on its side while running while wearing a bag stuffed full of everything I own. Train wheels have this suction effect, they just want to suck you under, and I know some people who don't have legs anymore and I know other people who are dead.

Once you get on a train, you can't get off until it stops or until it slows down enough for you to do something stupid, like jump off on the fly. People say you can tuck and roll. Some of those same people have broken their bones jumping off at speeds as slow as ten miles an hour and had to stumble, crippled, for miles. The gravel rips skin from flesh, and blood runs down into the earth. Some wounds you recover from, some wounds you don't.

◆

"If we can get across the river," I said. I was whimpering, falling out of mania.

"It can fly, too."

"Then the car."

"We're better off staying here," she said.

"For how long?"

"If we open the tent, it'll go faster."

She pulled my head to hers, forehead to forehead, and looked me in the eyes closer than my eyes could focus. That was it, then. The plane was falling.

A long, hard journey, coming to its end.

I tried to convince myself she was right, that I was ready to die. So much had hurt me in twenty years. There were so many wounds and scars, so much ugliness. So many lives I'd led were over. The forest was a fine place to die, a fine place to never leave.

There'd been sunrises over lakes in the mountains while I'd frozen in boxcars. There'd been strangers who'd fed me, there'd been people who'd loved me. There'd been summer nights by the fire as a bottle of Jack made its way around and we'd told every story that's ever been told. Maybe I'd lived enough.

Fuck it. I opened the tent and the forest came in, eight legs at a time.

I lay down. I was naked and warm and I'd been through a lot and Suzie curled up into the crook of my arm. I took deep breaths as the forest came over me, black and gray. I shuddered, but just once. They clamped onto me, they burrowed their heads into me. They took my blood, and I felt nothing.

Suzie put her hand up into my hair, held me tight.

I'd never worry again. I could leave myself to the earth, save myself the trouble of getting old, save myself cancer and hip replacements and failing at life.

I sat with that in my head for a while, as I grew weaker. The weaker I got, the easier it was to convince myself it was okay to die.

But I'd never even made it out of the country. Whole continents I'd never seen. There were caves to wander and abandoned warehouses to climb and trains to ride and there were people to fuck and people to love. There was all kinds of shit out there in the world of the living.

A tick went back into my ear and that just wasn't right. I dug it out.

"Get up," I said. My voice wavered.

"What?"

"Fuck dying."

"I'm staying here," she said.

"You said being alive is shit because it disconnects you from the world?"

She didn't answer me. I barely had the energy to talk myself.

"That's a load of crap. Even if you go in for shit like that, you're not separate from the world. The forest can't absorb you into it because you're already part of the forest, you're already part of everything. We're all made of the same shit. I don't believe in fuck-all but I bet you do and I bet whatever made you did it for a reason and you're in the body you're in because you're supposed to be. One day you won't be. Right now you're alive and I need you to stay that way because *I don't know how to fucking drive a fucking stick shift.*"

She closed her eyes, sighed. A few ticks crawled along her lips.

"Fuck you!" I said it to get my blood flowing as much as to condemn her.

I got her keys from her pants, staggered out to the car. Got into the driver side, turned the key. The engine sputtered to life. I lifted my foot off the clutch while my other foot was on the gas because that's what you're supposed to do and I stalled the engine. I was running on adrenaline, wishing I could get her car to run on it too.

I tried again, and the engine shook and stalled.

In the chittering silence, I heard Suzie's weak shout.

I got back out of the car, and bugs swarmed my face and ticks crawled between my toes. I made it to the tent. She was crying, her eyes were open and bright white against the parasites that fed on her brow and cheeks.

"Help me," she said. Or maybe her mouth just moved and her eyes did the talking, I don't know. But I helped her up and out of the tent and she stumbled a few paces before her own adrenaline kicked in. We made it to her car and I sat her down in the driver's seat. She turned over the engine and we tore down the gravel away from that hell.

◆

We stopped at an overlook and stumbled out of the car. The ticks were on us like scales, but we'd made it out from the forest of death and the swarms were well behind us. I scrounged through my pack. In the hidden pocket, with my lockpicks and the high-powered magnets I used to take off security tags in stores, was a short length of plastic tube. I knelt down in the gravel, stuck the hose into the gas tank, then wadded up a sock around it to keep pressure. Deep breath, deep breath, then I got my lips over the plastic and sucked in. Three times, breathing in through the tube. Saw the gas coming through, moved my face in time, and gasoline fell freely to the ground.

I was shaking, terrified. I barely remembered what terrified felt like. I wanted to live, and I probably wasn't going to, and my nerve was shattered.

"Come here," I said, and I bathed Suzie in gas. Gas kills ticks, even if it doesn't get them to detach.

I don't have much extra weight or blood to go around, so Suzie was holding up better than I was. When I finished hosing her down, she started on me. The fumes went to my brain, and I faded in and out.

Some of the dead ticks, the ones who hadn't gotten firm into us, started to drop off. The others were stuck, and Suzie and I went at one another with tweezers and pliers. It hurt. It hurt a lot.

It was mid-afternoon by the time we were done.

"How do we get them out of the car?" I asked.

"We don't," she said. "Leave it."

"Are we going to make it?" I asked.

But that's never really the right question, because the answer doesn't ever matter.

IT BLEEDS, IT BURROWS, IT BREAKS THE BONE

The land was beautiful, though the house was not. The house was as decrepit as only a house made in the eighties could be, carpet, paint, and mold. Too big, too empty. Sarah Nails herself was as decrepit as only a girl made in the eighties could be, skin, teeth, and aches. Too small, too empty.

The land was an endless field of snow with pines like iron bars, pines like a cage. Twenty minutes to a neighbor, an hour to a store, three to a city. That was Minnesota. The feds might not find her in Minnesota. They might not break her, they might not bind her. They might not throw her into a prison full of men. Trans girls, arsonists, they belong in prisons full of men.

Sarah watched the road through the window, the one over the desk, the one framed in spiderwebs and dead flies. Nothing ever came up that road, nothing but Darnell, once a week, with groceries.

"It bleeds," the walls of the house said.

"Not now, Josephine," Sarah whispered.

"It burrows," the walls said, louder now, more insistent.

"Please, not now."

"It bleeds, it burrows, it breaks the bone."

Sarah put her hands to her face, holding back tears. "Not now."

"Later," the house said. "When you sleep, when you dream, when it bleeds, when it breaks."

"Yes, Josephine, we'll talk tonight."

"I look forward to it," the house said.

Sarah, in her despair, did too.

◆

The bedroom faced west and the setting sun cut in through the window onto the bed and onto Sarah. No blankets, just sheets and a cranked up thermostat.

It wasn't even 4:30. A few days from midwinter, the sun scarcely bothered to rise at all.

A poster hung from a single thumbtack, lost among decades-old show flyers and political screeds. In photocopied high contrast, three punk women with nineties hair posed with guitars. Under it, cursive script read:

"We don't have to win. We just have to survive."

Sarah had always wanted to win, her whole life. She'd set that compound in Virginia on fire in order to win. She'd killed two neo-Nazis with little more than a gas can and a kitchen timer. She'd wrecked thousands of hours of their planning, plotting. A million dollar arsenal, gutted and twisted by flame.

The thing about killing Nazis is it's a net gain of human life. The other thing about killing Nazis is that for some indiscernible reason, it's illegal.

Friends within her movement found friends within an allied movement, who found friends within a third movement, and those friends hid her in Minnesota. The people who were hiding her didn't know why they were hiding her, and they didn't want to know, which is what friends of friends of friends are for. They hired someone to look after her, to show up once every couple of weeks with food and hormones and whatever she needed. And that was it. That was her life now. Hiding. Running. Minnesota.

Under the posters in the bedroom sat a chair. An ugly chair, steel-legged and upholstered with cracked vinyl. On the chair, her notebook. Nothing but tallies in that notebook. Days. Twenty-four hours reduced to a single tally. Her life was reduced to the passage of time.

"Now, Sarah?" the house asked.

"Now is fine, Josephine," Sarah said.

The ghost appeared in the doorway. She was hazy, only distinct wherever Sarah focused her attention. Sarah had read the news reports. Almost twenty years back, Josephine DeCleyre had disappeared at age thirty-nine, presumed dead of exposure somewhere in the pines. Search teams hadn't tried very long, and they never found a body. Survived only by an aunt and a cousin. The aunt had since died. The cousin, an environmentalist, inherited the house and donated it to the movement. Sarah wasn't the first person who'd been on the run at Josephine DeCleyre's house.

"The pines aren't angry," Josephine said, from the doorway. Straight black hair framed her beautiful face. She had crow's feet and green eyes that were always wet with tears and she had the smallest mouth, a doll's mouth, a mouth Sarah longed to kiss.

"What, they're not angry, they're just disappointed?" Sarah asked, trying and failing to get herself or the ghost to laugh.

"They are dispassionate," Josephine said. "They suffer, they sorrow, but they do not speak."

"I'm tired of riddles," Sarah said. "Tell me a story. Tell me about yourself. Tell me how you lived, how you died."

"You think I'm not real, Sarah Nails. You think I'm in your head. I can't tell you about myself, because you wouldn't believe me."

"Then why can I see you?"

"Two years is a long time to be by yourself," Josephine said.

"It is and it isn't." Sarah, on the bed, started to cry a little. "I wish you could hold me," she said.

"I wish I could too."

"Tell me about the pines, then. Tell me about dispassion."

"It bleeds," Josephine said, her countenance wavering in the last light of the day. "It burrows. It breaks the bone."

◆

Sarah didn't even bother trying to sleep at night anymore. Whenever she slept at night, she dreamt of police raids. Different, every time, but every time she was dragged away in handcuffs, or shot in the back as she ran, or shot in the front as she fought, or subject to things worse than violence.

So she was awake, sitting in the cold vinyl and steel chair, reading trashy romance when the wolves came. The same pack of seven. Two parents and their children. They circled the house, counterclockwise. Silent. Ten nights in a row, and they were always silent.

She put down the book and went to the kitchen.

◆

"Darnell?"

Before she'd moved to the house in the pines, Sarah hadn't held a landline in ten years at least.

"Yup," a voice said on the other end of the line. Distant and tinny. He was talking to her by speakerphone, like always.

"Can you come a few days early? I'm running low."

"Damn, girl, how'd you eat ten days of food in five?"

Darnell always accented the word "girl" when he was talking to or about her. A lot of cis people did that. It was sweet and it was irritating in equal measure, like Darnell himself.

"I gave it to the wolves," Sarah said, mumbling.

"You did what?"

"I… they were hungry. They're outside the house. They howl like the wind and they pad and they plod and they were hungry, and now…"

"Yeah," Darnell said. "Yeah, sure."

"Can you bring extra meat? Anything. A couple of pounds at least."

"I'm not sure this mental health sabbatical is doing you good."

◆

"Listen to me," the house said.

"Not now," Sarah said. "Company is coming. We'll talk tonight."

"Listen to me now, Sarah Nails."

"What?" She put down her quilting and turned her attention from the snow falling outside. Josephine wasn't there. She could talk anywhere in the house, but she usually only appeared in the bedroom. Only to watch Sarah as she slept, and as she didn't sleep.

It's why Sarah slept in that room.

"Under the house, a tunnel. At the end of the tunnel a path. Beyond the path a lake. On the lake a boat. Across the lake a bike. A bike lays open the world."

"There's no tunnel, Josephine. I've been over every inch of this house."

"Under the house, a tunnel."

"You're not real, remember?"

"Under the house a tunnel. At the end of the tunnel a path."

"Who built the tunnel, huh? The gods of the pines? Are they who is burrowing, bleeding?"

"You have company coming," the house said, then grew quiet.

Sarah turned back to the window and watched the truck come out from the trees, crawling through snow and ice in four wheel drive.

The truck stopped just outside, and Darnell stepped out with a heavy bag of groceries under each arm. He saw Sarah watching through the window and his smile crept up into his eyes.

He obviously thought she was crazy—he was probably right, whatever—but it was just as obvious he liked her anyway.

She went to the door to let him in. He stomped his big brown boots on the mat, then strode inside.

"You've got to let me get a couple of guys out here, fix this place up," Darnell said. He went in to the kitchen, sat at the table while Sarah put food away. Like he did every time he came. Her only living human contact, two years. "Look at this floor. The linoleum... I mean, it's coming up anyway, and... it's linoleum. It's a shame the old house is gone. You know a rum-runner house had to have had a good wooden floor."

As Sarah had heard it, the old house had burned down in the seventies, before the current monstrosity was built. Before Josephine had lived here. Bootleggers had used it on their way across the border. More fugitives.

He kicked at the floor. "I know a guy who can get us laminate pretty cheap."

"I don't own the place," Sarah said. "Besides, I'm just here..."

"Till you're feeling better," Darnell cut in. "Yeah, but for how long, Nails? Even when shit's temporary you've gotta make the most of it. Don't be afraid to settle in. Don't be living life like you're on the run. That's what my dad says."

"Your dad left you when you were ten."

"Yeah, but he wasn't afraid to settle in before he skipped town."

If Sarah liked men, she would have liked Darnell. He was handsome, smart. Never condescending. Self-educated. Alive.

She'd take a dead woman over a living man, which wasn't fair to any of the three parties involved.

"Hey, so, I got you something for Christmas," Darnell said.

"Solstice," Sarah corrected.

"Sure. Pagan Christmas, whatever." He reached into his pocket, pulled out a compass, set it on the table. "It's not much, right, but I was reading about how the lady who lived here, how she just disappeared into the snow one day. And I grew up not too far from here, and I don't go in much for woo woo shit, but the land here is cruel. Dispassionate."

"What did you call it?" Sarah asked, setting down a jar of pickles, trying not to look as startled as she was.

"The land don't care about us. So first I thought I'd get you a gun, but I couldn't really afford it, and besides, it uh... it might be... a bad idea. For reasons. Mental health stuff. And then I thought, get you a compass. You're ever lost, pick a direction and stick with it. Doesn't matter the direction."

"Dad teach you that too?"

"Yeah. And he's a piece of shit, sure, but he's right sometimes."

"Thank you," Sarah said. She picked up the compass. It was solid, came with a hard plastic folding lid. She slipped it into her pocket.

"I have something for you too," Sarah said. She went to the living room, picked up the quilt. She tied off a final thread and cut it.

"Yeah?" she heard from the kitchen. "Yeah, I'll be in town later. Tonight or tomorrow. Yeah, something came up. No, it's not a big deal. I'm fine."

He was on the phone.

Sarah walked back into the kitchen clutching the quilt to her chest.

"Yeah, hey, I've got to go." He hung up, put the phone on the table.

She stared at the phone. He stared at her.

"Oh, shit, sorry Nails."

"No cell phones," Sarah said.

"I know, I'm sorry. Here, look, I'm turning it off now."

"It might be too late. They might know where I am. You've got to go."

"If you're worried, let me stay over. I'll keep you safe."

"No. No sleeping over. You are friend-zoned. Friends get quilts, so don't complain. Now leave. Leave!"

She thrust the quilt into his hands.

"This is... this is amazing, Nails."

"Yeah it took a long time I'm glad you like it now go."

He cast a long look over his shoulder on his way out the door. It was obvious he was worried about her. That made sense—she was worried about herself too.

◆

The first time Sarah met Josephine was a summer night, not a week after the arson, while Sarah slept on her back in the bed in the house in the pines. In her dream, Josephine had been sitting on the ugly chair, gazing out the window. A bottle of pills balanced, precarious, on the sill.

Josephine had been crying. Maniacal, hysterical laughter sobs that shook the house. That shook the bed. That woke Sarah up. When Sarah woke up, and the pills were gone, because they were the dream, but Josephine was still there. Still ghostly.

"Hello?" Sarah asked. She was too scared to be scared.

"What's your name?" Josephine asked.

"Sarah Nails. I'm sorry I'm in your house."

"I'm not, Sarah Nails. I'm glad you're here. You're something new to look at, something beautiful. Like the land, like the snow, like the blood, like the birds, moths, deer, death, moon."

"Tell me something about yourself," Sarah said.

"I'm dead," Josephine said.

"Besides that."

"I'm lonely."

"Me too, Josephine."

Sarah had never seen ghosts, not once in her life. She hadn't believed in them, and she hadn't disbelieved in them. Most interesting was to realize that she wasn't afraid of them. The things she was afraid of were far worse than a dead woman.

"Will you come into bed with me?" Sarah asked.

"I can't," Josephine said. "I can't touch you." Josephine stared for a moment, her eyes glistening with life. "I can watch, though."

"That will do."

◆

A few pounds of hamburger weren't enough to feed a pack of wolves. Sarah knew it, and she was sure the wolves knew it. Still, she filled a big wooden salad bowl with raw pink meat and went outside. The moon was behind clouds, so she flicked on her keychain flashlight.

They were waiting for her, standing twenty feet from the door. The mated pair stood still, their children played in the snow. Teeth at throat, the same games everyone plays.

Years ago, Sarah would have named the wolves. It wouldn't have been right. They didn't have names, they didn't need names. They were not pets, not companions, not friends, not enemies. They were wolves.

She set the bowl down on the stoop. Every time they came, it was the same. First the mother came forward, skittish. Sarah didn't go back inside, but she didn't hold out a hand, either. The wolf grabbed the meat in her maw then darted back a few feet, then looked over her shoulder and met Sarah's gaze.

The pack trotted into the forest, and Sarah was alone again, with less food.

◆

"Hey, Sarah?" Darnell asked. He wasn't calling from his own number. That set her on edge.

"Yeah?"

"I don't know how to say this, but..." Darnell hesitated. "Some guys in suits came to my door asking about some guy. Said his name was Richard something. Hold on, I got it written down."

Richard Stillman. They were looking for Richard Stillman. Sarah knew.

"Stillman," Darnell said. "Said 'he' might be dressed like a girl. Might be hiding out. Said that if I knew anything about that, that I should let them know. That it'd be a good idea."

"What did you say?"

"I didn't say shit. Didn't say yes, didn't say no. I took their business card, yeah they're FBI, and I called a lawyer and now I'm calling you."

Sarah took a moment to still her mind. "Best if you don't visit anymore. Thanks, Darnell. Sorry for all the trouble."

"Yeah. Shit. I'm sorry, Sarah."

"Not your fault." It might have been his fault, of course. It might have been the phone thing, or god knows what else.

"Take care of yourself, yeah?"

"Same to you."

She hung up.

They were coming. There was no way they weren't. If they weren't here now, they'd be here soon. Contingencies. She's planned for contingencies. She went into the basement.

"Under the house a tunnel," Josephine said.

"Not now."

"At the end of the tunnel a path."

"There's no tunnel under the house."

There was no tunnel in the basement. She'd been over every inch of it, when she'd first arrived. She'd inventoried everything. She'd studied everything. The house was her own prison, and she'd searched every crack in every brick. The house was full of a lot of things, including a veritable pharmacy of expired prescriptions in the bedroom closet. Including ghosts. No tunnels.

Gasoline, though. There was plenty of gasoline. Sarah found the five-gallon jugs just where she'd first seen them. She picked one up and started towards the stairs. It was heavy enough to pull her to the side as she walked.

"You can't solve every problem with fire."

Josephine didn't usually talk to her in the basement. She didn't like the basement. Even ghosts were scared of basements.

"Watch me," Sarah said.

"Violence begets violence," the walls said. "You killed people, now other people are coming for you."

"What would you have me do? Just lay down and die?"

Josephine was quiet. She was thinking. "Yes."

"No. I refuse, Josephine. You hear me? I fucking refuse."

"Think about Darnell. What's going to happen to Darnell, if you kill the people coming after you?"

Sarah put down the jug at the base of the stairs and stood up straight.

"Nothing good," Sarah said. "Is that what you want me to say? Nothing good. They'll arrest him, and he'll have to prove in court he wasn't an accessory. Maybe he'll plea out and go to prison." It was never nice to get your friend locked up, and worse still to do it to a Black man.

"Exactly," Josephine said.

"I'm not going to prison," Sarah said. She picked up the jug and started, slowly, up the stairs.

"You don't have to go to prison."

"I'm not going to prison and I'm not going to just fucking kill myself, either!"

The walls were silent in response.

Sarah got four jugs of gas up the stairs. Two by the front door, for the most dramatic effect. The other two best positioned to bring down the building.

She'd had plenty of time to plan the whole thing, but never let it get overcomplicated. Two kitchen timers, some flares. That was it. Might not even kill anyone.

"What made you do it?" Sarah asked, as she took the cap off of the last flare.

"Same as you. End of my rope."

"I'm not at the end of my rope."

"I'm not going to argue," Josephine said.

Sarah sat down in her favorite chair, by her favorite desk, by her favorite window. She was going to miss that chair. She was going to miss watching the wind blow the snow in the winter and the grass in the summer and the pines all year round.

"A man was after me," Josephine said. Her voice was quieter than usual. "Eyes with fire behind them, hands with blood inside them, a gun a gun always a gun. A man who thought I was his."

"You should have fought him."

"He would have won, Sarah Nails. He would have won, and I would have been his, and he would be sitting in this house right now and I would have been sitting in this house right now and it's better to be eaten by wolves than be married, sometimes."

"Wolves?"

"So I took pills, more pills than other days, and I went out to the pines, and I gave myself to the forest, the snow, the moon. Yes, the wolves. I followed the wolves. I gave myself to the wolves. Not to the man."

"I'm sorry that happened to you, Josephine."

"I'm not sorry."

"It's not going to happen to me, though."

"Then the tunnel."

"There is no tunnel, Josephine. You're in my head."

"Of course."

◆

The sun set, and no feds had arrived. Not yet. Sarah wished Darnell had brought her a gun after all.

Sarah made herself tea, thick and black. Every light in the house was off. The half-moon lit up the world and the wind blew the shadows of trees against the wall behind her. Two flares sat on her lap.

The wolves arrived and circled the house. There was no meat for them. Not unless Sarah decided to die like Josephine.

"They bleed," Josephine said.

Sarah saw her reflection in the window, but didn't turn to look back at her friend. Her lover, of sorts.

"They burrow. They break the bone."

"Who?" Sarah asked.

"The pines, the land."

"Yeah, and the moon, and the snow, sure, sure," Sarah said. "And the wolves."

The wolves.

Sarah stood up and looked at Josephine. The ghost stared at her, her eyes moist with tears like they always were.

Headlights broke through the window.

"Shit," Sarah said. "I thought I'd have longer."

"Everyone always does."

Sarah looked at the gas cans, bright red and plastic and out of place by the door.

She couldn't do it to Darnell.

There were pills enough in the bedroom, of course. She could avoid prison, at least. She didn't want to die, but it was bound to happen eventually.

She walked up the stairs, her boots heavy on the ugly, faded carpet. She walked into the bedroom, opened the closet. Box after box of sleeping pills. A good night's rest. A long night's rest.

She turned and saw two things at once. Josephine, on the chair, by the window. And the poster on the wall, visible through Josephine's translucence. "We don't have to win. We just have to survive."

"Are you real?" Sarah asked. "I need to know, and I need to know right the fuck now."

"What do you think?"

"Are you real. Are ghosts real. Is the tunnel real."

A car door slammed.

Out of time.

"I love you, Sarah Nails," Josephine said.

That was real enough.

"I love you, too." Sarah sprinted for the hallway, careened down the stairs, and ran out of the side door of the house, grabbing her coat from the chair as she went. The flares and the pills spilled from her hands into the snow.

The wolves stood back, nervously watching her. Headlights came from the front of the house.

She followed the wolf tracks around back. The wolves followed her at a distance, curious. Dispassionate.

Sarah traced the tracks down into the gully that marked the end of the yard. They only ran another twenty feet before they stopped, suddenly, at the side of a boulder set against the ravine's wall. The wolves' den.

In the distance, there was shouting, then howling. Then shooting. Then a wolf screamed.

It wouldn't be long.

Sarah had always been small for a boy, and she got down onto her belly, and she squeezed between the rock and the earth and made it into the den though it ripped her coat and soaked her in snow.

She turned on her flashlight. There were the bones. Animal bones. Animal bones, and a human is an animal too, and there were the old bones, and the skull. Josephine was real, and she'd given herself to the wolves.

Past the midden was a tunnel. Waist high, cut by human hands into the earth, reinforced with old timber. Bootleggers.

"Tracks lead here!" a voice called from just outside. A man's voice, low and angry. People get angry, the land doesn't. "I can't fit, though."

"This will fit," another man said. Sarah heard gas and turned to look as a metal canister rolled into the den. Smoke. She turned her back on it and crawled.

She crawled through the tunnel, which was endless until it ended. She came up in a part of the woods she'd never seen before, and the half moon showed her the path. The path, too, was endless until it ended at the shore of the lake.

The lake was frozen over, and the rowboat had rotted through, and she set out on foot across the ice. It creaked and it cracked and it held.

The bike's engine turned over, and it filled the world with its roar, and Sarah Nails took off up a gravel road. She reached a fork, and she took out her compass. North.

Somewhere up north was a border, and beyond that border was hope.

Not a lot of it, but maybe enough.

THE THIRTY-SEVEN MARBLE STEPS

I grew up near the foothills of Appalachia, and there's something to these forests. The trees themselves aren't old, but the mountains are old. The mountains are old and battered and smoothed over, and what is a forest but the outbursting of life come up from the land. The trees themselves are not old, but the forests are old because these mountains are old.

I grew up near the foothills of Appalachia, and I remember when *The Blair Witch Project* came out, set close to where I lived, it didn't surprise anyone. Like yeah, the movie is a work of fiction, but there's still something to these mountains and these forests. There's still something there, something that the movie drew from.

My father told me this story, when I was a kid. He told me this story under the boughs and the stars and it's not something I'll ever forget. The next day, he took me to the place it happened. He took me to the marble steps.

◆

There are thirty-seven marble steps in the middle of the forest, far from any road. The steps climb steep and twisted up from a seasonal creek, up to a tiny concrete foundation peppered with stones. There's no house there anymore.

There is, however, a crack in the foundation.

The crack is narrow and long, and underneath there's nothing. Not soil, not rock, just nothing. You shine your flashlight through that crack and you see nothing. You slide your skinny arm through that crack and you feel nothing. You drop a coin through that crack and you hear nothing. I tried all those things.

There was a house on that foundation, years ago, years before my father was born, probably before his mother was born, maybe before her mother came over from the old country fleeing persecution. I couldn't tell you when, exactly, there was a house on that foundation.

It doesn't make sense for there to ever have been one, not out where there's no road, not out where whoever built it had to carry marble and concrete on their back or the backs of animals.

I can't tell you why there was a house, I can only tell you that there was one.

I can tell you about the woman who lived there, too.

I can tell you that she didn't have a name, that she didn't need a name. Names are not for yourself, they're for other people. You live alone in a house in the woods at the top of the marble steps and you don't need a name, because no one calls you anything. The people from the nearby town, they just called her the woman who lived in the woods.

This woman lived alone and she was ageless, like all women who live alone. She lived only five miles or so from that nearby town. That town is gone now too. It probably had a name, though I don't know it. The woman lived close enough that people hiking or hunting in the forest saw the smoke from her chimney and some saw the light in her windows. Sometimes people even saw her herself, wandering the forest. They saw her hair pinned up in a bun in the summer and under hats and hoods in the winter. They saw her gaze, alternatively blank and fierce. Sometimes they heard her sing.

It went like this. She walked paths through the woods, sometimes down even to the road alongside the town. She had a stick in one hand, a burlap sack in the other.

"Bad man, bad man, braise the bones," she sang, as she beat bushes with the stick. A good whack, a good thump against the branches. "Bugbear, bugbear, boil the broth."

Animals, all kinds of animals, would run out from the bushes and the brambles right into her sack. Rabbits, groundhogs, snakes. Possums, raccoons, mice. Birds and lizards. Every creature under the sun and every creature that hides from the sun would run right towards her and into that sack.

Once it was good and full, she'd twist the end closed, lift it like it weighed nothing, and beat the bag with the stick until the squirming stopped and the crying stopped and everything inside was dead or willing to pretend.

She'd throw that bag over her shoulder and walk away, whistling now instead of singing. That same tune. I know the tune, I could hum it to you, but I don't know how to write it so maybe that tune will die out one day, and maybe we'll all be safer when it does.

Dogs went missing sometimes around that town. Cats, too. Lambs and calves and chickens. Never children. One reason people in the town put up with that woman as long as they did is that whenever a kid went missing, they'd wind up back at home right in their crib, not crying, the blood of berries tinting their lips.

One day, a little girl, not yet seven years old, got swept away by the river. Surely she'd drowned, the parents thought. The whole town thought. That night, she walked up to her own house wearing a burlap dress, her hair brushed and braided, her belly full. She didn't say a word about what happened but everyone knew that the lady with the bag and the stick was watching out.

It went like that for years, for generations. Was it the same woman? No one could tell.

"Bruno, Bruno, bake the bread," she sang. "Boatman, boatman, baste the bear." A good whack, a good thump, and she had the animals, and off she went on her way. Never said a word to a soul.

This was fine, and this was good, and no one in town thought too hard on it. Until one day, it wasn't fine. It wasn't good.

People mostly want to let each other alone, and that woman wasn't hurting anyone.

A boy came up in that town, and he became a man while he was at school in a nearby city, and when he came back as a man he decided he wasn't going to be the sort to just let people alone.

John was his name, at least as I have it. Big John, they called him, because there were an awful lot of Johns and this John was the tallest.

One day in early March, John was walking home from the mill. The sun was near to set, and the wind was something wild and a little bit of snow was being thrown here and there. He saw the woman, and he heard the woman, and he saw a cat run into her bag and he decided enough was enough.

He waited until she was far enough distant and then he followed her, off through the woods. Up to that seasonal creek. Most people, they took one look at that house up on top of those marble steps, perched down over the gully, and they went right back the way they came. Big John, though, he waited until the woman went into the house, then he climbed each of those steps himself.

221

Smoke was pouring out the chimney and lamplight flickered through the unshuttered windows, and Big John went up to one of those windows and looked inside.

The woman was there, and she had the sack over one shoulder, and she went up to the middle of the bare concrete floor and she tapped her stick seven times. Tap, tap, tap. Tap, tap, tap, tap. She tapped her stick seven times and she stepped back and she waited, and a trap door was there where nothing had been, and she reached down and grabbed the iron rung and pulled it up and Big John heard a wailing, a keening, from within. He couldn't describe it better than that, in all the years he tried. Inhuman, inanimal. Demonic.

The woman upended the sack. Animals, including that cat, tumbled out, down into the darkness. Soon after, far worse sounds came from that trap door, and the woman smiled and cooed like she was tending a pet and she closed that trap door. She tapped on it seven times with her stick. Tap, tap, tap. Tap, tap, tap, tap. The trap door was gone.

On the wall, hung up with the coats and the cloaks, were animal collars and tags. Dozens of them.

Big John had seen enough, and he turned to go, but snuck in one last look and saw the woman at her stove, singing again, cooking what looked and smelled for all the world like vegetable soup.

◆

Big John snuck down those stairs as quietly and carefully as he could, but as soon as he reached the path by the creek, he ran all the way back to town. Five miles he ran, and when he showed up at the sheriff's house he was panting and sweating and pale and just worn out and his body was just about to give up on him.

He knocked on that door. Tap, tap, tap. The sheriff answered.

"The woman," he said. "The cats," he said. "The dogs."

He told the sheriff what he'd seen, and of course the sheriff didn't believe him about the trap door and he didn't believe him about the vegetable soup, but he believed him about the animal collars.

Everyone in town knew that the woman stole pets and livestock, anything with fur or feathers that was small enough to fit into her sack. Everyone knew it but no one had admitted it, because if they'd admitted it, they would have had to do something.

But here was Big John standing at the doorstep of authority and that authority decided to finally admit to himself what he already knew. It wasn't yet late, just past dinner, and the sheriff rounded up his posse and headed into the forest with guns and lanterns ready to find the woman and bring her to justice. Big John, though, he stayed at home. He'd used up all his nerve for that night, maybe for the rest of time.

Now, this is where you expect this story to go all wrong, and it will. But it doesn't go wrong the way it might have. The sheriff climbed the thirty-seven steps, his posse following. He showed up at the woman's door, banging with the handle of his revolver on the wood. Bang, bang, bang.

The woman answered, and the sheriff arrested her, and the posse tore apart the cabin looking for contraband. They found the dog collars and the cat collars, and that was enough, but they found nothing else besides. Hot barley soup on the stove, flavored strong with garlic and wild onion. No bones, no midden. No trap door, no basement at all. Big John had been seeing things.

They marched the woman five miles back to the sheriff's office and locked her into the town's one holding cell and by then it was the middle of the night, and the woman was steel-faced and unbroken.

"You have to feed her," the woman said.

"Feed who?" the sheriff asked.

"Someone has to feed her," the woman said. "Someone must go up there and feed my daughter."

"You don't have a daughter," the sheriff said.

And that was that, and the woman was sent to the city for trial, and no one thought much about her again, because what is a prison but a place to put those you wish to forget, those who make you uncomfortable. What is a prison but oblivion.

A week later, Big John was walking home in the evening out along that road, when he heard a terrible thing, a wrenching, a scream of wood and steel and a scream of animal throats and a scream of emptiness and horror.

Then... nothing.

Nothing happened.

Except from then on, children from that town, they weren't returned with berry juice on their lips when they went missing. When children went missing, they stayed missing.

And now there's a concrete foundation, peppered with stones, with a crack in it and nothing on the other side. And people don't camp there much, and people don't build towns there no more, and the forest is old and no one knows how those marble steps got there, and no one knows much of anything anymore.

◆

There's no moral to this, to be sure. I'm not here saying that you've got to let the little evils go unaddressed so you don't let out the big evil. I'm not even saying what was in that basement was evil, not for sure. I'm not saying it was right what happened to the woman and neither am I saying it's okay to steal cats and feed them to monsters. I'm just saying it happened. I'm just telling you about the thirty-seven marble steps, and that foundation, and that crack that goes off to nowhere.

CREDITS / PUBLICATION HISTORY

The Devil Lives Here
Rulerless (2021)
Edited by Byron López Ellington

The Free Orcs of Cascadia
Fantasy & Science Fiction (2019)
Edited by C.C. Finlay

Not One of Us Will Survive This Fog
Patreon.com (2018)

One Star
Vice (2015)
Edited by Claire Evans and Brian Merchant

We Won't Be Here Tomorrow
A Punk Rock Future (2019)
Edited by Steve Zisson

The Fortunate Death of Jonathan Sandelson
Strange Horizons (2018)
Edited by Cassie Krahe

Imagine A World So Forgiving
Fireside (2016)
Edited by Brian White

Everything That Isn't Winter
Tor.com (2016)
Edited by Diana Pho and Noa Wheeler

Into the Gray
Tor.com (2018)
Edited by Diana Pho

The Bones of Children
The Book of Three Gates (2020)
Edited by Simon Berman and Jennifer Shaiman

Mary Marrow
Patreon.com (2018)

Beyond Sapphire Glass
Strange Horizons (2015)
Edited by Julia Rios

The Northern Host
Patreon.com (2018)

Malediction
Shock Totem #10 (2016)
Edited by K. Allen Wood

Invisible People
Accessing the Future (2015)
Edited by Djibril al-Ayad

We Who Will Destroy the Future
Detritus Books (2018)

Men of the Ashen Morrow
Beneath Ceaseless Skies (2017)
Edited by Scott H. Andrews

A Reasonable Place If You're Careful
Grievous Angel (2016)
Edited by Charles Christian

The Name of the Forest
Strange Horizons (2016)
Edited by Catherine Krahe

It Bleeds, It Burrows, It Breaks the Bone
Patreon.com (2019)

The Thirty-Seven Marble Steps
Patreon.com (2020)

AK PRESS is small, in terms of staff and resources, but we also manage to be one of the world's most productive anarchist publishing houses. We publish close to twenty books every year, and distribute thousands of other titles published by like-minded independent presses and projects from around the globe. We're entirely worker run and democratically managed. We operate without a corporate structure—no boss, no managers, no bullshit.

The **FRIENDS OF AK PRESS** program is a way you can directly contribute to the continued existence of AK Press, and ensure that we're able to keep publishing books like this one! Friends pay $25 a month directly into our publishing account ($30 for Canada, $35 for international), and receive a copy of every book AK Press publishes for the duration of their membership! Friends also receive a discount on anything they order from our website or buy at a table: 50% on AK titles, and 30% on everything else. We have a Friends of AK ebook program as well: $15 a month gets you an electronic copy of every book we publish for the duration of your membership. *You can even sponsor a very discounted membership for someone in prison.*

Email **friendsofak@akpress.org** for more info, or visit the website: **https://www.akpress.org/friends.html**.

There are always great book projects in the works—so sign up now to become a Friend of AK Press, and let the presses roll!